Education

A Foreign Education

Craig Alan Williamson

www.CraigAlanWilliamson.com

ISBN 978-1-84685-694-5

Copyright © Craig Alan Williamson 2007

Edited by David Bagwell and Mark Hooper
Cover illustration by Clare Louise Mobbs
Author photograph by Robin Sandry
Cover design by Craig Alan Williamson

The right of Craig Alan Williamson to be
identified as the Author of the Work has been
asserted by him in accordance with the
Copyright, Designs and Patents Act 1988.

All rights reserved. No part of this
publication may be reproduced, stored in a
retrieval system, or transmitted, in any form
or by any means, without the prior written
permission of the author, nor be otherwise
circulated in any form of binding or cover
other than that in which it is published and
without a similar condition being imposed on
the subsequent purchaser.

For Dawn

ONE

I had never been more alone than at the top of those steps, yet my inner sense was one of total contentment. I turned to marvel at the view from my new home – a vast expanse of lush grass surrounded on all sides by buildings with matching red tile roofs and resplendent sandstone bricks. To my left was the arresting sight of the Rocky Mountain foothills. Their countless peaks were glowing orange from the intense rays of the late-August sun, providing stark contrast to the deep blue sky. The air was bubbling with the aroma of pine trees, while the only sound to be heard was the playful warble of finches in their branches.

It had taken years of hard work and careful planning to reach that day, and yet the past felt so much further away than a twelve-hour flight. Exactly what would the coming year have in store for me? More hard work? Undoubtedly. Good times? Certainly. Great friends? Absolutely. Promiscuous sex with a bevy of hot, young American girls? I could only hope so.

Removing my sunglasses as I entered the dark building, my eyes slowly adjusted to the cavernous reception area with a carefully aligned row of ten or more tables. Behind those tables sat a similarly well-ordered line of girls, each with a beaming beauty-queen smile full of brilliant white teeth that had my pupils constricting once more. Through the glare I could see one other person bravely approaching the lion's den and decided to head for the table next to his. Safety in numbers seemed to be the order of the day, as I saw every single bleached row of fangs follow me while I struggled with my suitcases.

'James Arriaga,' I overheard the other guy say to his designated set of gnashers. Before I could hear his reception, I was hit by the shockwave of my very own greeting.

'Welcome to the University of Colorado, and welcome to Cheyenne Arapaho hall!' My set of teeth definitely had a set of lungs on her too. She also spoke in the kind of ear-bleed inducing accent I had naively hoped to never encounter.

'Hi, I'm Ross Cooper,' I replied, once the ringing in my ears subsided.

'Oh my gosh! You have the sweetest accent! Where on *earth* are you from?'

'I'm from England.'

'No way,' was the deafening response.

'Yes, I'm afraid so.' I strained a smile whilst praying that a busload of fellow new students hadn't just walked through the door behind me to witness the humiliation.

'OH MY GOSH,' she beamed. I saw her eyes peer over my shoulder, and soon became aware that a busload of fellow new students had just walked through the door behind me to witness the humiliation. 'I've never met anyone from another country before! This is amazing! Do you even have electricity in England?'

Did she really just ask if we had electricity? Could I have mistaken her accent? I quickly tried to think of other words that could sound the same, but drew a blank. Nevertheless, I thought I had better give her the benefit of the doubt.

'No, we don't,' I hesitantly offered.

'Wow, this must be really weird for you then, even just being in here with all these light bulbs!'

Oh *my* gosh, she really did say electricity. I had to think quickly to follow that one up.

'Ah, I'd been wondering what you called those tiny candles in the glass balls,' was all I could manage.

'Well, let's get you sorted out with your room then, Ross.'

She began to work through her paperwork and then retreated to the back of the room to recover some more documents. The guy who had been next to me throughout the whole embarrassing affair turned to introduce himself.

'Hi, I'm James. Pleased to meet you.'

'Hi, yes I overheard your name earlier. I'm Ross, pleased to meet you.'

'I overheard your name too, and the rest of it! Welcome to America, Ross – the land of the free, and the home of the ignorant. Don't worry though, we're not all like that.'

'That's good to know. So where are you from?'

'Blackfoot, Idaho. I drove down today.'

'You drove? How far is that?'

'Oh, only about seven hundred miles, and I did set off pretty early this morning.'

'Shit, I'd think twice about a two-hundred-mile drive back home.'

'Ah, you'll get used to it soon enough. Everything over here is so spread out, so I guess long journeys are pretty normal.'

Our conversation was interrupted by James' allotted assemblage of pearly-whites.

'So, there are your keys, and here are details of your roommates. Neither has checked in yet, so you'll have the place to yourself. Chance to grab the best bed!'

'Thanks,' said James. He took the keys and looked over the roommate sheet he had been given.

'Nice to meet you, James,' I added before he left the desk. 'Hopefully I'll see you around.'

'Yes, good to meet you too, Ross,' he grinned while walking off to his room. 'I'll be sure to save the second best bed for you!'

My first lesson in UK-US language differences was a harsh one. Having been told my room was on the first floor, I laboured up the stairs with my two large cases and rucksack only to realise that my room number was nowhere to be seen and the corridors were, in fact, women only. A few more sensible and quieter comments about my accent from a particularly attractive lady lightened my mood, however, as she explained that 'first floor' actually meant ground floor. As much as I wanted to continue enjoying her company, I eventually stumbled back down the stairs and found the door to room 186.

'I thought I was gonna have to start on this without you,' said James, waiting for me with an impossibly large bottle of whisky and two paper cups.

'Yes, just a bit of confusion about which floor our room was on. Not to worry though, I did manage to have a brief sightseeing tour with an incredible girl in the hall above us.'

'Well, that definitely deserves a drink then.'

James poured as I brought my cases into the room. It seemed that we had a much bigger space than those I had briefly glimpsed upstairs, which had two desks and two beds in the same room. Ours was one of the few triple rooms, with a study area containing three desks in a U-shape and then a separate bedroom off to the right with a single bed, a bunk bed, and wardrobes. We were at the very front corner of the building and had a terrific view of the playing fields and the Rocky Mountains. As I took my belongings through to the bedroom, I could see that James' bag was already on the single bed.

'So,' I gestured towards the bunk bed, 'I have to decide whether I prefer being on top?'

James laughed. 'I thought you Brits were supposed to be reserved?'

'You're right, of course I should go on top – anything else would just be too kinky.'

'Dude, settle down,' he exclaimed while passing me a cup.

'So, where are all *your* suitcases?' I asked, noting that there was only one small holdall on his bed.

'They're still in the car. Do you mind giving me a little help bringing them up?'

'Not a problem,' I replied, downing the cup of foul liquid in a single, ill-advised mouthful.

'Well, at least the stereotype of you guys being heavy drinkers is right then.'

'You're just lucky I'm English and not Scottish.'

We headed back down the hall and through the reception area where the crowd of new students was subsiding. As we passed the tables, James motioned towards the dental technicians.

'Hey, Ross, maybe you could score a date with that girl this time?'

I hadn't really paid much attention to her looks during what would become known as the 'electricity incident', but this time I did notice that she was, in fact, rather facially challenged.

'Maybe after that bottle of yours has been emptied,' I offered rather callously. 'I suppose I could always ask her to keep the lights off. You know, because I'm a bit freaked out by the glass candles?'

'Yeah, you might be onto a winner there.'

My pace quickened and we walked back out into the sunshine and down the steps towards James' car. It was a red Ford Mustang that looked a little past its best, but nevertheless appeared to be his pride and joy.

'So, what do you think?' he asked expectantly.

'You drove seven hundred miles in this?' was not the kind of response he had probably anticipated.

'Hey, this is American engineering at its finest.'

'If that's the case, then I think your engineering industry might have a problem. Just open the boot and let's get your things out.'

'Just open the what?'

It took me a moment to think back through the phrases I had absorbed through many years spent watching American movies and sitcoms.

'Oh, sorry, the *trunk*.'

'Boot? And you say that we have problems.'

James removed the bags, and we began to make our way back inside.

'So I presume this is your first year here?' I asked.

'Yeah, it's my freshman year. I'm majoring in Engineering.'

'Oh, cool. Maybe you could work for Ford?'

'Yes, maybe,' was the ironic retort. 'So how about you?'

'Well, this is my second year – I'm doing a Physics degree back in the UK, but the course includes a year abroad.'

'That's awesome. I'd love to do something like that with a year in the Basque country.'

'The Basque country?'

'Yeah, it's a part of Spain where my family are originally from.'

'So you speak Spanish then?'

'Sí! My first name was actually Jakome, but it got changed to the English version when I was young. My friends actually call me Jak.'

'Oh right then, Jak it is.'

'So what made you come here to Boulder for your year abroad?'

'Well, I've always fancied living in America and, of the choices I had, this seemed to be the best location. I've only been here for less than an hour, but already I just love the atmosphere and the views – both of natural beauty and natural-looking beauties.'

'Yeah, I must admit I've been impressed on that front too. So I guess you don't have a girlfriend back in Britain then?'

I hesitated. 'Er, I'm not really sure.'

'You're not sure if you have a girlfriend? What's wrong with you, man?'

'It's kind of complicated. I mean, there *is* a girl, but we were only together for a few months before I left, and then we didn't really talk about what would happen when I came here.'

'So you just left her for a year without figuring out if you were staying together or breaking up?' It did seem rather strange when put in those terms.

'I suppose so, yes.'

'Man, that's crazy. If I had a girlfriend, I'd be flying back every weekend for some action.'

I clumsily changed the subject. 'So I wonder when our other roommate will arrive?'

'Yeah, what's his name, Todd Johnson? Well, it says he's from Colorado, so maybe he'll stroll in pretty soon.'

We arrived back at the room and proceeded to unpack our luggage while chatting some more and slowly working our way through the whisky. It seemed like Jak and I had much in common and it was a relief to have a kindred spirit as a roommate. We were actually both fairly similar in appearance – around five feet ten inches tall, short brown hair, not strikingly ugly, not strikingly handsome. We seemed to enjoy the same sense of humour and liked to talk about women – perhaps a little too much. At the age of nineteen, though, I think we could be excused.

The mysterious Todd Johnson didn't arrive that night, but it turned out that our entire corridor of around fifteen or so rooms was pretty quiet. It was only Friday though, so we assumed that Todd and everyone else would turn up over the weekend ready for lectures starting on Monday.

The remainder of the day soon passed, and we were both ready for bed around midnight. With the slightly misguided combination of jet lag and cheap liquor in my system, it wasn't long before I fell fast asleep.

Waking the next day in the heady heights of the top bunk, my pounding head was a rude introduction to life in Boulder with its elevation of over 5,000 feet. I had read the advice about drinking plenty of water and not too much alcohol, and was thankful that the 'I told you so' comments of my mother were thousands of miles away. Jak seemed to be suffering similarly, as I heard a groan from his direction. I moved to the edge of my bunk and looked down towards his twisted figure against the opposite wall of the room in his single bed.

'Morning, Jak.'

'Ohhhhh, morning dude,' he croaked back at me.

'This altitude's a bit of a pain, isn't it?'

'Ohhhhhhhhhhhh.' He began to sit upright and cradle his head delicately in his palms. 'I'm used to the altitude, but just not that much alcohol.'

'I didn't think we drank *that* much?'

'Maybe not much for an Englishman, Ross.'

He began to open his eyes with a look of excruciating pain cast across his face, and then gingerly craned his neck towards me. His expression of near-death was quickly exchanged by one of utter shock.

'HOLY FUCK! WHO THE HELL ARE YOU?' he yelled as his body involuntarily bolted upright.

'Well, that's not really the reaction I look for first thing in the morning,' I replied, somewhat bemused.

A third voice suddenly burst forth. 'Ah, hello! My name Kazuki Mori! I your roommate!'

I quickly swung my head down to look at the bunk beneath me. I now also yelled, 'HOLY FUCK,' as I saw a portly and naked Japanese man spread-eagle on top of the bed. He was proudly displaying an erection of, it must be said, quite magnificent proportions. 'Where's Todd Johnson? Did you eat him?'

'Todd is dead, so I here!' Kazuki said with an unnerving ear-to-ear grin.

'Did you fuck him to death?' Jak helpfully contributed.

'Good morning, day is wonderful outside!' was the innocent response.

Jak looked at me with an expression that said "You jump on him while I fetch my Swiss Army knife". I silently replied back with a glare that translated to "No, *you* fucking jump on him". Diplomacy now appeared to be our only hope. It was time to demonstrate some of that levelheaded spirit that we English are renowned for the world over. I looked our intruder straight in the eye – well, it was difficult not to – then looked him straight in the eyes and took a deep breath.

'Now, listen to me and listen carefully. First off, we are both rampantly heterosexual, so you'll have no joy with that thing in here. You might as well put it away before you have someone's eye out. Secondly, the police will be looking for you by now, so the best thing you can do is leave here and turn yourself in. Oh, but pop some clothes on first, there's a good chap.'

'I from Japan!' wasn't the answer I had expected.

'Look, buddy,' Jak now joined in, 'just get the fuck out of our room, NOW!'

'My name Kazuki Mori!'

The tension was at its peak. Our nerves were frayed and our arseholes were twitching with grim expectation. My heart skipped a beat as our room phone suddenly began to sound its bells of hope. Jak's eyes met with mine, and we tacitly acknowledged that it could be our last chance. With the phone situated evenly between the bunk and the single bed, Jak would have to be quick to beat this ruthless, naked, erect killer. He sprung out of his bed and picked up the receiver in one hurried manoeuvre. Kazuki sat motionless. Perhaps he had lost his nerve?

'Quick,' Jak implored down the phone, 'there's a Japanese guy in our room, and he's big...VERY big...what?' There was a foreboding pause. 'You mean? Oh my god!' Jak put down the phone with a calm look of resignation. Perhaps it had been Kazuki's accomplice, telling Jak that the room was now sealed along with our eye-watering fate.

'What, what, WHAT?' I asked of Jak.

'That was reception. Apparently Todd Johnson died a couple of months ago, and we should expect a Japanese exchange student called Kazuki in his place.'

'*My* name Kazuki!' came the enthusiastic response from our new roommate.

TWO

I took a mid-morning stroll around campus to soak up the atmosphere of American college life. I was accompanied by the sunshine and another cloudless sky while I admired the sheer beauty of the architecture. From the residence halls to the academic centres, every single building was immaculately finished and delicately interspersed with flourishing conifers. Thinking back to the concrete carbuncles of my university back in Lancaster, it was in a completely different class.

I stole a look at Folsom Field – the stadium where the university's American football team played. The contrast here was even more staggering – a purpose-built all-seater stadium in comparison to the muddy fields of Lancaster. The UK national sport of football might attract a crowd of ten or so resilient girlfriends at a top-level university game, whereas this stadium could hold more than 50,000 crazed fans.

As if my cup didn't already runneth over, there was also the sight of beautiful, young, supple, American women sunbathing on the field right in front of my residence hall. Don't get me wrong, such women also existed in England, but bikini weather rarely did. Arriving back at my room, my cup almost burst its banks when I realised that my desk overlooked the aforementioned women. Jak was already deeply engrossed in the view. He reluctantly turned away from the sweet shop, albeit briefly.

'Hey Ross, good walk?'

'Oh my god, Jak, this place is just paradise.' I joined him in admiring the finery on display. 'The campus is amazing, the stadium is amazing, the weather is amazing, and those women...'

'Aw, the women, dude, the women. If only you were a single man, right?'

'Meaningless sex with *any* of those women would make my life complete. You could kill me afterwards and I'd die a happy man.'

'I'll have a word with Kaz – I'm sure he could arrange your death by samurai sword.'

'Yeah, samurai trouser sword no doubt. Where is he anyway?'

'He's upstairs having brunch.'

'Just as well I persuaded him to put some clothes on then. Have you eaten yet?'

'Nah, shall we?'

We managed to peel our eyes away from the window and headed up to the canteen for Saturday brunch. Meals were provided for all residents, but the dining hall was pretty empty at that point due to the many late arrivals. It wasn't difficult to find Kazuki – his rotund figure was eagerly bobbing up and down as he worked his way through a mountain of pancakes.

'Hey, Kaz, good breakfast?' I enquired.

'I eating breakfast!' he replied, reading from a phrase book he had at the table.

'Ah, very good. We'll just get something and come join you.'

Cereals, fresh fruit, toast, pancakes, juices – it was a pretty impressive spread. We piled our plates high and sat down with our roommate.

'I studying English!' Kazuki greeted us on our return.

'Oh, thank fuck for that!' was Jak's reaction.

'That's great!' I added, a little more sympathetically. 'So when did your plane land last night?'

'I proud of my manhood!' Kazuki's fixed expression of joy still remained.

'Indeed you are, indeed you are,' was all that I could offer in return.

We returned to our food and eventually began chatting again about our background and how we had ended up there. Truth be told, Jak and I did most of the talking while Kazuki smiled earnestly and offered the occasional response to a question never asked. It had been an unusual introduction to our Japanese friend, but I was certainly warming to his innocence and unending enthusiasm.

'So, Ross, tell me about more about this "maybe-girlfriend" of yours,' probed Jak.

'There's not much more to tell really. She's called Chloe. We got together on the last day of term back in May, and then saw each other a few times during the summer. We've only really spent a handful of days actually "together", although I suppose we were friends for a bit before.'

'So how do you feel about her?'

'Well, we got on well as friends, but I'm not sure if she's really into me for anything more. I mean, we haven't even gone very far...'

'You mean you haven't even fucked her?'

'Well, I wouldn't have put it quite like that. I've just been a gentleman and not pushed things too fast.'

'Man, you've put in the hard yards and not even cashed in your pussy pass? What is *wrong* with you?'

'I know, I know, trust me I know. What I really need is a healthy amount of no-strings-attached sex with some gorgeous American girls – maybe that will sort me out.'

Kazuki looked up from his plate, and we were shocked to see his eternal grin swiftly turn into an expression of deep sincerity. He then spoke with a poise and profoundness we hadn't previously thought possible.

'True love is key to all happiness.'

There was silence. Jak and I looked at each other in disbelief. We then focussed our attention back on Kazuki, whose lips were about to impart further words of intimate wisdom.

'In Japan, I banged a whore!'

We returned from the dining hall to the sound of the phone ringing in our bedroom. Jak duly answered.

'International pussy palace, can I help you?' I prayed that it wasn't my mother. 'Oh, sure, just a minute...hey, Ross, it's Chloe for you.' I then realised I had made the wrong prayer. Oh shit, how to play it? Aloof man of mystery in a foreign land? Doting boyfriend, fighting back the tears of pain at being apart from my beloved? I took the phone with trepidation.

'Oh, hi Chloe,' was my nervy opening gambit. Jak and Kazuki left for the study room to give me some privacy.

'Hi Ross, how are you doing? How is everything going?' I could sense an undercurrent of nerves in her voice too.

'Oh, pretty good. The flight was OK, the campus is great, and my roommates seem like good fun.' Concise and non-committal seemed to be a sensible strategy.

'So, what's going on with me and you then?'

Oh shit, I didn't expect *that* so early on in the proceedings.

'How do you mean?' I sheepishly asked.

'What do *you* mean?' came the reply, rather angrily. 'We can't just go on like this. There are four bloody thousand miles between us now, and even less chance of you wanting to sleep with me than there has been for the last three months! I've been waiting for some sort of commitment from you. Hell, I've offered myself on a plate to you enough times, but you're not willing to give me anything in return. I'm beginning to wonder if you even *have* a dick.'

My heart was pounding, my brow began to sweat, and my balls shrivelled into a tight package of shame. My only consolation was that nobody else was in the room to hear her embarrassing revelations. OK, Ross, take it on the chin, maintain an inner calm, and get this mess sorted out.

'Did I tell you one of my roommates was from Japan?'

She continued apace. 'You're so pathetic that you can't even discuss your bloody feelings with me? That last girlfriend of yours really did a number on you, didn't she?'

Final chance, Ross. Get a grip, take control, be dominant.

'How's the weather over there?'

'OK then, Ross, fuck you. This thing is over, that's if it ever began in the first place. Until you can learn to talk about your feelings and satisfy a woman sexually, you're going to be a sad and lonely man. Don't even bother to keep in touch.'

The 'click' from the earpiece signalled the end of our relationship. The following 'click' signalled the existence of a second phone in our room. On my return to the study room, Jak's look of solemnity temporarily assured me that everything would be all right, until it burst into a look of wild amusement.

'So then, Mr Gentleman, you didn't want to push her?' he smirked.

'All right,' I conceded. 'So maybe things are a little more complicated than I let on.'

'Yeah, just a little.'

Kazuki now chipped in to complete my humiliation. '*I* satisfy women sexually!'

I laughed off the jokes, but couldn't hide from the fact that the relationship had finished horridly and it was entirely my fault. I had lost a good friend, and to top it all off my virility had been called into question. Several times if I was not mistaken.

I needed to escape into the fresh air to clear my head and regroup my thoughts. I changed into my running gear and headed out towards the hills.

The run was exactly what I had needed. It felt good to be hitting the streets again after a few days off, although the altitude took its toll and restricted my efforts. It did give me time to put things into perspective though. I had lost a girlfriend whom I wasn't particularly head-over-heels for anyway, and there I was – an Englishman with a cool accent in a foreign land. It was exactly the kind of edge my average looks needed to gain entry into the promised kingdom of high echelon one-night stands. It was going to be my time to shine – a new person in a new place, able to reinvent myself as a debonair English love machine. Breaking hearts and bra straps, campus-wide.

'Hi there!' rang the sweetest American accent I had ever heard. As she spoke, her lips pursed delicately to reveal the cutest dimples at the corners of her mouth. She was every bit as beautiful as I had remembered from the first floor/ground floor incident. 'Now we're all settled in I thought I should come and introduce myself properly.'

'Oh, hello,' I said, perhaps labouring my Englishness a little too much.

'I hope you don't mind me coming down here, it's just that I remembered your room number and things were a little quiet upstairs.' Her flowing russet hair was straight out of a shampoo advert, while her faultless bronze skin had featured on the cover of countless fashion magazines.

'Of course not. By the way, the name's Cooper, Ross Cooper.' You're not James Bond, Ross. Just calm it down, calm it down.

'Oh, well hi, Ross. I'm Fischer, April Fischer,' she mocked me, delightfully, while her emerald eyes glowed brightly. 'So are you going to invite me in?'

'Of course, how rude of me...' I beckoned her inside. 'So, do you pay follow-up visits to all the men who get lost on your corridor?'

'Only the foreign ones,' she smiled. 'We Americans have a thing for the British accent.' I knew it, I bloody well knew it! 'It's just a shame that yours isn't a *true* British accent.'

'Excuse me?'

'Well, you don't sound much like the Queen, do you?'

'Well, no, but neither do her sixty-one million subjects – only bad actors on American TV shows use that accent.'

'If you insist,' she teased. 'Next you'll be telling me that you don't even drink tea or wear a bowler hat.'

'And *you'll* be telling me that you don't have a therapist and you've never sued anyone.'

'Touché! So what are you studying, Ross?' Apart from her tranquillising loveliness?

'Physics, I'm afraid.'

'Don't say that!'

'Why not, are you studying Physics as well?' Surely fate hadn't dealt me such a wonderful blessing.

'No way, Physics is for geeks! I'm studying Creative Writing actually.' Fate *had* dealt me a kind hand.

'Oh, that's great. I'm actually taking the "Introduction to Creative Writing" course – I was allowed one free choice away from all the science and maths so I thought I'd do something completely different. I think my first class is on Wednesday.'

'Mine too. We're probably in the same group you know.'

'That would be nice,' I coolly understated. 'So how are you finding it here so far?'

'Pretty good, apart from missing my family and friends. How about you?'

'I just can't get over how beautiful the campus is.'

'I thought British universities were all architecturally grand and steeped in history?'

'Well, maybe Oxford and Cambridge, but Lancaster is steeped in concrete.' She giggled and I momentarily lost myself in her adorable schoolgirl-like innocence. 'Where is home for you then?'

'Actually, Southern California at the moment. Encinitas – a little place on the coast, hence the tan!' She playfully gestured towards her absurdly angelic face.

'Ah, I see.'

She strolled towards the window while admiring the view, allowing me the opportunity to move my gaze to her exquisite body. She was only a little shorter than me in height, with a figure that was in perfect proportion. Her plain white T-shirt feigned indifference as it held her ample breasts, but it couldn't fool me – that cotton blend knew full well that it was the luckiest combination of natural fibres in the entire world. Similarly blasé were the pale denim threads of her jeans – they tried to look casual, but simply couldn't hide their joy as they cupped her firm buttocks.

Her lips then softly opened once more. 'This view is awesome!'

'Tell me about it,' I enthused, with perhaps a little too much conviction. At that point I noticed Jak and Kazuki outside the window and my train of thought was momentarily broken. It was probably for the best, however, as my loose-fitting trousers weren't very forgiving with groinal excitement as I knew from bitter past experience. 'There are my roommates – it looks like they're coming back.'

'Oh cool. Are you making some good friends?'

'Yeah, Jak's great and Kaz is fairly harmless – he's from Japan so Jak and I are teaching him plenty of English phrases. I'm not sure about the rest of the guys on my hall though – they're all called Brad or Chad and seem to be heavily sedated by recreational drugs.'

'Yeah, I thought your hall smelt a bit smoky. Of course, the girls' corridor smells of rose petals and lavender.'

'Of course.'

Our banter was soon interrupted by the arrival of Jak and Kazuki, who duly made their introductions.

'Oh, hi. I'm Jak.'

'And I Kazuki. Can I drink your pussy juice?' Granted, it was rather an ill-timed foray into trying out one of our new phrases.

'Oh, well, nice to meet you both...I'm April,' she managed through her laughter. Not only beautiful in mind and body, but also able to appreciate a juvenile smutty joke – perhaps she really was the perfect woman. 'Well, I'd better be going anyways.'

'OK then, thanks for calling in,' was the more

reasonable alternative to getting down on my knees and begging her to stay. With that, she walked out of our room and left my mind in a state of utter chaos.

'Oh my god, oh my god, what did you think of her?' I demanded of Jak while he nonchalantly carried on with his business as if the world remained unchanged.

'Oh, April? Yeah, she seemed nice.'

'Nice? *Nice?*'

'Well, yeah, she seemed nice. I think I saw her down in reception yesterday.'

'And you didn't think she was the most incredible woman you had ever met?'

'What? Have you been smoking with the Brads and Chads? Dude, you need to get laid before you end up humping some farmyard animal because you thought she looked hot.'

'Farmyard animal?' I couldn't quite comprehend Jak's reaction. Was he trying to save April for himself, or did he really not see this alluring young woman in the same light that I did? I really needed a third opinion. As misguided as it may have been, I asked Kazuki.

'Hey Kaz, this is really important, OK? So I want you to think very long and hard before answering, and feel free to consult your phrase books and dictionaries, OK?'

'OK,' nodded Kazuki keenly, his fingers itching to open his books and begin the research.

'April...' I made a shapely sign with my hands and pointed at the door, '...the girl who was just here. Was she attractive?'

'April a tractor?'

'No, is she *attractive*. You know, was she...' I kissed and cuddled an imaginary April right there in front of me, '...or was she...' I then looked the figure up and down and pulled a face of disgust.

'Aaaaaaah!' A million light bulbs glowed brightly above his head. He then feverishly thumbed through his books to find words that would adequately describe her magnificence.

Jak joined back in as we were awaiting the verdict.

'So you thought she was something special?'

'Er, *yes*!' I exclaimed.

'Well, I guess she's OK. Her looks are a bit plain; she has a fat ass and a flat chest. But other than that, I suppose she was pleasant.'

I was dumbfounded. It had to be a wind up. Kazuki then looked up from his books with a raised finger of success.

'April...is...ordinary,' he proclaimed.

'What?' I begged of him.

His head sank down into his books once more. He spoke slowly, word-by-word, as he read aloud what he had discovered.

'Not special in any way. Un...how you say...un-im-press-ive.'

I was astounded.

'Amazing! Unbelievable!'

'No, I think he said "ordinary",' quipped Jak.

'Was she really ordinary-looking?'

'I'm afraid so, my friend. Still, if you're into her then that's great. You've got to start playing in the Little Leagues before you can get signed up for some Major League action. So get her banged, get it out of your system, then move up to the next level.'

Usually I would have laughed at Jak's comments, perhaps offering a few crude additions of my own. But April was somebody special – so pure and heavenly that I couldn't even think of her in such an animalistic fashion. My only wish was for us to grow old together, sipping homemade lemonade on our porch in the Southern Californian sunshine.

'I'm sorry, man,' said Jak, sensing my unease. 'I'm

sure she's a really nice girl, but are you ready to try for a relationship so soon? I just think that maybe you need a bit of time to sort yourself out before making any big decisions.'

'You know what, Jak, you're absolutely right. I just lost myself there for a moment. Probably a rebound thing.'

'Hey, no sweat, dude, I'll always be here for you.'

'Thanks, thanks a lot.'

'It's my pleasure. Better to get some hitting practise with a few relief pitchers before ramming one down the throat of a starter, if you know what I mean.'

THREE

By Wednesday afternoon my brain was at breaking point. My Physics courses were supposed to be equivalent to those I was due to take back home, but it had become clear that there was a serious mismatch going on and it was most definitely not in my favour. It also appeared that every student in my class was a potential Nobel Prize winner with a flair for brown-nosing. So my courses were tough, the competition was ruthless, and my impeccable university grades up to that point were soon to be a distant memory. For the first time since my arrival, I was longing for life in Lancaster with more manageable lectures and fellow students who really didn't give a shit.

The morning had been a blur of quantum mechanics and thermodynamics, with the only prospect holding me back from a campus-wide killing spree being that of my Creative Writing course. Now that time had arrived, I made my way to Norlin library where the designated classroom was located. All attempts to contain my excitement had failed miserably as I hurriedly climbed the library steps to discover my destiny.

A small group of students were timidly waiting outside the room. A cursory glance revealed no foxy minxes of the April variety, but I did recognise a guy from my residence hall – thankfully not one of the chemically adjusted ones. I felt it my duty to break the silence shrouding the group and make myself known to him.

'Hi!' was my greeting, perhaps a little too loud considering we were in a library. Fifty 'shushes' flew in at me from all angles as I realised we were next to a set of study booths. Twenty-five were probably from my fellow physics students who were frantically working to disprove Einstein's theory of relativity.

I tried again, this time in more hushed tones. 'Hi, it's Brad, isn't it?' I couldn't actually remember his name, but the odds were in my favour.

'Oh, hi Ross,' came the muted response. 'It's Brandon actually. I didn't know you were taking Creative Writing too?'

'Just this one course, unfortunately. It seems the rest of my time will be spent having my arse hole ripped wide open by Physics classes.'

'That bad? I'm majoring in English so this is just part of my normal classes.'

Our whispering was interrupted by the arrival of an unfamiliar man who unlocked the door and soundlessly summoned us in. I guessed that he must be our teacher, although his possession of the door key was the only clue to his identity. He was African-American, probably only a few years older than me, and scruffily dressed in loose jeans and a hooded top that provided shelter to an impressive set of dreadlocks. It was certainly a breath of fresh air compared to the elbow-patched, bespectacled lecturers I had encountered up to that point.

'Afternoon all,' was his welcome in a slow, rasping voice. He pulled down his hood to set free the dreadlocks and reveal a pair of sunglasses that were testament to a past evening of excess. 'Find yourselves a desk and wait for the others to show up. I'm just gonna head to the bathroom and throw up again.' He calmly strolled outside.

Tables lined the walls of the room, with fifteen chairs all focussing inwards towards our esteemed teacher's desk in the centre. Brandon and I sat opposite the door, and by the time everyone else was seated I counted eight empty chairs of hope. Our teacher soon returned.

'Man, thank the lord for my hood – trust me guys, you don't want vomit in your dreads.' Seven innocent heads looked around at each other, not quite sure what to make of it all. He glanced down at a sheet of paper. 'Looks like we're expecting ten.'

I opened my notebook and began dating the first page. Just as my pen had made contact with the paper I heard the heavy wooden door swing open, and I glanced upwards to see two eager male faces. Damn their penises! The likelihood of April joining our group was becoming more remote as the new arrivals settled into their seats.

'OK guys, let's get started then. I'm Kenny Fox, and I'm gonna be your teacher for this intro' to Creative Writing class.' Every word seemed to be inflicting pain within his head as his brow furrowed deeply. 'I'm a grad student in the Creative Writing department here, and my head is pounding like a bitch.'

'We never doubted it,' Brandon whispered in my ear.

'Before we get started, I thought we could introduce ourselves. So if you wanna give your name, where you're from, and then say something *fictional* about yourself. I don't mind starting...so, my name is Kenny, I'm originally from North Carolina, and I struggle to bring women to orgasm.'

Brandon and I laughed raucously while the other

students looked somewhat startled. I definitely liked Kenny's style and could tell that his classes would be the highlight of my week.

He took his seat. 'OK then, let's work our way around the table, starting with you.' His finger was pointing right at me. I wasn't generally a good performer when under pressure, but Kenny's lead inspired confidence.

'Well, my name is Ross, and I'm from England.' Several female voices in the room all cooed appreciatively and my self-assurance swelled even further. I rashly decided it was time to test how well the English sense of humour travelled across the Atlantic. 'At weekends, I enjoy wearing nothing but a silk g-string and a pair of high heels.'

As tumbleweed rolled across the classroom floor, it was clear that the English sense of humour suffered from travel sickness. The female voices now muttered amongst themselves in disgust, while Brandon sniggered and Kenny flashed me a wry smile of consolation.

Mercifully, the door then opened once more and everyone's attention turned to our tenth and final student as she entered apologetically. Oh my god, it was her – it was April. In a moment of panic I frantically looked down towards my notebook, not allowing my eyes the time to unravel my earlier impression of the perfect girl. At least she hadn't just witnessed my mortifying introduction to the group.

'Hi, take a seat,' said Kenny. 'You haven't missed much, just Ross here telling us how he enjoys kinky cross-dressing on weekends.' Oh, shit. 'Don't worry though, we're just introducing ourselves with our name, where we're from, and then something fictional about ourselves. Do you want to go next?'

'Sure! Well, my name is April, and I'm from

Southern California.' My eyes were still firmly facing downwards, but there was no escape from her bewitching dulcet tones. 'I won ten million dollars on the lotto last week.'

Her conservatism sat better with the audience, and the introductions continued around the room in a similarly tame vein. Once everyone had participated, Kenny took charge again.

'OK, we've just had a little bit of creativity from all of you there. Now let's see how well you can write.' He got up out of his chair a little delicately and began wandering around the room. 'I want you to spend fifteen minutes writing about whatever you want. Maybe it's your thoughts on college life so far, or even your thoughts on this class. Whatever it is, just start writing and keep on going. Don't worry too much about form or style for now; just write what comes into your head. I'm going out for a shit, but I'll be back soon.'

On that unnecessary note, fifteen minutes of quiet followed with only the scratching of pen nibs and heads to be heard. I somehow managed to focus on my writing while fending off every agonizing urge to look April's way. It was as if I was in the middle of a glorious dream, and seeing her face would be like waking up to realise that none of it was real. I wrote a cunningly crafted page about my flight over from England – cleverly entwining a murder and a love story. I couldn't wait to read it out loud.

'OK, time's up,' was the gargled call from Kenny, as he frenetically downed a bottle of water in record time. 'Now I don't give a rat's ass what you just wrote – the whole purpose of that exercise was just to get you writing. So screw that bitch up and throw it in the bin.' The no-good bastard. 'However, for the next assignment, I do care what you write cuz you're gonna read them to each other in pairs afterwards. So have another fifteen minutes, and now write about something related to love. Maybe romance, maybe joy, maybe heartbreak...' he looked in my direction, '...or maybe even g-strings and high heels. I really don't give a shit, just write descriptively in any style that you like – prose, poetry, whatever you want, it's up to you.' He paused while clenching his belly in anguish. 'Damn! I shouldn't have drunk that water so fast. I'll be back in a minute.'

This time he rushed to the door while his cheeks gently swelled. He left us with the prospect of another hushed quarter of an hour, and another nine hundred seconds for me to fend off the ever-increasing desire to look at April.

The clock ticked on as if twenty sumo wrestlers were strapped to its hands, resisting its every move. While my stomach knotted tighter with the indecision, my mind moved on to the task in hand. I made the painful journey back to my one brush with love and shared the emotions openly with the page in front of me.

It had only been ten minutes when Kenny returned with water dripping from his face.

'Right, time's up. I know, I know, you didn't really have fifteen minutes, but I like to see raw writing. Now let's get you paired up to read to each other.'

Brandon, the treacherous swine, turned away from me to pair up with the other guy next to him. This set off a domino-like flow of partnering that left two people on opposite sides of the room without partners. One of those people was me, and the other was the very girl I had been trying to avoid, and the very girl whom I really didn't want to read my piece to.

Amongst the hum of conversation I reluctantly walked my notebook over to April's desk, still bowing my head as if the additional two seconds would make all the difference.

'Hey, Ross, are you OK?' she enquired, perhaps a little bemused by my lack of communication thus far and my hunchback approach.

'Oh, not too bad,' I replied pitifully, as I pulled my neck straight and gave a hopelessly artificial expression of pain. 'I just slept a little funny and cricked my neck I think.'

Through squinted eyes I caught my first true glimpse of her since our last meeting. Her brightly glowing expression drowned me in the same emotions I had felt during that encounter, and my pulse raced wildly once more.

'Oooh, looks painful,' was her wonderfully sympathetic response as she rose to join me perched on the edge of her table.

'I think I'll survive.'

'I suppose we'd better get started then.'

'OK, you first.' I desperately needed time to concoct a new piece in my head. After all, the words I had confided in my notebook were never intended for *her* ears.

'All right then, here goes.' She took a breath so deep that she rose up on her tiptoes. It was completely adorable. 'Love is the ultimate joy, love gives us life. Love makes our worlds whole and makes the sun shine through the darkest of clouds. It gladdens our hearts when in the depths of despair, and never fails to restore lost faith. Life gives us love. The ultimate joy is love.'

Her heartfelt words left me speechless. I sat frozen – firmly ensnared by her sentiment and the endearingly hopeful smile that had followed. After a considered pause, I gave my critique.

'That was terrific!'

Her dainty lips turned upwards in appreciation.

'Gee, glad you liked it! Come on then, your turn now,' she eagerly demanded.

In the heat of the moment I didn't have the opportunity to fabricate a new piece, so it was going to have to be improvised. My head bowed to my notes and I prayed that my mind would be magically impregnated with inspirational musings worthy of accompanying her own.

'Love...is a funny thing...' My stumbling introduction wasn't promising. '...it can bring sunshine through dark clouds...' oh shit, that's what she said, '...and light a fiery glow inside the loins...' oh bollocks, '...love....'

'Are you making this up?' she interrupted.

'Could you tell?'

'Yeah, just a little. Why don't you just read what you wrote? Surely it can't be as bad as "fiery loins"!'

Again she was mocking me, but in the most marvellous way. Perhaps I should just go ahead and say the words I had written? It was no time for doubt or hesitation – I just needed to go for it full throttle. Head down in my book, I began.

'L.O.V.E.: four simple letters that ruthlessly conceal a very serious message. L is for the emphatic Loneliness that inevitably follows love. O is for the callous ways that love Obstructs true happiness. V is for the elusive Vaccination that may one day prevent the crippling disease of love. E is for the brutal End to life caused by love.'

It was a little dark, perhaps even a little disturbing, but I was sure that April could handle it. I cautiously raised my head to face the consequences.

'Did you prefer my fiery loins?' I offered.

April wore a look of complete astonishment. 'I...well...it...' She was struggling to find the words.

Kenny broke up our moment of awkwardness. 'All right everyone, back to your seats, let's move on.'

April sat back down in a daze, as I retreated to my desk with the unresolved issue looming large.

'Great work guys, great work. I was listening in to some of your work and I think we've got some real potential here. Hey, April and Ross?' He flashed us each a glance. 'I especially enjoyed your pieces.'

I tried to catch April's eye so that we could bask in the warmth of the compliment together, but her state of bewilderment couldn't be broken. Brandon must have recognised the tension and leant in to pass on his whispered comment.

'Hey Ross, what did you say to that poor girl?'

'Oh, I had to pass on a message from her mum – her dog just died.'

'No wonder she looks so bummed.'

It wasn't the time to be pointing out humour in American English, so I settled for an inward chuckle at Brandon's use of the word "bummed".

Kenny continued, 'OK then class, I wanna finish up this session by reading you a passage from the book I've chosen as our first text – *Master Trojan Warrior* by J C Jenkins. It's a bit different to anything you've probably read before, but I think it holds a message for us all. I want you to read the first three chapters before our two-hour class on Friday. Here's something from later on that'll whet your appetite.

'"The day was unlike any other..."'

I tuned out the story whilst frenziedly contemplating my options. I had left myself completely exposed, revealing a part of me that was never meant to be shared with her. Had I given her the wrong impression? Or maybe the right impression? I really wasn't sure *what* I had just done. What was crystal clear, however, was that I needed to turn things around.

My deliberations were rudely halted as my ears

suddenly found interest in Kenny's story. '"...and he then straddled his gay lover with deep and intimate passion." OK, guys, that's it, so get out of here and I'll see you Friday.'

I had to ask Brandon, 'What on earth was that book about?'

'Oh, just a couple of gay Chinese Monks going at it. Who'd have thought bald guys could be so sexually creative?'

It was a bizarre end to the day, but my mind was only focussed on clearing the air with April. I saw her hurriedly leaving the room and swiftly made my apologies to Brandon.

I rushed to exit the door and found myself in a sea of people leaving the library from adjacent classrooms. I fleetingly spotted April amongst the masses, but she disappeared as I advanced through the crowd. I forlornly made my way out of the building and began the short walk back to my room in solitude. The sun was still shining, but it now appeared a little less bright, while the sky was a little less blue.

It wasn't long after four p.m. when I arrived at my room and the academic day was over. Jak and Kazuki were studying keenly at their desks as I entered.

'Hey, Ross, good day?' enquired Jak.

'Well, it started off badly, got slightly worse, then finished off pretty shit.'

'Sorry to hear that, dude. Hey, it'll get better on Sunday night – I joined the Spanish Club today and they're having a house party. It should be awesome and you're coming with.'

'Maybe. Unless I get a better offer.'

'Yeah, like that's gonna happen. Oh, and I nearly forgot – there's a message for you on the machine.'

I pressed the 'play' button and a slow, whiny,

incredibly annoying female American voice spoke.

'Hey Ross, my name is Kristen Weber and I've been assigned as your buddy by the exchange student office. Anyways, if you wanna meet up, maybe have a coffee or something, then just give me a call on 2-6572. Bye.'

'Jesus Christ!' I reacted. 'How ugly did *she* sound?'

'I know, I thought the exact same thing,' was Jak's reply.

'I think she was struggling to get her words out through the moustache.'

'Are you gonna call her back?'

'Er, I don't know. Possibly. I don't suppose today could get much worse.'

Kazuki abruptly closed his books and got up out of his chair. He then beamed at me, 'No worry! It Wednesday night, so we drink!'

I couldn't fault such impeccable logic, and neither could Jak. Kazuki broke out a bottle of what could well have been Japanese paint stripper, and we each took a single, vile, mouthful.

FOUR

'Well, wish me luck,' I asked of Jak while I tied my shoelaces.

'Dude, I think you'll be needing lots of that.'

'Probably. The question is, will she be ugly of face but with a tidy body, or ugly of body with a tidy face?'

'My money's on ugly both. Have you packed the heavy lifting equipment?'

'Hey, you never know, she might be a slender eight stone.'

'What the hell's a "stone"?'

The language differences were becoming fewer as the days passed, but there was still the odd surprise.

'Oh, sorry, a stone is fourteen pounds.'

'Man, I thought you Brits were all metric now?'

'Not quite – weights are in stones and, more importantly, beer is in pints. Right then, I think I'm ready. I'll see you later.'

And so I left to meet with my "buddy" Kristen. She was supposed to be an 'emergency friend' – an American student designated by the foreign exchange team to meet up with me and offer to talk through how things were going. I didn't feel any nerves; just a slight trepidation at what beastly creature awaited me.

Our meeting place was Farrand Hall. Kristen had told me that the basement room was converted into a coffee lounge on Friday evenings, and there were free drinks and snacks for students. It was only a stone's throw from my own dormitory, so it appeared to be the perfect venue where a quick escape could be easily orchestrated. I soon arrived at the basement entrance and flashed my student card to the guy at the door.

I had wondered what the evening entertainment would be like on a campus where the drinking age was twenty-one and there were many thousands of underage students. I was impressed to find a vast room with sofas and coffee tables, randomly scattered amongst free-flowing non-alcoholic drinks and copious quantities of cookies and buns. Students sat around chatting, reading books, and playing board games. This appeared to be the cultured alternative to life back at Lancaster where students would get lashed at the nine bars on campus and then finish off the evening with a kebab and a fight.

I was wearing a brown short-sleeved shirt as we had arranged, and Kristen was to be wearing a pink T-shirt bearing the word 'Juicy' on the front and 'Babe' on the back. Worst-case scenario, I could always just ask around for the bearded lady and somebody would have undoubtedly pointed me in the right direction. The lights were down low which made the identification parade difficult, but I eventually saw 'Babe' on the back of a pink T-shirt at one of the coffee urns. Initial impressions were favourable, but this was only from behind. Her blonde hair was resting atop her cropped T-shirt, which teasingly revealed the small of her back above a cute silver skirt. I sidled up alongside her and poured myself a coffee while she looked at a basket of sweet delights.

'Those buns looks tasty,' I commented innocently in her direction.

'You bastard!' came the reply, somewhat louder than I had been prepared for. She swiftly turned with the look of a lion about to tear the stripy flesh off an innocent zebra.

'Woa, woa!' I pleaded, rather shell-shocked, 'I'm Ross, I'm Ross!'

Her angered face unfurled slightly as she barely apologised, 'Oh, Ross, sorry, I'm Kristen.' She was vaguely attractive and her accent wasn't quite as bad in person either.

'Well, it's nice to meet *you* too! What's with the hostile reception?'

'Well that's how I normally react when a guy gives me such a vulgar compliment.'

'But all I said was...oh, wait...you call them "muffins", don't you?' I pointed towards the buns in the basket.

'Aaaaah!' came the knowing reply as she finally softened.

It really wasn't the best of introductions, but I'd rather be savaged by a semi-attractive Kristen than kissed by a bearded one. With the violent greetings out of the way, and my false image of her blown out of the water, we collected our drinks and "muffins" and found an empty sofa. The atmosphere was still a little awkward, so I attempted to break the ice.

'Would you like to nibble on my buns?' I asked cheekily.

'Maybe later, if you're lucky,' she replied, indicating that the thaw was well under way.

'So what made you volunteer to be one of these "buddies"?'

'Well I'm gonna be studying in Spain next year, and figured I'd like to have a friendly face to talk to when I'm over there, so I'm happy to do that for someone here.'

'Well, that's very kind of you.'

We paused for a drink and a nibble, of the muffins, and I had time to admire her with a little more thought. Her face was fairly attractive, with a cute little nose and a bright smile. Her body wasn't catwalk-model slim, but I certainly found the tight T-shirt and short skirt quite tantalising. As I placed my cup on the table in front of us, I sneaked a look at her midriff and caught sight of a tiny heart tattoo and a belly-button ring. This girl's dress sense was confident and rather provocative.

'I like your belly-button ring,' I commented, possibly a little inappropriately.

'Oh thanks. There's more where that came from.' Her wink told me that nothing was going to be inappropriate. I couldn't let the subject change.

'Oh yes, I see your ears are pierced too,' was my deliberately naive follow-up.

'*And* my clit, if that's what you were wondering?'

I was a little flustered by her openness, but enjoying the blatant flirting nevertheless.

'It never even crossed my mind!'

She changed the subject with a wry smile. 'So what's the strangest thing about American life so far then?'

'Hmmm. Well, this may sound a bit weird, but it's the toilets I'm struggling to get used to.'

'How do you mean? A toilet is bound to be the same anywhere in the world.'

'You'd think so, wouldn't you? You Americans don't seem to worry about privacy though. Your cubicle doors have huge gaps down the side that you can see out of while you're sat there – it's really quite distracting. Didn't anyone ever think to overlap the door with the frame so you couldn't see through?'

'I can't say I'd ever thought about it, to be honest. It's quite cool when you can watch people having sex in a cubicle though.' Now she really was teasing me.

'Well, I'd maybe enjoy watching a little lesbian sex in the ladies toilets, but I really don't want to know what goes on in the gents. It's not just the doors though; I mean your water levels are all wrong too. When you sit down your arse hairs are practically dipping in the water it's so high.'

'Well, firstly I don't have a hairy ass, and secondly I think you'll find that it reduces splashing.'

'Fair enough, but splashing is the least of your worries when your turds bob back out of the water and scrape your bum cheeks.'

'This is a really disgusting conversation, you know?' Her laughter indicated that she was enjoying our candid discussion as much as I was.

'Oh, sorry, let's get back to talking about your piercings then.'

'No way! Tell me what you like to do for fun, and *try* not to be rude.'

'OK, OK. Well, I enjoy running.'

'Oh yeah, how long have you been doing that for?'

'Well I've been running seriously for the last couple of years now.'

'Wow, so do you do long distances then?'

'Yeah, I usually run about ten miles at the weekend, and shorter distances during the week. I never race or anything, I just enjoy being out there on my own. I like to get outside, enjoy the fresh air, clear my head, that sort of thing.'

'That sounds awesome. So are you going out tomorrow then?'

'Yeah, but probably just for four miles or so – I'm really not used to the altitude yet.'

'Well, would you mind if I joined you? I normally run on the treadmill in the gym, but it would be nice to have some company.'

'Sure, that sounds great.'

We continued chatting at length, interspersing deeper subjects like US politics with rather crude and transparent flirtations. Although we were supposed to be meeting as friends, it did almost seem like we were on some kind of date. Kristen wasn't as stunningly beautiful as April, and she certainly didn't send my head in a spin in the same way, but she was extremely sexy and we were getting on well. Maybe things could develop into the sort of relationship I really needed? After all, the way April had ignored me since that Wednesday pretty much indicated nothing would ever happen between us. Kristen was an ideal opportunity for me to try to get April out of my system.

Time passed effortlessly, and it was soon time for the lounge to close its doors. We finished our fourth cups of coffee and made our way out into the warm evening air. Kristen's hall was on the other side of campus, so I walked with her while we continued our conversation.

'So, I'm gonna see you again tomorrow then?' she asked hopefully.

'The run, of course, looking forward to it.'

'I'll come round to your dorm if that's OK?'

'Sure, outside Cheyenne Arapaho at around six p.m.? It's better to go in the early evening while it's still light but not as hot.'

'OK, Chey-Ho at six it is.'

With the plans made, it wasn't long before we arrived at her room. I had feared an awkward moment where I didn't know whether to kiss her on the cheek, hug her, shake her hand, or ravish her madly. In the end she dashed through the door before I could do anything.

'See you tomorrow!' she called as the door shut

behind her.

'Bye!' I said to the closed door.

It was almost midnight when I arrived back at my room. Kazuki was fast asleep, but Jak was still in the study room, deep in his homework.

'Thank god you're back,' said Jak. 'I thought she'd swallowed you whole! Was she a real beast like we thought?'

'Well, *there's* a funny story...'

'Dude, you mean she was hot? Was she hot? Tell me she wasn't hot. Oh my god, she *was* hot!'

'All I'm saying is that she has a heart shaped tattoo that I have seen, and a piercing that I hope to see.'

'Dude, you lucky bastard! Shit, I think *I* need to pretend to be a foreign student – that's the only way I'm ever gonna get laid.'

'No, the only way you'll ever get laid is if you stop doing homework on a Friday night.'

'You might be right, Ross, you might be right.'

'Of course I'm right. I don't really blame you though. I've got shit loads of homework too, but I figure that my grades are going to hell anyway so I may as well try and enjoy myself.'

'Man, why didn't we study an arts subject? Those guys have half the classes that we do, and practically no homework. I guess we're too smart for arts classes though.'

'When you put it like that, it sounds like we're too stupid.'

'Anyway, tell me about this Kristen. What's she like?'

'Well, she's not as good-looking as April...'

'You've really got to forget about that chick, man. She goes all funny on you in that class on Wednesday and then completely ignores you since – you don't need that shit; trust me. And, for the last time, she's really *not* that good-looking.'

'OK, OK, well Kristen is just sexy as hell.'

'Big boobs? Large titties? Enormous jugs? Juicy nips?'

'Would you settle down! She just has a really sexy body and flirts constantly. I tell you, I was almost busting out of my undercrackers by the end of the night. We're going for a run together tomorrow night.'

'Aw, I like your style man. Get her all hot and sweaty – you know chicks love that.'

'I'll have to take your word for it.'

That Saturday, Kristen introduced me to a running route I had yet to explore. It took us off campus and out towards the Flatirons – the distinctively angled rock faces that overlooked the city from the edge of the Rocky Mountains. After a couple of miles, we reached Chautauqua Park from where a meadow trail would lead us right into the foothills. We found ourselves completely alone as we paused for breath in the still considerable heat, admiring the hills and Boulder from afar.

'Wow, this place is incredible,' I enthused.

'I know,' agreed Kristen. 'I normally just walk up here, but it's nice to get here a bit quicker. Can you see the letters "C.U." that have been written on the face of that one Flatiron? The local students go climbing and write it on there.'

I looked high into the early evening sunshine and saw the chalked letters.

'That's cool; I'd never noticed that before. Why isn't it U.C. for the University of Colorado then?'

'I don't know, everyone just seems to call it C.U.' She now pointed further south down the range. 'And can you see the rock down there that looks like a penis?'

'Oh my god, yes. These local students *are* busy then, aren't they – climbing, writing, and carving phallic symbols out of the rocks.'

'I think that one was nature's doing, actually.'

I gestured to the north of the range. 'Well, who made that huge pair of tits down there then?'

'I'm not falling for that!'

'Spoil sport.'

We had picked up right where we left off the previous evening – enjoying each other's company and flirting outrageously. Kristen's figure was inviting, with her tight Lycra shorts and sports bra leaving very little to my highly active imagination. She made no attempt to hide her bodily imperfections, but carried it off with a very attractive confidence.

'So, shall we head up into the hills?' she asked.

'Yeah, I'll race you,' I said, marginally before I began sprinting up the trail.

'Hey, that's cheating!' was her distant response as she tried to catch up.

We were soon in the midst of trees and rocks, and continuing to run became impossible. We slowed to a gentle hike through the undergrowth, not really knowing where it would lead but enjoying the shade nonetheless. Not a word was spoken as we basked in the natural beauty and walked ever higher. I offered my hand to Kristen as we climbed one particularly steep path, and our hands somehow remained connected even after the route had levelled out.

Yet again our encounter had evolved into something resembling a date, as our bodies gravitated ever closer. While there was no doubting how my penis felt about the whole situation, things were a little less clear in my mind. Even there, in the great outdoors with a voluptuous half-naked girl whom I liked, April was on my mind.

While advancing upwards, we stumbled upon a small level clearing that was lush with grass. It was as if the geological events of millions of years ago had taken place purely to create that opening for us to enjoy. While still gripping my hand, Kristen playfully threw herself down onto the perfect lawn and pulled me on top of her. Our bodies sandwiched together tightly and our lips were within millimetres of connecting.

'What are we doing?' I thought out loud.

'Enjoying ourselves, just relax,' she whispered.

My hands had naturally fallen around her waist, and her skin was delightfully soft to the touch. She wrapped her arms firmly around my buttocks and pulled me even closer. There was no hiding the excitement that was exploding proudly from my running shorts.

'So, shall we make use of that hard thing pushing against my leg?' she propositioned.

Our lips were now within a hair's breadth of satisfying their desire. It took every ounce of my will power to resist giving in to their lustful needs.

'Well...' I stuttered, 'I'd love to, I really would...oh my god I *really* would, but...'

'But what?' she softly reasoned. 'We both want it, so why deprive ourselves?'

Our chests thrust back and forth with their heavy breathing.

'But, it would just be sex. Probably the best fucking sex of my life, but nevertheless, just sex.'

'I know. It would be no-strings-attached, raw sex. Do you have a problem with that?' she demanded with a wicked smile.

They were the words every man dreams of hearing. Even if they had been spoken by a toothless eighty-year-old grandmother with tits down to her ankles I would have been aroused. As it was, I was outdoors in the fresh air of the Rocky Mountains, with the late summer sunshine falling on my exposed skin, and a highly sexed young temptress underneath me. It was time for a mental cold shower. I tried frantically to imagine my prime minister taking her president roughly from behind. It took a little while, and the mental scars would last for eternity, but it bought me a little time.

I then attempted a different approach. She may have turned out to be the filthy siren of my dreams, but I still wagered that deep down she was a sensible girl who didn't want my unquestionably fertile sperm getting her pregnant.

'But...but...we don't have any protection.' I felt sure that this bombshell would halt proceedings. She relaxed her vice-like grip from my left buttock and fumbled around the front of her sports bra.

'Not a problem,' she declared while revealing the condom she had been holding with her right breast. You had to marvel at her incredible foresight.

I giggled nervously. 'Well, that's a relief. Since we set off I'd been thinking you had one bloody huge nipple there.'

'Just shut up and kiss me.'

I had exhausted all reasonable avenues of resistance. The situation was perfect – exactly what I had wanted ever since I had landed in the country. So why couldn't I follow up my words with actions? The grim realisation then struck me – this really *wasn't* the kind of man I was. I couldn't just have sex with women I had no feelings for – not then, not ever. And I certainly couldn't have sex with Kristen when my heart was aching to be with someone else.

I rolled off Kristen's taut body and lay next to her. We both looked skyward while our panting subsided and our sexual excitations ebbed away. The burden had been lifted, and I felt wonderfully liberated.

Kristen broke the silence.

'You know, most girls would take that personally.'

'Listen, I'm truly sorry. You are amazing, probably the sexiest woman I have ever known.'

'But?'

'This just isn't the sort of man I am. You're funny, we get along really well, and we enjoy flirting together, but we don't *love* each other.'

She turned to hug me, indicating that she understood my feelings and didn't begrudge my morals.

'So, who is she then?'

FIVE

'YOU SAID WHAT?' Jak yelled at me in astonishment.

'Well, I just realised that I wasn't that kind of man.'

'ARE YOU OUT OF YOUR FUCKING MIND? *OF COURSE* YOU'RE THAT KIND OF MAN. WE'RE *ALL* THAT KIND OF MAN!'

He was clearly having trouble getting to grips with my account of events in the foothills.

'I know, I *thought* I was that kind of man, but trust me, when you're faced with that situation you really find out exactly who you are.'

'Man, if I had a face full of flaring pussy, I just know my morals would be going to the trash.'

I could only laugh at Jak's unique turn of phrase.

'Jak, just calm yourself down. Now hurry up or we'll be late. We've got to be at the radio station for eight.'

Eight to ten p.m. on Saturday nights was to be my weekly slot on KVCU, the campus radio station. It was slightly more prestigious than the two to four a.m. show I had during my first year at Lancaster, but if that experience was anything to go by then listeners would be thin on the ground at any time of day. I'd had my training on the equipment earlier in the week, and my 1980s British pop CDs were at the ready. Despite the lack of listeners and the lousy hours, I really enjoyed student radio. It was a great chance to unwind, play my favourite tunes and talk about nothing in particular. I had asked Jak to join me for the first show to see if we could strike up some kind of double act.

'So are you gonna let me play some of my music?' Jak asked while I waited for him to get changed.

'Of course. We just have to play a disclaimer first, warning of all the bad language.'

Jak was a big fan of gangsta rap. Being white and from Idaho, I never quite figured out where the obsession came from, but I suspected it had something to do with the plentiful references to 'bitches' and 'hoes'.

'Can I play *Pussy Ain't Shit?*'

'Yes, Jak, you can play anything you like.'

'Awesome, this is gonna be awesome!'

The radio station was in the basement of the UMC – the University Memorial Centre – a bit of a bizarre multi-use building including a bank, bookshop, bowling alley, and food court. The small reception room of the station was walled with shelves of tightly packed records and CDs. A fragile-looking table held a music system tuned to the station's frequency, and we arrived just in time to hear the previous show signing off.

'And that was *Mystic River of my Dreams* by the Moondancers,' came the brusque female voice from the speakers. 'Well, I'll leave you with my final track, but you'll have to guess what it is and I'll reveal all next week. Goodnight C.U., see you next week.' And with that, all we could hear was static. However, KVCU was only on medium wave so perhaps the aerial was just a bit dodgy. We thought nothing more of it, and waited for the DJ to exit the windowless studio room so we could get set up.

When she did emerge, it was clear that she was a hippy with a hygiene problem. The buzz from the stereo was replaced by the hum of her dreadlocks as she made her way past us.

'Later guys, have a good show,' she offered as she exited the station without looking back.

Jak and I glanced hesitantly at each other, neither of us wanting to discover the foul stench that awaited us in that sealed booth.

'You first, Ross, you're the DJ.'

'Oh, thanks,'

As I entered, it appeared that most of her odour must have been firmly encrusted on her body – mercifully it was probably many months since it had been in liquid form and able to absorb into furniture. We both let out a sigh of relief and settled into our chairs. Putting on our headphones, it became clear that the 'static' we had heard outside was, in fact, supposed to be a song.

'What's this crap?' asked Jak.

I looked around and found the CD sleeve.

'Just a minute...' I flicked the switch that made my microphone live, and slightly faded down the music. 'If anyone is still listening to this utter shite, I'll put you out of your misery right now and tell you that it's from a new CD called *Wilderness Chanting Instrumentals Volume Two*. The first person to come down to the station reception in the UMC can take home their own personal copy! Just collect it from the rubbish bin in reception.' The studio door suddenly flew open, and I quickly muted my mike and faded the "music" back up. Oh shit, she was back, and she surely must have heard what I had just said.

'I forgot my coat,' she stated through gritted teeth,

whilst picking up a multicoloured pile of fabric from the corner of the room and shooting me a deadly glance that was distinctly lacking in peace and love.

Jak turned to the wall to hide his laughter, while I smiled politely until she left the room and the door swung tightly shut behind her.

I shared my relief with Jak. 'Bollocks, I thought she was going to wrestle me to the ground there!'

'Very smooth, Ross, very smooth.'

'Hey, pass me one of your classics. I think we need something hard hitting to kick us off.'

'With pleasure dude, with pleasure. Set up track six.'

I cued up the disclaimer on the tape machine, and prepared track six of Jak's CD. I was finally ready to get that crap off the air and start the show properly. I cut the 'song' dead and switched on our microphones.

'Welcome to KVCU at eight o'clock on this warm and moist Saturday evening! I'm Ross Cooper...'

'...and I'm Jumpin' Jak Arriaga...'

'...and we'll be with you for the next two hours with the perfect antidote to whatever that last crazy chick was playing you.'

I activated the disclaimer and switched off our mikes.

I shook my head sorrowfully in Jak's direction. '"Jumpin' Jak"? What *were* you thinking?'

'Sorry dude, I don't know what came over me.'

The disclaimer finished it's warning of impending naughtiness, and I hit the play button on the CD machine. After a few brief and heavy beats, the chorus of *Pussy Ain't Shit* kicked in.

'So this is the famous song then, eh Jak?'

'Aw yeyah!' It seemed that Jak had temporarily transformed into a gangsta. 'Just listen to the words man, it's a lyrical master class!'

Jak rapped along to himself whilst waving his arms wildly. As the song came to a close, I kicked off our discussion live on air.

'So that was *Pussy Ain't Shit* by Funkdoobiest. A veritable master class in lyric writing according to our very own Jumpin' Jak.'

'Too right,' agreed Jak. 'Show me any other track that rhymes "pulsating" with "masturbating" – I tell you, it's breathtaking.'

'Yes, and don't forget "diaphragm" with "frying pan". But I think the real Einstein moment must have come in the recording studio when they realised that "Funkdoobiest" actually rhymed with "uterus". That's sheer creative genius, right there.'

The time flew by as we played an unconventional mixture of 1980s pop and gangsta rap. Our distaste for each other's musical selection provided fertile ground for frivolous discussion, and it soon became clear that Jak would be a permanent fixture on my sixteen weekly shows up until Christmas.

'Hey, Ross, why don't we run that competition for our last half hour?' Jak was referring to the instructions we found on the mixer desk indicating that we had some free CDs to give away on the show.

'Well, I'm estimating that our listenership is ten, at best. And most of those people are probably picking us up involuntarily via the metal plates inserted in their skulls. But what the hell, let's give it a try.'

I gently faded down *The Reflex* by Duran Duran and then courted our lucky listeners with an overly ironic voice.

'So, you're probably sitting there wondering where on god's green earth you can get hold of a copy of the new CD by The Flying Muffters.'

'Who *exactly* are The Flying Muffters then, Ross?' Jak was playing the script perfectly.

'Well, I'm glad you asked that, Jumpin' Jak,

because The Flying Muffters are the hottest new rock band from our kind and generous sponsors over at Bedraggled Records.'

'Oh shit, *that's* The Flying Muffters? Fuck me, I've been waiting to get hold of that CD for months!'

Jak's sudden expletive-laden improvisation caught me a little unawares.

'Well,' I stumbled on apprehensively, 'wait no more! The first lucky caller to answer a simple general knowledge question will be the blessed recipient of that very CD. It really is that simple, so just call in now on 2-5822!'

We had made the pitch, now for the waiting game. I played the next song and carried on chatting with Jak.

'You know if we do get a call, it will probably be from an irate record label executive having a go at us for swearing during his promotion.'

'Chill man, chill.'

We spent the next three minutes and twenty seconds staring at the telephone and waiting for its red indicator to begin flashing. Needless to say, it didn't.

'Well, just a reminder about our competition,' I offered once more. 'Just call us now on 2-5822 for the chance to win the fantastic new CD by The Flying Muffters!'

Four minutes and three seconds passed without a call.

'OK then, we're fighting through all the calls that have been flooding in, but you still might be lucky if you pick up the phone right now and dial 2-5822!'

Nothing.

'Look, I'll level with you here. We don't even really have to ask you a question, so don't let that put you off. Just call us on 2-5822, now!'

Another song passed by.

'OK, OK, I'll cut the bullshit. The CD is pretty crap, but it's free. And all you need to do is pick up that fucking phone and dial 2-5-8-2-2. So what are you waiting for? As an extra special bonus I'll even bring the disc right to your door, anywhere on campus, straight after the show. So come on, *please call us!*'

I sought Jak's opinion as the next track played. 'Did that sound a bit too desperate?'

'Nah, don't worry, man, you lost your self-respect a long time ago. We've only got ten minutes left anyway so let's just give up on it.'

'I tried not to get my hopes up, but a little piece of me secretly hoped that we had thousands of people listening to us out there.'

'Let it go, Ross, just let it go.'

At that moment the studio abruptly glowed with a gorgeous redness that threw our mouths wide open in amazement.

I looked skyward like a born-again Christian and cried out, 'Praise the Lord!'

My hand moved delicately towards the phone, not wanting a rushed move to cause it to cut off our valued listener. I removed my headphones and gingerly raised the receiver to my ear, savouring every single joyous moment.

'Hello, KVCU?'

A female voice replied, 'Oh, hi, I'm calling to put you poor guys out of your misery.' She sounded vaguely familiar, but I couldn't quite place her.

I continued tentatively, trying to charm the lady with my English accent. 'Well thank you so much, you are too kind.'

'No problem, but first of all you have to answer a general knowledge question for *me*, OK?'

I looked quizzically at Jak, but he couldn't hear her side of the conversation.

'Well, OK then, I suppose. You American listeners are very demanding, you know.'

'OK, if you can answer this simple question then I have won the CD. Are you ready?'

'As I'll ever be.'

'Right, what do the letters L.O.V.E. stand for?'

Holy fuck, it was April. I pressed the mute button and animatedly told Jak.

'It's April, it's April, it's April!'

The receiver spoke once more, 'Are you still there?'

I pressed mute again. 'Hi April. Yes, I'm still here.'

'Look, you don't really have to answer that question. This is just my lame attempt to apologise for freaking out on you this week.'

'I'm really sorry if you were...well, a little shocked by what I wrote. Things haven't been too good for me in the past and...'

'You don't have to explain. I don't know what my problem was, really I don't. I mean it was only a little creative writing exercise, after all.'

'Exactly, exactly. I'm sorry if I upset you though.'

'Let's just forget about it, OK? I kind of had this sense that we could become good friends, and I really don't want to stop that from happening.'

'I had exactly the same sense.'

'Well great, OK then. Now, how about that CD?'

'Consider it yours! Shall I bring it to you?'

'Tonight's not really good, but how about Sunday night? You could come up to my room, meet my roommate and hang out for a while?'

'That sounds good.' It sounded incredible.

Sitting back in my chair, I closed my eyes and silently revelled in the world of possibilities that had just opened up before me.

In a quest to expend some of my nervous energy on

that Sunday afternoon, I found myself making the short journey down the hallway to Brandon's room. During Friday's writing class we had pledged to play a game of table tennis, after I had regaled him with captivating tails of my stunning victories in division seven of the Lancaster Thursday night league. Now seemed like the perfect time to brush up on my skills.

Working my way down the corridor, my progress was slowed by a huge hulk of a man whose arms were flailing about his body, rap style. His shaven black head was bouncing up and down as if listening to one of Jak's CDs, but there was no music within earshot and no headphones in sight. While we approached each other I could only hear a mild humming along to the tune in his head, while his huge smile indicated there was no cause for concern. However, as our paths neared and his glance rose to meet mine, the humming intensified and his face unexpectedly assumed a look of fierce graveness.

'Afternoon!' I cheerily acknowledged.

The humming strengthened further until he was within inches of passing and his lips finally opened.

'...boom, boom...I fucked yo' momma up the asshole...boom, boom...'

It was over as quickly as it began, as I looked back to see his goliath figure bobbing and humming as before. Slightly startled, I carried on to Brandon's room, where I found him with the door open, sat at his desk.

'I think a big black man just fucked my mum up the arse.'

'Oh, you saw the Hall Rapper?' he asked with excitement, rushing to join me at the door. 'I've heard legends about that guy.'

A glance down the hall revealed no sign of the mysterious musician. 'He's...he's gone.'

'Damn. So what are you up to anyway, Ross?'

I hesitantly moved on. 'Well, I just wondered if you fancied a game of table tennis?'

'Ping-pong? Sure!'

'No, not "ping-pong". That makes it sound girly. "Table tennis" is much more masculine.'

'Whatever you say, whatever you say! Let's go then, I'll just get my paddle.'

'It's a *bat*, for Christ's sake. We're not going in a boat.'

'Wow, you British sure are serious about your ping-pong!'

We were soon in Cheyenne Arapaho's games room where our manly joust would be fought. I analysed the layout of the room and judged that there was just enough elbowroom for my rasping forehand smash, and barely sufficient height for my formidable topspin recovery lob. Brandon became excited when he saw the red balls I had brought for us to play with.

'Wow, nice balls! So you British play with these so you can see them in the snow?' he laughed.

My game face was firmly in place. 'No, we use them because they don't discolour with the blood of our opponents.'

'Oh, er, right.'

'Shall we play?'

Brandon wore a look of apprehension as I served the ball over the net. It soon became clear that his previous boast of "Yeah, I've been playing ping-pong for years" actually translated to "I've played it once...with my two-year-old sister...and we used frying pans for bats". My uniquely engineered rubbers justified their price tags with accurately glided forehand strokes and wickedly spun backhand shots, while Brandon's two dollar "paddle" bore scars that were testament to the strength of my smash and the speed of his face-protecting reactions.

It didn't take long for him to beg for mercy, and I soon switched to playing left handed which evened up the game considerably. As we timidly tapped the ball back and forth, my thoughts turned to April once more.

'I'm going to see April later.'

'Oh, the chick from our writing class?'

'Yeah. What do you think of her?'

'She's OK, I suppose.'

There it was again, I could hardly believe my ears.

'Everyone keeps saying that she's "OK", but I think she's amazing.'

'I'll let you in on a little secret, Ross. Your true soul mate in this life is the one who appears perfect through *your* eyes. Screw what anyone else may think.'

I took a few shots in silence while I digested what Brandon had shared. I hadn't necessarily been seeking approval for my interest in April, but I had been concerned that nobody else could see her as the incredible young woman that she clearly was to me.

'I suppose you're right,' I tentatively agreed.

'Of course I'm right. Look, man, you should see this as a blessing. I mean, if nobody else finds her that special then at least you'll have no competition.'

'Another very good point.'

'Just don't end up in the "friend zone" or you'll have no chance of getting laid.'

'But all my previous relationships have been built on good friendships.'

'Yeah, but they all obviously fell apart in the end, didn't they? So, why get to know each other as friends when you can get to know each other on dates with the chance of some action too?'

'I hear what you're saying, but I really hate that whole American dating thing. Asking someone on a date is like setting up a bloody job interview. Then if you pass the interview, what's your reward? More and more interviews until you finally decide whether you actually want to be boyfriend and girlfriend. It sounds like a lot of hard work to me. What's the point?'

'The point *is* that you're in America now and you're interested in an American girl. That's the way the game is played over here, and April has home field advantage.'

I hadn't been prepared to play the whole dating game. My only intention was to spend time with April so that we could get to know each other better, but Brandon had me doubting my approach.

'So, what you're basically saying is that if I don't ask her out on a date we'll only ever be friends?'

'Exactly.'

'But I've never asked anyone out on a date before.'

'Time to start learning then.'

In my frustration, I switched the bat back to my right hand and let rip a ferocious swing.

'Oh, shit,' I yelled at the prospect of asking April out on a date. 'OH SHIT!' I yelled again as the bat slipped from my grasp and headed violently for my face.

SIX

I knew full well that I looked a million dollars in my best trousers and favourite shirt. If Brandon's wisdom turned out to be true, then it was no time for conservatism. I had to state my intentions clearly and dress to impress.

I took a deep breath as my trembling hand moved hesitantly towards the door. It clenched clammily into a timid fist and gently knocked. After an unfeasibly long wait, of what must have been at least five seconds, the handle began to turn and light streamed forth through the ever-increasing crack between the solid oak barrier and its frame. A small, imp-like figure looked me up and down and began laughing heartily.

'Lime green! With brown! Wow, you must be the British guy!'

It wasn't the reception I had been hoping for. I then heard a more friendly voice in the distance.

'Hey Laura, let the poor guy in!'

The door opened wide to reveal a welcoming bed against the far wall, with April sat at its foot. The bed appeared to be raised off the ground by building blocks, and April's feet swayed playfully above the ground.

'Hey Ross, I'm glad you came,' she beamed.

'I wish I could say the same,' I remarked light-heartedly as I looked at Laura.

'Sorry Ross! I'm Laura – April's roommate.' She was one of the shortest girls I had ever met, with a rather cute smile set-off beautifully against her Asian skin. It was just a shame she had an eye for colour co-ordination that apparently eluded me.

'Hi, pleased to meet you.' I gestured towards my finery, 'Do these colours not match?'

Laura continued to laugh. 'Are you kidding?'

'Hey, leave him alone!' defended April.

'Well, I'm glad that *you* like what I'm wearing,' I said with a wry smile.

'Well, I wouldn't say I *liked* it. It *is* brown and bright green after all.' April now began giggling with her roommate as I absorbed the humiliation with uncharacteristic cool.

'You know, I only dressed like this to break the ice.'

'Whatever you say, Ross!' replied Laura through the tears. 'Anyway, I've got to head out for a while so I'll see you guys later.'

She swiftly left the room and pulled the door shut behind her. April's chuckling subsided as she invited me to sit on Laura's bed against the room's left wall. I looked around to admire the various pink and girly trinkets adorning the walls and shelves, unaware that April was looking intently at my face.

'Oh my god,' she exclaimed. 'What happened to your eye?'

By now my right eye was swelling nicely as a result of my wayward table tennis bat.

'Just a sporting injury.'

'Oh, right. Football? Basketball? Hockey?'

'Er, table tennis actually.'

She laughed at me again, and for quite a sustained period of time. 'Oh, ping-pong is a very dangerous game!' She leant down to the portable fridge beneath her bed, removed an ice pack and threw it over to me. 'Here, it looks sore – use this.'

I dabbed the soothing pack against my eye.

'Does this thing soothe bruised egos too?'

'I think you've handled yourself well enough, Ross Cooper. You British guys obviously have pretty thick skin.'

'Thick, but fairly pale – unlike you Californian girls. So tell me about your home in Encinitas then. What's it like there?'

She talked at length about her life back in Southern California – her town, her family, her two dogs, her three cats, her friends. She spoke with an uncommon liveliness that made it a real pleasure to listen.

'...I love it *here* too, but I do miss my pets and my family so much. Even my annoying brother.'

'Yes, I can appreciate that,' I agreed. 'I've got one older brother and my parents back home.'

'Don't you find it difficult to be so far away? I mean, I'll be flying home at Christmas, but I guess you can't even do that?'

'No, I won't be returning until my year here is over, but I really haven't let it bother me so far.'

'I think you're really brave to come all the way out here on your own.'

'Especially when I get laughed at so much and nobody even listens to my radio show.'

'Ha! Hey, that reminds me – where's my CD?'

'Oh, I forgot to bring it back for you, sorry. Trust me though, you really didn't want it.'

'How could you forget?' she asked with mock hurt.

'Well, after I put down the phone to you we had the station controller walk in and have a bit of a go at us. Apparently we're not allowed to swear on air, and we're not allowed to play whatever music we want – they have this "playlist" that we have to pick five tracks from every hour.'

'And how many *did* you play?'

'None. They were all so bad and I really didn't think anyone would bother to see if we stuck to the rules or not.'

'Well apparently they do.'

'Yes, it would appear so. And as our reward we've been moved to two a.m. on Monday nights.'

'Ouch.'

'So does that mean we've lost our one and only listener?'

'I'm not making any promises.'

We smiled together and shared a rather lengthy pause, but without even a hint of awkwardness in the air. April delicately swept her lengthy auburn locks behind her ears while I lowered the ice pack from my face to allow a better view. I could see the deepening dimples at the edges of her mouth as they threatened to swallow me whole, while her emerald green eyes were twinkling brilliantly.

Our wordless conversation was then rudely interrupted by a sharp knock at the door. April ignored the intrusion and held my gaze. I felt a sudden surge of electricity run through my body, although on reflection it was probably just the static from my trousers.

'Come in,' called April to the intruder, finally looking towards the door as it opened.

'Oh, hi, April!' came the reply from an attractive female figure, albeit with small breasts and short boyish hair. 'Did you slap him for his dress sense?' asked the flat chest with one nipple pointing to my swelling eye while the other was directed towards the ice pack in my hand.

April summarised the whole situation very succinctly: 'No, he's British.'

'Oh, right. So what's going on with you two then? Are you about to fuck or something?'

My word, this girl didn't pull her punches.

'No, we've just finished actually,' replied April with a deadpan look.

'Do you have any cigarettes?' I helpfully chipped in.

'Hah, nice!' spoke the tiny tits, not buying our charade for a second. 'I was just looking for Laura anyway. I'll pop back later.'

The door clicked firmly shut once more.

'Nicely handled,' I complimented April.

'Thanks. I'm sorry I didn't introduce you, but I only know her as "Doggy Style" and I could hardly introduce her as that! She's in the room next door, but all I know about her is that her roommate walked in on her with this guy once, in a certain position, and hence the nickname.'

'I see.'

I resumed my silent admiration, wondering if I had imagined the brief moment we shared before Doggy Style had entered the room. There was then a most unexpected development, not even foreseen in my wildest and wettest dreams. April's dancing vocal chords conjured up the following, magical words: 'Take your top off.'

Zero to six inches in less than a second – it was a truly remarkable, world-speed-record-breaking erection that followed. Unfortunately, the rush of blood to my groin had left my brain ill-equipped to respond with a coherent sentence.

'Oh, er...what...I mean...'

'Hey, relax!' she laughed. 'I only mean for a massage!'

And that was supposed to calm me down?

'Well...I...er...how...you know...' Beads of sweat must have been cascading down my forehead by this point.

'*For your neck*! In our writing class you said you cricked your neck – as I'm a trained masseuse I thought maybe I could give you a quick neck massage. Don't be so shy!'

In all of my life, one simple little white lie had never brought me such astounding benefits. I resolved to find the person who first declared that honesty was the best policy and laugh in his naive face.

'Oh, my neck, yes! Well, it has been better over the last few days, but maybe it *is* still a little bit stiff. A trained masseuse, eh?'

'I'm full of surprises,' she added mischievously.

I removed my lime green shirt and laid it across my lap, concealing the swelling from my other stiffness. April sat alongside me on the bed, directing me around until my back was leaning towards her and my legs were stretched along the mattress.

She rested a pillow against my lower back and quietly instructed me to close my eyes. I then heard a squirt of liquid that had me briefly wondering if I had lost all control of myself, until she added, 'I'll just use some lavender oil – it's good for stress relief.'

Her warm, soft hands worked their soothing way around my neck and shoulders, while the calming aroma of the oil slowed my heartbeat and cooled my excitations. I mused that "April Cooper" had rather a nice ring to it, and began pondering names for our unborn children. Delicate, almost tender strokes were followed by deep kneading that released a world of tension. This tension was soon replenished, however, as my mind snapped back to the present day and contemplated asking her out on a date.

I tried to spur myself on with inspirational

thoughts of England – Winston Churchill, Geoff Hurst, James Bond. Ah yes, that was the stuff. Of course I could do it, of course I could ask her out. But while my heart was boldly attempting to make its way to my sleeve, my withered testicles were frantically scurrying back into my body. Maybe later.

The blissful treatment must have lasted for ten minutes or more, after which she made a business-like retreat to her own bed before my eyes had even opened.

'How does your neck feel now?'

'Wonderful...amazing...thank you,' I replied, groggily returning to the real world while putting my shirt back on.

'What were you thinking about?'

There was no time to improvise. 'Oh, er, Winston Churchill.'

'Really? So you like men with big cigars? That's a worry.'

'Well, he did save my country from Nazi Germany.'

'I thought *we* saved your country?'

'Oooh, you've done it now!'

A good-humoured political debate ensued, as we explored the far reaches of UK-US relations. Things soon degenerated into a nationalistic slanging match with cheap shots being freely exchanged.

'Well at least we speak proper English in England. None of this "waaaaadder" instead of "water" or "veydamin" instead of "vitamin".'

'You'd be speaking German if it wasn't for us!'

'OK, OK, let's stop this nonsense then. Let's just agree that England is best and be done with it.'

'Oooh, *you've* done it now!'

'Yeah, well take this!'

I threw a pillow at April, a little stronger than I had intended, but she duly caught it with a look of excited surprise.

'Oh, it's like that, huh? Well you're forgetting that I've got a brother and I ain't afraid of brawlin'!'

With that she pounced on me, returning the pillow in the form of a glancing blow across my head. I reeled backwards, managing to grasp another pillow before landing my own clout across her radiant cheeks.

There followed a brutish melee on Laura's bed as we bounced around and pounded each other with the pillows. I frantically reached for more ammunition, and soon found it in the form of an oversized teddy bear at the foot of the bed. It connected satisfyingly across April's back before bursting open into a vast cloud of feathers. We couldn't hear the door opening above our raucous laughter, but we could certainly hear Laura's distressed shrieking as the stuffing from her cherished childhood teddy poignantly rained down on her.

Our night ended rather abruptly, as all offers to clear up the mess were roundly spurned by Laura. Even the free use of my extensive needlework skills was rejected out of hand, although maybe that was for the best as my expertise hadn't truly been tested since I made an outdoor shoe bag at primary school. As April tried to comfort her distraught roommate, my options were reduced to volunteering my handkerchief to stem Laura's flood of tears, and then getting the hell out of there.

I was left with both a disappointment and a relief that the evening had come to such a sudden close, which made it a real struggle to lull myself to sleep that night. When I did finally find myself in the midst of a massage-laden dream, however, it wasn't long before I was stirred by some intense whispering coming from the study room.

A female voice was urging, 'Sh, quiet, you'll wake them.'

The male reply came, 'They're my roomies, I love them!'

'SSHHH!'

'Have I been a naughty boy?'

'Look, just be quiet and let's get you to bed.'

'I love my bed.'

The bedroom door creaked open and I rose to find Jak on all fours. Much to my surprise, he was being dragged into the room by Kristen.

'Oh, I'm *so* sorry,' whispered Kristen.

'What's going on?' I asked.

'Jak had a bit too much to drink at the party so I wanted to make sure he got home safely.'

'The Spanish party? You guys met there?'

'Can I undress him for bed? Please let me undress him,' she begged. 'Go on, let me do it.'

'Maybe you should go now – I can handle it from here.'

'Damn you.' She turned her attention to Jak's slumped figure. 'OK Jak, I'll see you later, OK?'

'Thank you, Mommy!' was Jak's slurred acknowledgement.

'You're welcome Jak, you're welcome.'

She lovingly stroked his hair before kneeling down to kiss him, ever so delicately, on the cheek. Jak returned her tender affection by vomiting abundantly in her face.

'YOU LITTLE FUCKER!' she instinctively screamed, causing Kazuki to emerge confused from his slumber.

'Go back to sleep, Kaz, there's nothing to see here,' I reassured him. Kazuki dutifully put his head back on the pillow and fell back to sleep.

Staring in nauseating displeasure at the expanding pool of effluent on the carpet, I called Kristen back.

'Maybe you *could* put him into bed?'

She barely managed a sarcastic smile as the ex-contents of Jak's stomach dribbled down her face, before leaving me to clear up the mess and put Jak to bed.

Luckily, neither Jak nor I had any lectures that Monday morning. I woke early and cleaned up the patches of carpet I had missed in the dark of the night, while Jak slept soundly with the foul crust still on his face. I just hoped that he enjoyed whatever he could remember of the house party, and that Kristen would be willing to give him another chance. It was around ten o'clock when Jak finally began to show signs of life, not long after Kazuki had left for his first class of the day.

'Uh, oh, aaah,' he mumbled while struggling to lift the heavy weight of his eyelids.

'MORNING JAK!' I cruelly bellowed.

'Woa, man, woa, just give me a minute.'

'Good night last night?'

'Er...shit...I'm not sure.' He scratched his itching cheeks and felt the stale product of his over indulgence flake off in his palm. 'Is that vomit?'

'It certainly is, my friend.'

'Well then I *must* have had a good night. Just a shame I can't remember any of it.'

'You can't remember *anything*?'

'Well...' he paused while running his hands through his hair, '...I remember getting to the party, speaking a bit of Spanish with a few guys, having a few drinks...shit, I think that's about it.'

'And you saw Kristen, right?'

'Kristen? Why would I have seen her? I thought she was *your* chick?'

'So you didn't see her last night then?'

'No way, man. I'd have remembered that after

what you told me about her. Dude, I wish she had've been there cuz I don't remember any good-looking chicks at all.'

'Oh, right. So you definitely don't remember Kristen bringing you home?'

'FUCK OFF! No way, dude, no way.'

'I'm afraid so.'

Jak's eyes widened with the realisation.

'Oh my god, I don't even remember meeting her.'

'Well, I'm pretty sure that you made quite an impression on her.'

'Oh, man. Tell me I didn't blow chunks on her. Please, tell me I didn't. Please, tell me.'

'In her face.'

'IN HER FACE? No, no, no! I'm such a fucking idiot.' He buried his head under his pillow and let out a muffled scream. There followed a knock at the door, and he quickly emerged with a look of panic.

'Shit, that better not be her.'

'Relax, Jak, I'll go see who it is.'

I headed out to the study room and opened the door to find a fraught-looking April. My voice went rather high-pitched as I nervously greeted her.

'Oh, hi April!'

'Hey Ross. I'm really late for class so I can't stop. I didn't get chance to ask you last night, what with you destroying Laura's childhood memories an' all, so I just wondered if you'd like to go ice-skating tomorrow night?'

Holy shit, was April asking me out on a date? The frequency of my voice now reached glass-shattering levels.

'Oh, er, yes, that sounds...great.'

'Cool, OK...' She became distracted as her nose twitched enquiringly. 'Can I smell puke?'

I was too dazed to provide a detailed explanation.

'Er, yes, that's puke.'

'Oh, right, anyway, come up to my room around eight tomorrow night then?'

'Great, I'll see you then.'

April dashed away to her class while I was left to piece together our conversation, as well as various items of glassware.

'Did April just ask you out on a date?' croaked Jak's stooped figure as he joined me in the study room.

'Possibly...perhaps...I think...'

'Man, I guess you guys had a pretty good night too then. Hey, why do you smell of lavender?'

'Er, that might be massage oil.'

Jak simply shook his head in disbelief and shuffled disconsolately back to his bed. '*I* vomit all over my one chance at getting laid, and *he* gets a fucking massage,' he muttered to himself. 'I'm such a fucking idiot.'

SEVEN

'Dude, I can't believe it's only three a.m. I'm not sure I can survive another hour.' Jak was clearly struggling with our radio show's new time slot.

'Hey, it's not my fault you got hammered last night, Jak.'

'I just want my bed.'

We were in the middle of the new feature we had created to cater for the radio station's policy of including five playlist songs every hour. Rather than allowing ten records of dubious merit to taint the entirety of our show, we crammed in half immediately before three a.m. and then half straight afterwards. We christened the feature 'Don't Blame Us'.

'OK, that was *Car Wreck* by the Finger Dolls – yet another classic from the playlist. What was your verdict, Jumpin' Jak?'

'Crap. What did you make of it, Ross?'

'Truly dreadful. But don't worry listeners, just another few tracks of questionable quality to go, and then we'll be back to some decent music. Here's the next one...'

Perhaps we weren't following the true spirit of the playlist, but at least we couldn't be accused of breaking the rules. With the next disastrous song playing, my thoughts turned back to Tuesday night.

'So, Jak, are you sure you don't mind me inviting Kristen around tomorrow?'

'Not at all, man. I'll just make sure I'm not in.'

'You don't have to do that.'

'Oh yes I do. There's no way I can face that chick after what you've told me about last night. Besides, what if she realised I couldn't even remember her?'

'I'm sure she'll be fine about the whole thing, don't worry so much. And besides, I need her help picking the right clothes for my ice-skating debut.'

'Fine, but I'll be long gone by the time she arrives.'

'So, what time is Kristen arriving?' Jak asked for the third time.

'Seven o'clock,' I replied, putting him at ease for the third time. 'Don't stress, there's another thirty minutes yet.'

'You better not have tricked me.' Jak's relaxed face quickly tightened into a look of blind panic as there was a tapping at the door. 'You bastard!'

I was as surprised as Jak at the early arrival, but I maintained a roguish air as I approached the door and opened it wide.

'Oh, hi! Good to see you again!' I greeted the bewildered stranger in the doorway like an old friend. 'Come in, come in, we've been waiting for you.'

She nodded obligingly and came into the room. She was quite a short girl with a horribly disfigured nose and an incredibly large wart on her right cheek. I had never seen her before in my life.

'Jak, come and say hello,' I generously offered.

His meek figure shuffled towards the girl to meet his fate.

'Hi,' was his sheepish salutation as he looked worriedly at the girl. 'Ross,' he whispered in my direction, 'could we just have a quick word in the bedroom?'

'Sure, sure,' I replied. 'Please excuse us for a moment,' I said to the girl as I accompanied Jak, firmly closing the door behind us.

'Holy fuck, Ross, you never told me she was *that* ugly,' he said frantically.

'Chill, chill. She's a really great girl, just give her a chance.'

'But that nose, man – I'm not sure I could live with that nose.'

'Listen, there isn't exactly a queue of women waiting for a chance to be with you, is there? Now Kristen obviously likes you, so why not give her a chance?'

'You're probably right,' Jak grimly accepted. 'And I suppose once you're inside, it's all the same.'

'Wise words indeed. Now get out there and show her a bit of the old Jumpin' Jak magic.'

Jak purposefully strode out into the study room where the girl was politely waiting.

'I'm sorry about that,' he began, 'and I'm really sorry about last night too. To be honest, I don't remember much, but Ross filled me in on parts of it. I can't believe I barfed in your face. I'm just so, so sorry. I woke up this morning with it all crusted on my face...actually...' he closely inspected her cheek, '...oh, god, you've still got a little bit on your face too. Here, let me get it for you...' He reached over to her cheek and began scratching with his nails to try and remove the offending lump. 'Shit, it's a bit stubborn, isn't it?' He scraped harder until the increasingly frightened girl finally pulled away from him just as Kazuki entered the room.

'Castalia!' Kazuki excitedly greeted the girl.

'Kazuki!' she replied in terrified relief.

'Castalia my study partner!' Kazuki explained.

'She from Greece!'

'I from Greece,' Castalia agreed, while giving Jak a reproachful glance. 'We go study upstairs, Kazuki,' she hastily pleaded before dragging Kazuki out of the door.

'Bye!' I called to them both, before falling to my knees in uncontrollable hysterics.

'Ross, you little shit!' said Jak with relief. 'You know, I only believed she was that ugly because she was prepared to sleep with you.'

'That was a wart on her cheek, Jak, a *wart*!'

Half an hour later, and with Jak long gone, Kristen arrived to help me with my wardrobe selection. She introduced me to the tried and tested female method of clothes selection – wearing every single item in every conceivable combination. Once that torture was over and my wardrobe had been ridiculed to an inordinate extent, the final selection was made – a pair of black jeans with a grey T-shirt. I retreated to the privacy of my bedroom to change back into the winning outfit, while Kristen waited patiently in the study room.

With my jeans securely zipped, but my bare chest still on proud display, I heard Kristen greet a visitor in the study room. A quick look at my watch revealed that eight o'clock had been and gone, and April must have got bored of waiting for me upstairs. I pushed my ear to the door to hear the conversation.

'I'm Kristen, so you must be April?'

'Oh, yes, nice to meet you. Ross told me all about your buddy thing.'

'Oh, he told you all that? Yeah, he's a nice guy. Just a shame he wouldn't *do* me up in the mountains!'

'Well...maybe he didn't tell me *everything* then.'

'Er, he's just in there anyway, he won't be a

minute. I've just been helping him get changed...oh, shit, not like that...we haven't just been doing it in there or anything...I was just helping him pick out some clothes.'

'Oh, well I should definitely thank you for that!'

I threw my T-shirt on and stumbled out of the bedroom before Kristen could put her foot any deeper down her throat.

'Hi, April! I'm really sorry I'm late.'

'Hi! No problem, Kristen explained it all. I'd rather you were late but dressed nicely.'

I turned to Kristen, while opening the door wide for her overdue departure.

'Well, thank you for your help. I'll see you later?'

'Oh, sure,' she replied, rather reluctantly. 'You guys enjoy the skating.'

It might have been a little rude, but I wasn't taking any chances – there was no telling what havoc she might have wreaked if left in that room with April for another minute. As the door closed behind Kristen, however, it seemed that the damage might already have been done.

'So, what exactly happened in the mountains with you and Kristen then?'

I played innocent. 'Oh, we just went for a run up there.'

'Oh, is *that* all?' April laughed.

I didn't expect her to pop Kristen's eyeballs out with a rusty spoon or anything, but a little jealously wouldn't have gone astray.

'Yes, it was quite a nice run actually. It really is beautiful up there.'

'Oh, I see. It's just that Kristen said something about you not wanting to "do" her up there?' I searched for some resentment in April's voice, but found nothing. If anything, she seemed to be enjoying the tease. 'I think you're crazy to have passed up the chance – I mean, she seems like a really great girl.'

Had I just heard her right? Was this some kind of twisted first date test that Brandon hadn't told me about, or was this not even a date at all? Could I really have misread the whole situation so horribly?

'Yeah...' I hesitated, 'she *is* great. But just as a friend.'

'If you insist! So, have you ever skated before?' The subject change was effortless, further compounding my fears.

'Er, no...no I haven't,' I stuttered, trying hard to put our previous exchange out of my mind. 'How about you?'

'Oh, just a few times. It's been a while though so I'm really looking forward to getting back on the ice. Are you nervous?'

About our date? Yes. About the prospect of it not even being a date? Certainly. About ice-skating? 'Not really – it can't be that difficult, after all.'

'Ah, right. Well we'll see about that!'

We arrived at the sports centre and made our way to the busy ice rink. We duly exchanged our shoes for skates that were far fouler smelling than anything I had ever encountered at a bowling alley, and tied our laces on a wooden bench next to the ice. I looked out at all of the other sweaty-footed bastards sliding around in their own filth, and momentarily forgot my predicament.

Until, that is, April yelled, 'Oh, look, there they are!'

'*They?*' I asked quizzically.

She pointed to a group of girls making their way around the ice to meet us. I recognised Laura and Doggy Style, who were skating with three other girls I had never seen before. Laura skidded to a halt in front of us.

'I thought you guys weren't gonna make it!' she said.

'Oh, Ross was just a little late, but we're here now,' explained April.

'Well great, get out here then.'

Bloody marvellous. That just about answered all the questions that were swimming around in my head. It took every ounce of self-control to hide my anger, disappointment, and abject misery at the whole situation. When would I learn my lesson and just stop trusting these women? And to top it all off I was about to make a fool of myself again, but this time on the ice. *And* I would probably contract a whole range of exotic fungal infections into the bargain. Bloody marvellous.

'Come on Ross, are you ready?' beckoned the evil witch.

'Just about.'

I stood up on the pencil thin metal blades for the first time, before crashing down in a heap on the floor. All six girls giggled extensively while I stumbled to my feet once more, not affording myself any time to dwell on the rapidly deteriorating state of affairs. I took baby steps towards the ice, and then apprehensively prodded my right foot onto the frozen water. The skate instinctively slid away from me while my left foot was still firmly rooted to the carpeted ground. My stance involuntarily widened to eye-watering lengths until I could bare the pain no more and fell backwards on my arse. One cheek nestled comfortably on the carpet, while the other began to soak up the melted ice and the humiliation through the seat of my jeans.

In the midst of my undignified demise the giggling reached unprecedented levels. I briefly closed my eyes, trying to prepare myself for however long I had left to endure in that wretched place. I then slowly opened my lids to find April kneeling down and offering her hand to me in salvation. I could no longer hear the laugher, nor could I see any of the girls that I knew were still surrounding me. I only had eyes and ears for the angelic beauty that was April.

She smiled at me sweetly and whispered, 'Here, let me help you.'

The absurdity of the situation helped to clear my mind as I was unexpectedly captivated by this amazing girl all over again. So what if it wasn't a date? I never really wanted to get into that whole pantomime anyway. There I was, with the opportunity to spend time with an incredibly beautiful and enchanting young woman. *That* was exactly how I had wanted things to be – relaxed, laid back, getting to know each other, having fun, and building a solid friendship. *That* was surely the key to our future. We had a lifetime to spend together, so there really was no rush.

'Thank you.' I gingerly reached for her soft hand and enjoyed the lingering contact as she helped me to my feet.

'You're welcome. Now, let's try getting you on the ice again.'

She turned to face me, and then held both of my hands as I ventured forth into the frosty arena. She skilfully skated backwards while pulling me along and being amused by my mock-look of terror. My confidence built slowly, while she patiently taught me how to move my feet. I gradually managed to make some progress under my own steam, albeit with a few falls in between. Then she moved to my left side and held my hand as we made circuits of the rink together. I tried not to read too much into the hand holding – as without it I would have been flat on my back – but the touch of her skin was exhilarating nonetheless.

We were soon joined by April's friends, who had been whizzing by at regular intervals. Laura held my other hand while the rest of the girls joined at either side and we circled together in a wide line. They all seemed like fairly strong skaters, although April had a flair and a poise that hinted at a little more experience than she had previously let on. The line naturally split before long, and I took the opportunity to take a break.

'Do you mind dropping me off at the seats?' I asked of April. 'I think I need a rest.'

'Sure.'

April slowed us down neatly as we approached the seating area, and I made an awkward jump off the ice and onto a bench.

'Now you go and show me what you can *really* do,' I encouraged her, fully aware that babysitting me for the last half an hour probably wasn't the best fun in the world.

'Alrighty, if you insist.'

She skated backwards while waving at me, her feet making graceful figures of eight on the surface. She built up an impressive speed before taking off in a mini jump-twist to point herself forward. She then swirled and twirled her way around the rink at breakneck speed, making impossible turns and elegant manoeuvres that had only previously been witnessed during the Winter Olympics. A quick glance at the random staggering of the other skaters confirmed that April was indeed in a completely different class.

Time passed readily as I was completely absorbed in her performance. She took the occasional break to skate with her friends, but soon broke away from their timid skills to excel on her own once more. I was left speechless when she returned to see if I was ready for more.

'I'd forgotten how much I enjoy skating,' she beamed.

'You're amazing. Honestly, that was phenomenal.'

'Thank you.'

'How did you learn to skate like that?'

'Well, me and my boyfriend were State champion figure skaters.'

'Oh...er...'

'Yeah, we started five years ago and finally won State in our last year together.'

Last year together – thank god for that!

'Oh, I see. So you broke up after that then?'

'No, I meant that was our last year *skating* together. We're still together, together.'

'Oh,' was my crestfallen acknowledgement that the bottom had just fallen out of my world. My heart sank deeply into my soggy arse, and the numbness of my infected feet spread rapidly across my entire body. Marvellous, just bloody marvellous.

EIGHT

'You need to get back out there, man. You've been a boring tool for the last few weeks.'

Jak was right. I really had been no fun at all since the date that never was.

'No, I'm just gonna stay here and get through this physics homework.'

'Dude, you've been throwing yourself into your studies but your grades still suck.'

He was right again. Even with no social life and an unhealthy dedication to my classes, my grades were still deep in the shitter.

'I know, I know. But physics is logical, predictable, and dependable. It's exactly what I need.'

'No, Ross, what you need is to get the hell out of here, get stupid drunk, and end up screwing some hot Spanish chick.'

'Chicks are off the menu. If someone like April could turn out to be as evil as the rest, then I'm just not interested anymore.'

'So you want some man-love? OK, dude, as your friend...' Jak bent over and thrust his arse in my face. '...come on, stick it in me, right here, right here...'

'Put it away!' I turned my head away in disgust,

but failed to hold back my laughter.

'There you go! I knew the real Ross was still in there. Now let's go get wasted.'

'Do you ever shut up?'

'Not until my butt-fucking buddy agrees to go out with me tonight.'

'Hey, I've chosen a life of solitude, not sodomy.'

'But that doesn't mean you can't have a night of debauchery with the guys. Now put that scientific calculator down, retract the lead back into your pencil, take a shot of Kazuki's "Vodka of Death" and let's get going.'

Jak had finally worn me down. It was by no means his first attempt to jolt me from the melancholy in which I was so deeply ensconced, but on a miserable Saturday night in September I suddenly felt in need of some light relief. The pages of meaningless equations could wait, and the self-pitying could stop, if only for one night.

'I just know I'm gonna regret this.'

'DUUUUUUDE! Welcome back! Now take this.' He passed me a shot of the putrid liquor and I made sure that it didn't touch the sides.

'I'm gonna need another of those.'

'Coming right up.' He then called theatrically to the back of the empty room, 'Another shot for the British gentleman on the eve of his return to civilisation!'

'Just pour.'

I took the second shot, picked up my wallet and headed out of the door. I no longer cared what I was wearing or what I looked like.

'We've got to get Brandon first,' Jak motioned down the corridor as we walked together.

'Are you wearing aftershave?' I sniffed, noticing a musky fragrance in the air.

'Mountain Delight. What do you think?'

'I think Kristen needs her head read for going out with someone who thinks *that* smells nice.'

'Tonight might just be the night.'

'How long has it been now?'

'Only three weeks.'

'Three weeks since you officially started dating, and you've still not had any action? She met me, and wanted some of the old Ross magic only hours later. What does that tell you?'

'You were a plaything, I'm something more serious.'

'You keep believing that, Jak. Just keep believing.'

We pushed Brandon's door open to find him downing a bottle of beer.

'Hey guys, I'm ready to par-tay!' he gurgled.

'Onward, to the house of España!' called Jak.

We walked through the cool evening air heading towards the Hill – an area of shops, restaurants, beatniks, drug dealers, and student houses just across the road from campus. It was a famed district for out of control student partying, and a magnet for Boulder's Police Force who were ever-keen to punish underage drinking to the fullest extent of the country's backward law. Jak had told tales of moving houses several times a night in an effort to evade capture and follow the keg of beer that provided the firm foundation of all the best parties. It was going to be my first time drinking outside the relative safety of our room, but in the mood I was in, I felt no fear.

We strolled across the open spaces of the university, treading the well-worn route of many of my runs. It was quiet, save for the occasional student with a rucksack full of books on their back or the odd dreadlocked skateboarder failing miserably at his tricks.

As we approached the underpass that lead out to

the Hill, there was a noticeable change in the atmosphere. A group of edgy-looking youths manned the entrance, offering cigarettes and more as we passed them by. We emerged on the other side of Broadway to join the bustling sea of students looking for some Saturday night entertainment. Anyone who was old enough to drink was already in the bars, so the rest of us were under twenty-one and looking for a party.

Jak directed us towards the Spanish Club gathering. '1095 13th Street they said. It can't be much further...'

'So what makes you Spanish such a bunch of drunkards anyway?' I asked.

'We just know how to party, and that's all I know.'

Brandon joined in. 'So do you think there'll be some hot chicks for me?'

'Brandon, there will be more than enough to go around. Especially as our British friend is leaving it to the real men tonight.'

'I've already got all the Creative Writing chicks to myself,' Brandon added, while rubbing his hands together greedily. 'That reminds me, Ross. Kenny keeps asking when you're gonna be back in his class?'

'Well he can keep on asking.' I had been careful to avoid all contact with April, which involved passing on a string of excuses to the colourful Kenny Fox. 'Has he turned up for a class without being hung-over yet, anyway?'

'Not yet, but the law of averages says that it's gotta happen soon.'

Brandon suddenly nudged me indiscreetly while nodding even more obviously at two scantily clad girls walking towards us. We all stopped talking and admired the gorgeousness as it came ever closer. We were walking three abreast on the pavement, but as we neared it became clear that our three against their four was never going to fit. Especially when their four were so pert and fulsome.

Jak and I moved over to the right, allowing the two girls room to pass, while Brandon roamed in a daze with his view firmly locked on to the delights in front of him. It all happened so quickly, but it seemed as though the girls tried to separate to go around him when one of them stumbled into the path of his grateful hands. He caught her firmly by the left boob and, after she finally steadied herself, she landed a well-aimed slap on his cheek and stormed onwards.

'Did you see that? Did you see that?' Brandon demanded with undimmed enthusiasm.

'Yeah, great catch,' Jak complimented.

'Those chicks wanted me *badly*.'

I had to give the boy a reality check. 'Brandon, all they wanted was to get from A to B. And I'm sorry to break this to you, but A was not your scrotum and B was not the tip-end of your penis.'

'I'm on fire tonight, let's get to the Spanish chicks.' My words had clearly washed right over him.

'OK, I think this is it,' proclaimed Jak with a triumphant glow.

"It" was a detached two-storey wooden house with a large porch boasting an oversized C.U. flag next to a more modest Spanish one. From the exterior there appeared to be little going on apart from some muffled Spanish music, with the heavy curtains successfully blocking out any silhouettes of illicit drinking activity. Jak led us up the steps and knocked harshly on the door. It opened just enough for his Spanish words to sneak through and unlock our passage into a night of revelry.

The door swung wide and a cloud of smoke and hops welcomed us in. Jak introduced us to his countless friends on our way to the keg that was situated in the back room.

Keg parties weren't something I had ever experienced in England, but appeared to be the done thing in American college towns. I hated beer, but there seemed to be an endless free supply, so I grabbed a half-litre disposable cup while waiting for Jak and Brandon to fill their own. When my time arrived, I picked up the hose that coiled outwards from the vast steel drum and pushed the button on the tap at its end. The watching crowds were undoubtedly impressed by the five hundred millilitres of pure froth that I poured myself.

Jak saw my plight and took pity on me. 'Here, let me show you...you've got to pump it first, like this...' He pumped the blue rubber button atop the keg several times, before pouring me a perfect cup of beer.

'Cheers,' I thanked him as we left to find the source of the Spanish music in the basement of the house. Bodies were crowded into every room and hallway – drinking, smoking, and mostly speaking in Spanish. The cramped stairs to the basement opened up to reveal a cavernous space with yet more people tightly packed in.

The god-awful music could now be heard in all of its rancid magnificence. As the castanets and tambourine echoed piercingly within my skull, I mused on how the Spanish may well have been party animals, but they were certainly not renowned for their musical tastes.

We forged through to the back of the room where a self-appointed DJ was firmly in charge of two record decks and a CD player. I had hoped that our purposeful journey would conclude in a thorough and conclusive beating of the DJ, but the possibility became more remote as we made it to a small clearing where people were gaily circle dancing with

Spanish abandon.

'This is great!' shouted Jak before joining the circle and spilling increasing amounts of beer with every move.

Brandon and I looked at each other, shook our heads, and carried on towards the greasy-haired DJ.

'Hey, Mr DJ,' I called above the din.

'Hello, my friend!' he bellowed back at me in a heavy Spanish accent.

'This music – it's complete shite, isn't it?'

Granted, it wasn't the most diplomatic approach, but the Vodka and few mouthfuls of beer were urging me to rectify the situation.

'The music is what?' he queried while leaning his ear in closer.

Brandon interjected, 'Great music, man, great music,' before firmly pulling me away.

'Hey, I was just trying to sort out the music,' I defended.

'I know, man, but mere abuse is no way to solve this.'

'So what did you have in mind?'

'Watch and learn, Ross. Watch and learn.'

Brandon turned back to the DJ, engaging him in conversation once more.

'So, what's this you're playing?' he said while pointing to the twelve-inch record rotating on the turntable.

'Midnight Sardana,' came the loud and proud response.

'Cool, cool,' mumbled Brandon, before unleashing himself like a coiled spring and ripping the record from beneath the needle that was injecting its poison out to the masses. A loud scratch was followed by an abrupt silence that brought a thousand questioning eyes in our direction.

I turned away from the baying crowd and

whispered quietly in Brandon's ear, '*What* are you doing?'

'Don't worry, don't worry,' he gently responded through gritted teeth, as if stray bilingual lip readers were our most pressing concern. 'I know exactly what I'm doing.' He then waved the record above his head, making two full back and forth movements that seemed to last longer than the music itself.

All eyes were following the sacred record on its mystical journey, when Brandon suddenly threw it down on the hardwood floor and screamed, 'OPA!' at the top of his voice while the vinyl shattered into several thousand pieces. You could have heard a mouse fart, as a shocked silence swept through the partygoers.

'OPA, OPA, OPA!' Brandon repeated, with a simple expression of joy that was truly admirable under the circumstances.

I leant in to his ear once more, whispering a little more intensely this time, 'That's the *Greeks* you dickhead, and they do it with *plates*.'

His brow furrowed as his ventriloquism act continued. 'I thought they did it in Spain?'

'Nope.'

'Oh, fuck.'

'Yes, "oh fuck" indeed.'

My body tensed in preparation for the inevitable hiding we were about to receive at the hands and feet of our drunk and incensed Spanish hosts. In the glare of Brandon's stupidity, I had been blind to Jak's approach from the dance floor. Without warning he joined us, record in hand, and began waving it in the exact same style that Brandon had done earlier. At the end of his second swing he brought the disc down firmly across Brandon's head and yelled out, 'OPA, OPA, OPA!'

As the record splintered spectacularly, Brandon

looked confused while the crowd laughed wildly and chanted along, 'OPA, OPA, OPA!' Moments later, the infernal music started up again and everyone went back to their dancing and drinking.

'Sorry, man,' Jak explained to Brandon, 'but Spanish pride was at stake.'

'No problem, dude,' he accepted. 'You did what you had to. Now, how about another beer?'

Every cup of the amber brew tasted slightly less objectionable than the previous one. I soon lost count of how many had found their way to my lips, but I certainly had time to perfect my keg-pouring technique. I found myself perched on the stairs to the basement chatting to Kristen, who had been a late arrival to the occasion.

'I'm so happy that you and Jak are together,' I slurred.

'Yeah, I think it's going really well. Apart from the sex, or lack of it.'

'But Jak talks about sex all the time.'

'That's the problem. He talks the talk, but can't bone the bone.'

'I should be boning April,' I said to myself and, unfortunately, to Kristen.

'Would you just get over that girl! You've talked about nothing else all night long.'

'But she was so special and then she turned out to be exactly like Bethan. Whores – they're all whores.'

'Calm down, Ross, you don't mean that. Who's Bethan, anyway?'

'But she led me on, then ripped out my heart and danced all over it with her ice skates.' I stomped my feet on the stairs for effect. 'Fucking State champions – her boyfriend's obviously gay anyway...'

My intoxicated ranting was broken up by a shrill cry from above.

'COPS, COPS!'

'Oh, shit,' muttered Kristen. 'Come on, we've gotta go.'

She strode quickly up the stairs while I delicately rose to my feet and saw the stairwell spinning wickedly before my eyes. The next step just wouldn't stay still for long enough for me to plant my foot on it. A rush of bodies flew upwards past me while I gingerly sat back down to await my fate.

Dejected figures soon began to pass me on their return to the windowless basement. Two policemen completed the stream and swept me down the stairs with them. I saw Jak amongst the small group of successfully rounded up cattle, and staggered over to stand next to him.

'You're a foreigner, you don't speak any English,' he firmly implored me.

'OK, OK,' I managed while steadying myself against a chair.

'Against the wall, ALL OF YOU!' ordered a walrus moustachioed cop.

'And no fucking talking until we speak to you,' barked a handlebar moustachioed cop.

I suddenly wished that I was sober so that I could fully enjoy the moment in all of its stereotypical splendour. The Handlebar stood at the foot of the stairs to prevent any foolish notions of escape, while The Walrus greased his whiskers before pulling out a leather-bound notebook.

'OK then, you first,' he snarled at the timid little Spanish girl who looked like she had only recently stopped suckling from her mother's teat. 'How old are you?'

'Twenty-one?' she tried bravely.

'ID?'

She reached into the rear pocket of her jeans and passed him a driving licence – probably for the plastic tractor she drove in her back garden in Madrid.

'Hum...er...' he studied the document, '...ah...oh...appears to be in order, you can go.' He moved down the line. 'Next, how old are you?'

Shit, I knew that fake IDs worked on TV, but I never imagined they would actually work in real life. If I'd had one, maybe there would have been a way out. By the time The Walrus reached Jak, the first four people had all been dismissed having proved to be over-twenty-one, which I only believed to be true for one of the guys at most. Regardless, it was now our time to shine, and I knew that Jak didn't have any fake ID to rely on either.

'Now, son, how old are you?'

I cannot hope to replicate the fluent stream of Spanish that flowed from Jak's mouth, but it was impressive to say the least.

'HOW...OLD...ARE...YOU?' repeated The Walrus. Yes, slow and loud, that should make all the difference.

More Spanish poured out of Jak, and he even managed to land some spittle on The Walrus' moustache, which was particularly commendable.

'Shit. Bob, Bob!' he called to The Handlebar.

'Yeah, Billy?'

'Is Vasquez on the Hill? We need a Spanish translator.'

I felt Jak's knees tremble as the unexpected twist unfolded.

'No, he's down on Pearl Street tonight.'

'Shit,' The Walrus grumbled to himself. 'It's not worth the paperwork. OK, OK, go, go, vamos, vamos.'

'Ah, sí, sí,' Jak nodded innocently and scurried up the stairs to freedom.

The Walrus' glare was now firmly on me. 'OK,

now how old are you?'

All I had inside me was Jak's advice and a little too much Dutch courage. 'I'm English, I'm frightfully sorry, but I cannot understand you.'

'OK, wise guy, how old are you?'

'I'm English!' I smiled ignorantly.

'Last chance, tell me your age.'

'I'm English; I cannot understand a word you are saying. By the way, you have the bushiest moustache I've ever seen in my entire life. Do you have any woodland creatures nesting in that thing?'

'OK, Bob,' he shouted to his partner. 'We've got one, you can let the rest go.'

It was as if every single noxious odour I had encountered during my nineteen short years of life had been bottled at source and re-released on that very evening in celebration of my arrival. While the bare brick walls exuded stale sweat and urine, the concrete floor oozed vomit and excrement. The rows of benches carried the bloodstains of countless convicts who had sat there before me, while the steel toilet bowl dripped the desperate brown splatterings of the unfortunate few who just couldn't hold on until morning.

If the sights and smells didn't kill me, it seemed inevitable that one of my cellmates would. All five possessed manic glints in their eyes, and I appeared to be the only one with an ounce of mental stability. At the other side of a set of impenetrable bars sat a generously proportioned officer, keeping an eye on our foul chamber during the advertisement breaks of the shows on his portable television. I had little faith that he would rush to my rescue should one the crazies break off a bench leg and sink it through my chest, but I didn't particularly care. As I wallowed in my April-induced depression and the filth of a thousand inmates, the only fear I felt was one that my bowels wouldn't make it to daybreak. I could handle a brutal murder at the hands of one deranged criminal, but dropping my trousers and taking a dump in front of five of them was another matter entirely.

It would only have taken someone with a few hundred dollars to bail me out, but I refused my phone call and decided to wait until morning. I deserved to be there amongst life's losers and besides, I'd have a better story to tell if I made it through the night in one piece and without any skid marks on my underpants. Several hours passed in a tense atmosphere of silent intimidation and self-willed constipation, as I made the steady transition into sobriety. While one by one the others fell asleep, I tried hard to deny myself the privilege. Instead, I dwelled on April's evil deception and the crushing blow she had dealt to my chances of ever being able to love again. Resistance eventually proved futile, however, as my bloodshot eyes could handle the self-pity no more, and I fell soundly asleep on the floor against the cold bars of our cell.

'Ross, Ross.'

I felt a nudge against my back, but decided I must have dreamt it. After all, who else would be in my bed?

'Ross, wake up.'

The nudge became a gentle shake as I began to doubt my dream theory. I then became aware of the hard concrete against my cheek and realised I was not in my usual bed. The events of the previous evening rapidly flashed through my mind, leading to the numbing conclusion that a nudge in the back was probably the prelude to some jailbird man-love. I snapped into action, jumping up onto my feet and twisting towards the source of the bodily contact in one swift, chastity-saving manoeuvre.

'Get the fuck away from me, I'm English,' was my instinctive cry, in as manly a tone as I could muster.

'Sh, sh, it's me, don't worry, it's me...' The voice rang softly and without a hint of impending arse-rape. '...quiet, it's me, don't worry...it's April.'

I looked upward from my defensive stance to see April's face riddled with horror and concern as she wondered if hers wasn't the first backwards nudge I had received that night. All of my pre-sleep bravado appeared to have deserted me as the savagery of my plight suddenly seemed clear.

'Oh, April, thank god, thank god,' I welcomed her with desperation.

'Don't worry, I'm getting you out of here.' She offered her hand through the bars and I gladly accepted. 'They're just processing the bail – it won't be long now.'

'Thank you, thank you, thank you so much. How did you know I was here? How did you get here?'

She reached her other hand in to stroke my arm. 'Don't worry about that now. Let's just get you home. How are you doing?'

'Yeah, I'm OK. Not as OK as I thought I was, but I'm OK.'

NINE

The taxi was waiting for us outside the jail, and we hopped in the back to begin the journey to campus. The freedom felt great, and I couldn't conceal my joy.

'Did I say thank you?' I asked with a beaming smile.

'Just a few times,' laughed April.

'Well I really do mean it.'

'Hey, I'm just glad I could help.'

'Yes, but coming out to this hellhole at four a.m. with a wad of cash is a little more than help.'

'Let's just say we're even.'

'What do you mean?'

April shuffled uncomfortably. 'Well, just the confusion that I might have...maybe...possibly caused.'

It was my turn to shuffle uncomfortably. 'No, please don't say any more.'

'But I feel that I ought to. You see I've been thinking about what happened between us, and I *can* be a bit naive at times. I think I was a bit unfair to you. Like, maybe I gave you the wrong signals?'

'Let's put it behind us,' I suggested, as much to end the awkwardness as anything else.

'Are you sure you can forgive me?'

'After what you've just done for me?' I offered my

hand across the back of the taxi. 'Friends?'

'Friends,' April agreed with her beautiful smile as she shook my hand. 'Does that mean you'll be back in Creative Writing on Wednesday then?'

'I'll have you know I've been very ill for the past few weeks which is why I haven't been able to attend,' I lied, rather blatantly. 'Just ask Kenny.'

'Oh yes, our tutor was telling me only an hour ago how ill you looked when he saw you being carted off in a police car on the Hill.'

So *that* was how she had discovered my predicament.

'Well why did it take him so long to get to you, and then what the hell have you been doing for the last hour?' I teased.

'Oh, you know Kenny. He had a few more drinks after he saw you, then thought he'd better knock on my door at three a.m. to tell me the good news. He seemed to think that we were good friends or something.'

'Well that explains his tardiness, so how about yours?'

'Well, I did have to get dressed, find out exactly where you were, figure out how much bail they needed and then pull together the $600.'

'$600?'

'Yeah, as they threw in "resisting arrest" with "minor in possession" it was apparently a bit higher than usual.'

I sank deeper into the upholstery with shame.

'Did I say thank you?'

'I hope you at least had a good night, apart from the ending.'

'It wasn't bad, I suppose. It was the first time I'd been out for a few weeks so I made the most of it.'

'Oh yeah, that illness must've been bad then!'

'Oh, it was. The worst.'

Chatter was exchanged freely and it felt as if we had never been apart. At that very moment I had forgotten all the woes of the evening just past, and all the angst of the previous month. It seemed utterly irrelevant as I simply enjoyed being with the wonderful April once again.

As the car pulled up outside the deathly quiet Cheyenne Arapaho, I reached in to my pocket to help April with the taxi fare.

'Here, I've got ten dollars left if that's any good?'

The taxi driver shook his head at the felon, and then addressed the sweet young girl. 'That's $142 please, lady.'

'Here you go,' she said while passing over a pile of notes. 'Keep the change.'

'Oh, my god...' I said to her as we walked up the stairs towards untold home comforts.

'Don't say it, don't say it...' she pleaded in good humour.

I stopped her at the top of the stairs and we faced each other. The words "thank you" no longer seemed enough, so I leant in and hugged her tightly.

'You're welcome,' she whispered softly in my ear. 'Now get off me – you stink!'

'I was waiting for your call but must've fallen asleep. Sorry man.'

It was the morning after my night in prison, and Jak was trying to explain himself while I was feeling somewhat put out.

'*Waiting* for my call? Why didn't you just come and find me?'

'Well, I *was* pretty wasted to be honest. That second party got really lively.'

'*Second* party?'

'Oh, er, you know, the one we were at, the one that got busted,' he backtracked clumsily.

'No, that would be the *first* party. Where the fuck were you partying while I was locked up with five lunatics?'

'Well,' he stuttered, 'the keg made it out to this house down the street, so me, Kristen and Brandon kinda ended up there. Dude, you can't leave the keg!'

I wanted to be angry but there was a simplicity to his reasoning that broke my will and brought out a wry smile.

'Unbelievable.'

'How did you get out anyway? I never heard you come in.'

'April bailed me out at four a.m.'

'April? You're shittin' me, April? "Evil Bitch" April?'

'I've dropped that title now. From this day forward she will be known as "April, the saviour in Ross' hour of need when his best pal abandoned him for a keg".'

'So does that mean you two are back on?'

'Not "on", just friends again. I'm telling you, it was pretty special what she did for me last night.'

'Well she obviously cares a lot for you, man, even if it's just as friends.'

'That's exactly what I thought. I'm gonna see how this friendship thing works out and take it from there.'

'Why don't you ask her out tonight then, as friends? Kristen mentioned this line-dancing place out towards Denver that's over-eighteen on a Sunday night. You should ask April if she wants to come – a group of us are going.'

'Maybe I will, maybe I will.'

I was told that the dress code was quite strict – possibly stricter than any club I would have ever been to before. Initially I was unfazed – after all, I was experienced with dressing smart for English nightclubs where only a shiny pair of shoes, non-denim trousers and a collared shirt would get you past the bouncers. Or a cracking pair of tits. Anyway, this was a very different dress code, and it had me slightly concerned. As I stood at April's open door with a bunch of flowers in my hand, I knew that I looked rather absurd.

'Oh, hey Ross. You look...like a lumberjack!' she scoffed.

April looked stunning in a tight pair of jeans and a cute checked shirt tied in a knot above her belly button. I, on the other hand, in my faded jeans and the bright red checked shirt Jak had lent me, apparently looked like a feller of trees.

'Here, I chopped these down especially for you,' I said while handing her the flowers. 'They're just to say...well, you know.'

'They're wonderful, thank *you* so much. I haven't received flowers in years.'

'It's the least I could do. And I insist on buying all your *non-alcoholic* drinks tonight too.'

'Well, we'd better get going then.'

I walked April down to my room where Jak and Kazuki were still readying themselves for the night of cowboy-esque entertainment. We entered the study room to find Kazuki standing proudly to attention, emphasising his new outfit. His short, stout frame was all-but exploding out of a pair of denim dungarees that made him look like he was heavily pregnant. I no longer felt as ludicrously conspicuous, and April and I had to momentarily turn away to staunch our giggles.

'You like, you like?' Kazuki feverishly asked.

Both April and I bit our lips as we turned back and tried our hardest not to hurt his feelings.

I ventured first into the minefield, just managing to extract, 'Great, Kaz, just great,' from my mouth before I let out a wild spray of suppressed laughter firmly in his direction.

April attempted to calm the situation. 'You look wonderful, Kaz, you are...' she quickly brought her hand to her mouth to forbid the mocking smile to break through, '...you are really...blooming!'

'Ah, blooming, yes, Kazuki like to be blooming!' he replied with his confidence intact. Until, that is, Jak emerged from the bedroom.

'Come on guys, let's go. Better let Kaz ride shotgun with me – I don't want his water breaking on the backseat.'

We drove to Kristen's hall on the other side of campus and then followed her car-full of girls out towards the US-36 and onwards to Denver. The Spittoon was our destination – an out-of-town country music dance bar where, legend had it, the local cowboys drank, danced, fought, and rode mechanical bucking broncos, often all at the same time. I thought it sounded like an unmissable opportunity to see some authentic cowboys and make fun of their primal ways, but April clearly had other ideas.

'I'm so excited to try line dancing,' she enthused, while trying to get comfortable in the back of Jak's Mustang.

'You're not actually going to dance, are you?' I questioned. 'I thought we'd just find some rednecks and laugh at them instead?'

'No way, Ross. We're getting up there and having a go with the real cowboys. And we've got to try the bronco too, that sounds like fun.'

'In a break-your-back kind of way, maybe.'

'Don't be so chicken! Just think where you were twenty-four hours ago. You really should make the most of your freedom.'

'You might have a point there.'

'And besides, you're treating me tonight and that includes doing exactly as I say.'

Jak briefly glanced over his shoulder like a parent chastising his children in the rear of the family car. 'Listen to her, Ross, you owe her big time.'

'I know, Dad, leave me alone. You just make sure that Mummy is comfortable up front. She really shouldn't be going dancing in her condition.'

Kazuki looked quizzically at me while April gave me a firm dig in the ribs with her elbow.

'Ow,' I playacted. 'What was that for?'

'You know what that was for,' she smiled. 'You're hardly qualified to be giving out fashion tips anyway.'

'Oooh, that hurts. So what do you think this place will be like? Have you been to a country dancing club before?'

'Never, I've only ever seen them on TV.'

'Me too, I wonder if they all wear cowboy hats and huge shiny belt buckles? That would be hilarious.'

'Just as long as you remember they all have shotguns too, Ross.'

'And lassoes? Do you reckon they've got long lassoes? That would be amazing. I might try to ask a guy in a Stetson if I can look at his big, long lasso. Do you think I would make it out alive?'

'After what you said to those cops last night, I'm just glad there'll be no drinking.'

I continued my train of thought. 'I could ask him at the urinals, now there's an idea.'

'I don't have any money left so just leave it for tonight, OK Ross?'

'*Now* who's being chicken?'

The journey passed swiftly and we were soon extracting ourselves from the Mustang as Kristen and her three girlfriends were making for the entrance of The Spittoon. The late September evening air was cool, the car park was brimming with pick-up trucks, and I suddenly felt very nervous. A glance at April and Jak confirmed that they also appeared a little on edge, while Kazuki merely hung his thumbs behind his dungaree straps and looked as excited as an unsuspecting child on his way to the dentist.

We hurried to catch up with the girls and then strategically walked behind them through the saloon-style doors. I estimated that stray gunfire would cause a 50% attrition rate in our first wave, so with any luck it would just be two of Kristen's friends lost and we could simply step over the bodies and get to the bar.

I was comfortable enough with our first encounter – the grotty inner-entrance pay booth that was a classic characteristic of all clubs. I began to think that maybe The Spittoon wouldn't be so scary after all, as I handed over a twenty-dollar bill for April and me. That soon changed, however, when we walked through the next set of doors and I was immediately pounced upon by a burly Stetson man who gruffly demanded, 'Hey, shirt,' while pointing at my groin.

'Oh, sorry,' I apologised, while pulling aside the tails of my shirt and pulling up my zip. How impressive, I thought – a man at the door to check that men have their flies done up. What a classy joint!

The beast then quashed my naivety with a rather rude and loud command. 'HEY, I SAID SHIRT!'

I turned to Jak in bewilderment but he looked as confused as I was.

The rudeness and loudness then stepped up a notch. 'TUCK YOUR FRICKIN' SHIRT IN, DICK WAD.'

I duly tucked my shirt in as if my life depended on it, and we were then permitted to enter the other world that was The Spittoon.

The corridor opened up to reveal a veritable showcase of all things American. We paused to soak up the atmosphere, admiring the huge wooden dance floor that formed a figure of eight in the centre of the vast space. A bucking bronco was situated in each of the two inner islands, with the remainder of the room taken up with seating, pool tables and bars. Our ears were being afflicted by the twanging guitars and whining fiddles that were the unmistakable hallmark of all of the world's worst music, while the lyrics were telling their well-worn stories of "cheatin' and fightin'".

The place was positively crammed with brawn and boobs. The brawn were fully clad in Wrangler jeans and shirts worse than my own, while the boobs wore matching Wranglers and smaller, tighter shirts using considerably less material. The multicoloured lighting above the dance floor put on a splendid show as it sparkled enthusiastically from the men's oversized belt buckles and the women's oversized cleavages.

'This is awesome!' remarked April as she looked around in fascination.

'This is awesome!' agreed Jak, while staring rather intently at one particularly impressive cleavage at the edge of the dance floor.

Kristen noted Jak's gaze and duly rebuked him. 'Hey, pop those eyes back in.'

We continued to the bar where the men bought the soft drinks and the women swooned at the display of buttocks on the dance floor. Jak and I actually did the honours as Kazuki could barely see above the wooden frontage or, for that matter, get the remainder of his body close enough once his belly button had touched the edge.

'Here you go, ladies,' I said while handing out the Diet Cokes to a sea of appreciative thanks.

'OK then everyone,' Kristen instructed, 'just one drink and then we're on that dance floor, agreed?'

The girls concurred, while Kazuki smiled and nodded without a particularly firm understanding of what he was committing to. Jak and I must have had apprehension written on our foreheads, as we were roundly barracked from all angles.

'Come on, you guys. Where's your sense of adventure?' started Kristen.

'Yeah, come on!' continued April. 'Ross, you owe me, and Jak, you owe me too for bailing out your buddy when you left him for dead.'

'Hey, that's a bit harsh,' defended Jak.

'But accurate, I think you'll find,' I added. 'OK then, this one drink then we'll have a little dance, I promise.'

'Goody!' the girls gushed in unison.

I sensed a night of very slow drinking ahead of me, but then all five girls suddenly downed their own beverages in some sort of pre-agreed frenzy of thirst.

'Right then, let's go!' Kristen smugly declared.

'Bollocks,' I muttered in defeat, before opening wide and draining my own glass. Kazuki followed my lead, although he only succeeded in pouring half down his throat while the remainder dribbled shamelessly down the front of his shirt. Our attention then turned to Jak.

'They've won, Jak,' I reasoned. 'Give it up, man, give it up. Just get in your Spanish dancing zone and you'll be fine.'

'I could dance to that because it's *good* music, but country? All this geeeetar stuff is freaking me out!'

'Calling Spanish music "good" is debatable, but I do agree with you about this shite. Nevertheless, are you really going to leave these lovely ladies exposed to the charms of Denver's wild cowboy folk?'

'You're right,' Jak confirmed, and dutifully sank his Coke. 'Let's go and show these hillbillies how this shit goes down in Spain.'

With agreement all around, we moved onto the dance floor and joined a line dance that was already in full flow. Our row of eight slotted in nicely behind a group of buckles and breasts whose every move we mimicked avidly. The dance progressed around the figure of eight as if it were a racing car circuit, affording us an ever-changing view of the ladies around the hall and a crossover point that was ripe for collisions.

Most of us just about managed to pick up the routine before the song changed and we had to start learning all over again. Kazuki, on the other hand, soon abandoned the country dancing in favour of a freakish backwards moonwalk around the floor. The locals loved it, and applauded him heartily as he made his way across the room. After several circuits even the bronco rides had stopped as their operators became similarly captivated by his performance. Kazuki thrived on the attention and started to throw in the odd twist and turn just to spice up the show.

We could see that he was losing his balance as we approached the crossing point for the umpteenth time, but we were all somehow powerless to prevent his fall. There followed a slow-motion sequence in which he fell backwards onto a tall and badly aged country gal who was heading in the opposite direction. Her well-worn hands managed to catch him on his way down and sweep him back to his feet. What we witnessed thereafter could only be described as a most disturbing moment, as their eyes locked together – his at a tender nineteen years old and hers probably the wrong side of fifty. She smiled broadly through her bedraggled straw-like hair, revealing a missing front tooth, while Kazuki graciously took her hand and kissed the back of it delicately in thanks. They then carried on dancing together and we were left to continue as a Kazuki-less line of seven.

We interspersed our dancing with a few games of pool and some surprisingly uneventful rides on the bronco, while occasionally catching sight of Kazuki with his scarecrow pensioner as their perverted mating rituals continued. During one of the girls' communal journeys to the toilet, Jak and I found ourselves a quiet booth in the corner.

'So Ross, are things going well with your "friend"?' he asked, teasingly.

'I think the "friends" thing is definitely going to be a bit of a challenge. But I suppose it's better than nothing.'

'And you never know what might happen in the future.'

'How do you mean?'

'Well, long-distance relationships usually break up at college so there's some hope right there. All you have to do is be the perfect gentleman, spend time with her, don't get involved with any other women, and wait patiently for your opportunity.'

'Maybe, maybe. Enough about April, anyway. I'll only end up frustrated again. Maybe now's a good time to talk about why you haven't shagged Kristen yet?'

Jak looked a little surprised. 'What? I don't know what you mean,' he defended.

'Listen, Jak, Kristen told me that the sheets are still dry on your relationship. Now, after all the shit you and Kaz gave me about me not sleeping with Chloe, I would be well within my rights to make some horrendous fun of you. But us ex-jailbirds have a more mature approach to life, so I'll give you the chance to explain first. *Then* I'll give you some abuse.'

'What did she say then, exactly?'

'Just that she was getting a bit bored of waiting. So what *is* your problem?'

He looked nervously around our table and then leant closer to me. 'I'm a virgin,' he whispered.

'What?'

'I said, I'm a virgin,' he repeated in muted tones.

'You're a virgin?' I exclaimed at excessive volume.

'Sh, sh. Quiet down, dude!' he urged.

I smiled. 'Of course you're a virgin, I never assumed otherwise.'

'What? How could you tell?'

'Listen, I'm sure Kristen must know too, so what's the problem?'

'I just know that she's experienced and things are going so well that I really don't wanna let this affect things.'

'Sure, she's probably had quite a lot of sex in her life. But if this thing between you really *is* that special, then I'm sure she'll break you in gently and only introduce the butt-plugs when you're absolutely ready.'

'Dude, don't be sick,' he grinned.

'Look, are you ready to go to that next level with her?'

'Of course I'm ready. I've been ready for the last nineteen fucking years!'

'So, just let things happen naturally and don't stress about what might go wrong. Remember that practise makes perfect and, besides, I bet she's never had Basque sausage before.'

Jak laughed zealously, and visibly relaxed before me.

'How did a virgin like you get so wise about sex

then, Ross?'

'What makes you think that I'm a virgin as well?'

'Well, you talk about sex as much as me, and I presume that's how you guessed my secret?'

'Jak, there are two types of people who talk excessively about sex – those who yearn for their *first* experience, and those who yearn for their *next* experience so that they can forget about the last one.'

'Right then, spill,' he demanded, while I wished I had just pretended to be a virgin.

'Who's that?' I stalled, while nodding to a female figure approaching our table.

Jak's gaze remained firmly on me. 'Don't change the subject now, just tell me exactly what your story is, Ross Cooper.'

'But she's coming! Look, here, she's coming...' I tailed off as the girl in question reached earshot. As Jak heard her boots on the hardwood floor, he then joined me in looking upwards at the pretty twenty-something cowgirl with her bright red lipstick and plentiful bosom.

'Hi guys!' she greeted. 'Which one of y'all is gonna kiss me then?' Jak and I shared a quizzical glance that solicited further explanation. 'It's my friend's bachelorette party and I've been dared to kiss one of you guys, so who's it gonna be?' she asked forcefully.

'My girlfriend's here,' Jak excused himself fretfully, 'but *he's* available, so go for it!'

Before I could enter into any discussion, the girl's lips were clamped firmly around my face and her cigarette-tainted tongue was probing the inner reaches of my mouth in keen exploration. Teeth, tongues, tonsils, epiglottises – they all clashed impossibly during the ten-second mauling.

When it was all over she rudely wiped her mouth on her sleeve and declared, 'There's plenty more where that came from, handsome,' before turning around and leaving me completely stunned.

'What the...?' I stuttered in disbelief.

'Awesome, just awesome!' enthused Jak wickedly before his face froze solid. He then muttered urgently, 'Shit, shit.'

'What's wrong with you? I'm the one who's been violated here.'

'Three o'clock, three o'clock.'

I looked to my left. Digital watches had ruined me.

'Not nine o'clock, you tool, *three* o'clock,' he corrected me.

I looked to my right and caught April's distant glare with a look of disappointment and disapproval washed right across her beautiful face. She turned to Kristen and they talked hurriedly.

'Oh, shit,' I said to myself, and to Jak, while we watched on intently.

A consensus between the girls appeared to be reached, and Kristen then walked over to deliver the jury's verdict.

'April's coming home with us,' she frostily stated. 'I'll speak to you later, Jak,' she added with a kiss on his cheek and a shamed look in my direction. My eyes then followed her as she re-joined April and the others, and they swiftly departed The Spittoon.

'Oh, shit. What just happened there?' I wondered out loud in exasperation.

'Chicks, man,' explained Jak, 'chicks.'

TEN

Our drive home from The Spittoon was a lonely one – April had deserted us in a mist of misunderstanding, and Kazuki didn't wish to be prised from the claws of his besotted cow-grandma. As Jak and I sped home on the I-25 out of Denver, I was still in a state of confusion.

'Don't worry about it,' consoled Jak.

'I know I shouldn't be worried and I shouldn't be bothered because I haven't done anything wrong. But I just hated seeing April looking so hurt.'

'Dude, don't you get it?'

'Get what?'

'*This* isn't really a problem. In fact, it's quite the opposite. Why do you think she seemed so upset after seeing you kiss that chick?'

'I thought she was just a bit annoyed that I was snogging some country bird after she had only left us for five minutes.'

'Yeah, but *why* would that bother her? Have you thought about that?'

'Well, she probably thought it was a bit rude when I was supposed to be treating her to a night out.'

'Let me spell it out for you, Ross – J.E.A.L.O.U.S.Y.'

Jak's idea put a whole new complexion on the

events that had transpired that evening. Perhaps April was developing some feelings for me and she really was jealous? But then again, maybe she was just disappointed that I had turned out to be the sort of jerk who couldn't spend one evening with her as a friend without trying to get some action elsewhere.

'I just need to explain to her what happened so we can smooth things over,' I decided.

'That's the last thing you need to do, my friend,' countered Jak. 'She's the one who jumped to conclusions and she's the one who needs to explain herself. There's no benefit in you telling her what really happened – what you really need is for her to find out for herself. That way she'll come crawling to you to apologise, and it's all good.'

Jak seemed to be speaking sense.

'Perhaps you're right. It isn't my fault that she took what she saw the wrong way, is it? Maybe I will wait this one out.'

'Damn skippy!' he agreed. 'Now, while you're waiting it out, you can tell me all about getting laid you non-virgin bastard.'

I'd hoped that conversation had passed, but in the comforting warmth of the Mustang I felt more at liberty to share than I had done earlier.

'Bethan Vidic.'

'Ah, the mysterious Bethan chick.'

'How do you know about her?'

'Oh, just something you must have slurred to Kristen back at the house party. Anyway, tell me more.'

'Well, our first time was well over a year ago now. We'd been going out for a couple of months.'

'So where did you fuck her?'

'In her parents' house.'

'Nice.'

'While her family were having a party downstairs.'

'Sweet.'

'On Easter Sunday.'

'Dude, you rock!'

'Yeah, well it sounds better than it actually was. Trust me, don't expect too much from the first time. But things do get better – that I can say for sure.'

'So what happened with you two in the end? Did you pound her so goddamn hard that you both crashed through her bedroom floor and into the middle of the party, where her furious daddy was waiting with a baseball bat?'

'Your imagination really is weird sometimes, Jak, do you know that?'

'So they tell me, so they tell me. Well then, what happened?'

I was comfortable in the Mustang, but not comfortable enough to dredge up *those* painful memories.

'It just ended, that's all. It just ended, and so did my life. Well, for a while anyway.'

'Man, she really screwed you up, didn't she?'

My concentrated silence gave Jak his answer.

'Anyway,' he finally said through the quiet, realising that my limit had been reached, 'I wonder whether Kaz is getting some country lovin' at the moment? How old do you reckon that woman was?'

'She had to be at least fifty. I just hope he doesn't put her hip out.'

'Can you imagine their hot throbbing bodies writhing up and down against each other in some back alley near The Spittoon?'

'Jak, stop,' I pleaded with amused disgust.

'I bet he shoots a really powerful load, that boy.'

'I said stop!'

'She'll be, like, "Oh Kazuki, baby, let me blow you like you've never been blown before..."'

I joined in, 'Yeah, and then she'll take her teeth

out.'

'You know it's true,' he laughed with me. 'We've just got to hope he can control himself though. I had a friend who just couldn't handle his bodily functions. He'd be getting a blow job then suddenly piss in the girl's mouth. It was really nasty.'

'Jak, there's no need for that.'

'I know,' he continued, 'and there's no need for him to follow-through when he farts in people's faces either, but he just can't help it.'

The abrupt end to Sunday night at The Spittoon made our radio show a little less tiring than it could have been, but we nevertheless relied on heavily caffeinated cans of Jolt Cola to make it through.

'You are tuned to KVCU at three-thirty a.m. on this Monday night/Tuesday morning, and you really need to get a life, even more so than Jumpin' Jak and myself.'

'That's right,' he added, 'now...BURP...oh, sorry, that Jolt's really hittin' the spot.'

'Thanks for sharing.'

'No problem, Ross. So, as I was about to say, here's another fine joint from Cypress Hill and then we'll be back with something a little bit special.'

As the music played and our microphones muted, I shook my head in dismay. 'Joint?'

'Hey, dawg, it ain't my problem if you're not street.'

Gangsta Jak was unstoppable at the best of times, but with a hundred milligrams of caffeine per can in his system, he was pure entertainment. The 'something special' to which he referred was a sugar-fuelled rap he had been preparing throughout the show and was about to unleash onto the world. I read through the scrawled lyrics in front of me and sought clarification.

'So, as I'm not "street", could you explain what a "J" is?'

'Dude, it's a joint...of marijuana.'

'OK, and what's a "forty"?'

'A big forty-ounce bottle of beer.'

'Cool, I think I've got it now. Are you nervous?'

'Dude, I was born for this shit. Now pass me another can.'

The eight cans of Jolt had all gone, just like Jak's perspective, and I was preparing for car-crash radio at its very best. Only sheer determination prevented me from wetting my pants with the anticipation, no matter how hard the litres of fluid swelled within my bladder.

The three minutes thirty-three seconds of *Insane in the Brain* took an eternity to pass, and I then played the swearing disclaimer to facilitate Jak's expletive-littered rap to conform to station policy. Next, I started the hard-hitting instrumental Jak had chosen as his accompaniment, and sat back in my chair.

To my left, Jak rose up from his seat and pulled his microphone from its stand. He closed his eyes and started bouncing to the beat, while moving his free hand rhythmically up and down like a cross between a traffic cop and a chicken. Blessedly, his eyes remained tightly shut throughout the performance, thus shielding him from my futile attempts to staunch the free-flowing tears of laughter.

With his game face firmly in place, he began in his best rap tongue:

'Rollin' with my homies, chillin' in the sun, grabbin' me some pussy and loadin' up my gun.'

It was a solid start, with a good number of rap clichés to kick things off.

'The shit goes down, my boots are brown, no need

to frown, cuz my ass is in town.'

Did really he just talk about his boots being brown after the shit went down?

'I'm gonna freak it like this, freak it like that, freak it like a mother fuckin' caaaaaaaat.'

Like a cat? Oh god.

'So roll up a J, whip out a forty, grab some bitches and have yo'selves a party.'

End it now. Please, Lord, end it now before my sides explode.

'I said roll up a mother fuckin' J, whip out a forty, grab some bitches and have yo'selves a party.'

He opened up his eyes and let out a triumphant whoop of delight. I rapidly composed myself and lowered the volume of the music.

'Well, you heard it here first, folks. That was Jumpin' Jak's rap debut, and I think we can safely say that you will never have heard anything quite like it before in your lives.'

'Thanks, man,' added Jak sincerely, as he took to his seat once more. 'Kristen, that one was for you, babe.'

'Yes, and that segment was brought to you by Jolt Cola – making white guys think they can rap since 1985.'

While the next song played, Jak sought more detailed feedback.

'So, what did you *really* think, Ross?'

'Honestly? I thought it was complete crap, but very compelling and very amusing crap.'

'I put my heart and soul into that,' he laughed, as the penny seemed to finally drop that he had no future in the music industry. 'Screw it, I had fun anyway.'

'That's all that counts,' I comforted.

We were then unexpectedly interrupted by the harsh red flashing of the studio phone.

'Record producer?' asked Jak, optimistically.

'Mental hospital?' I reasoned.

I removed my headphones and picked up the phone.

'Hello, KVCU?'

'...boom, boom...white guys should stick to rock...boom, boom...I sucked yo' daddy's cock...'

The line cut off and I was left aghast.

'Ross, dude,' said Jak, 'who was it?'

'It...it was that Hall Rapper guy again, it had to be.'

'What? I'm sure you're just making that guy up.'

'No, honestly, I'm sure. It had to be him. I think he was making some point about your rapping and then...well, then he talked about my daddy.'

'Wasn't it your mom last time?'

'I feel violated.'

The studio phone began flashing again.

'Right,' said Jak. 'I'm gonna answer this time. I'm sure you're making this shit up.'

'Be my guest, just prepare for your family to be desecrated.'

Jak eagerly grabbed the phone.

'Hello, KVCU?' he began expectantly. 'Oh, Kristen, hi...'

Kristen was no doubt calling to give him some moral support and massage his ego a little after his performance. The conversation appeared overly one-sided, with Jak only giving the occasional acknowledgement in between the doubtless words of pity. As the call came to a close, Jak began to look somewhat mischievous as he occasionally glanced towards me, and by the time he put the phone down I had the distinct impression that something was afoot.

'So what did Kristen have to say?'

'Oh, not much,' he lied rather obviously. 'She was just saying how she was enjoying the show while tucked up in bed. She couldn't sleep so she's in bed listening to us...in bed.'

The third time he mentioned 'bed' confirmed that Kristen was definitely not in bed. I couldn't figure out exactly what was going on, but I had a feeling that things were about to become clearer as Jak reached across to the mixer desk and faded out the music.

'Well, I hope you all enjoyed my little rap there, folks. It is with great regret that I have to announce my retirement from the rap world, but we will always share that very special moment.'

'You're bringing a tear to my eye, Jumpin' Jak.'

'Thanks, Ross. Anyhow, we're now about to start a new feature called "What we did last night", where Ross and I tell you listeners what crazy shit we got up to on Sunday night. So, Ross, why don't you start?'

I looked questioningly at his roguish face. We hadn't discussed any such feature and I had a feeling that this was related to his phone call from Kristen in some way.

'Well...' I hesitantly started, 'we went country dancing.'

'That's right. Ross and I went country dancing. And did anything strange happen while we were out country dancing?'

'Where do I begin?' I joked.

'How about anything strange involving Bachelorette parties?'

'Well, there *was* a crazy girl from a Bachelorette party who was dared to kiss one of us. She just about swallowed me whole for ten seconds while I was powerless to stop her!'

As soon as the words left my mouth, Jak's plan suddenly dawned on me. Kristen had undoubtedly been tasked with making April listen to the show, and her phone call must have been the signal for the little charade to begin. Jak said April needed to find out for herself what really happened, and she just had.

'OK, thank you, Ross. Now that feature's over, let's play another tune.' Jak faded out our microphones and then turned to me. 'How do you think the new feature went, Ross?'

'You sly bastard,' I grinned. 'You wonderfully sly bastard!'

As we arrived back at Cheyenne Arapaho not long after four a.m., the caffeine-induced high was subsiding and I was thoroughly prepared for bed. I was not, however, prepared to see April waiting in reception. She was curled up in a ball on an uncomfortable-looking chair, wearing a pink towelling dressing gown and dribbling uncontrollable down it as she slept.

'I'll leave you to it,' said Jak with a knowing smile, as he continued onwards to our room.

I took a moment to admire April's innocent beauty as the string of saliva continued its relentless passage into the absorbent towel. She was as radiant asleep as she was awake, even without her brilliant green eyes on show.

I noticed a small cardboard box on the floor next to her with a pile of serviettes on top. I reached for one of them, folded it into a small square, and began wiping her mouth delicately while crouched beside her. She began to purr adorably and raised her hand to the other side of her mouth like a kitten cleaning its whiskers. Her eyes began to open ever so slightly as she became conscious to the situation and gently took the serviette from my hand to continue wiping herself.

'Oh, god, I'm such a drooler!' she spoke softly

while her eyelids opened further.

'Don't worry,' I reassured her, quietly. 'At least now I know why you have a towel dressing gown.'

'Very funny. What time is it?'

'Just after four. What are you doing down here?'

She began to straighten herself out and release her legs from the knot they had formed on the seat.

'Well, I *was* supposed to be waiting to talk to you, but apparently it didn't quite work out like that.'

'Well I'm here now, so let's talk.' I sat down on the floor right next to her.

'I heard your show. Well, some of it anyway. Kristen started banging on my door at some ridiculous hour.'

'Oh, right.'

'Yeah, she brought these cookies,' she pointed to the box on the floor, 'and insisted Laura and I ate them with her before she would leave. I thought it was a bit weird.'

'I can imagine.'

'We saved some for you and Jak, by the way – help yourself.'

'Thanks.' I opened the box and selected one with chocolate chips. 'So what did you think to Jak's rap then, being an established student of creative writing?'

'Oh, truly world class!' she said with heavy sarcasm. 'But you guys really do put on an entertaining show.'

'Well thank you. It's just a shame that people only listen when they are tricked into it with a box of cookies.'

'Hey, I listened to your first show. It's just that your new slot isn't exactly primetime, is it?'

'Maybe not.'

'Anyway, as well as the rap I also heard your so-called "new feature".'

'Listen, it really wasn't my....'

'Don't worry, don't worry,' she interrupted, 'Kristen explained afterwards that she and Jak came up with the plan.'

'Good.'

'I just feel like such a dufus about the whole thing.'

I wasn't about to let her off lightly. 'About *what*?'

'You're not gonna make this easy, are you? About last night.'

'What about last night?' I prolonged her agony.

'Well, about me acting like a spoiled child and leaving you there at the club.'

'You, a spoiled child?' I beamed.

'Anyway, I'm sorry for jumping to conclusions,' she continued earnestly. 'Obviously I took it the wrong way – I just thought it was a bit rude of you to be hooking up with someone else when you were there with me and the other girls. But I realise now that I was wrong and I'm really sorry.'

'Apology accepted. At the risk of repeating past speeches, let's just forget it, OK?'

'Why *do* we keep doing this to each other do you think?'

'*We*?' I teased. 'I seem to remember a lot of apologies coming from *you*, actually!'

'Hey, that's not fair!' she pleaded while her dimples flared delectably.

'Maybe we're just destined to have one of those difficult relationships?'

'Perhaps you're right, Ross. Roosevelt and Churchill, maybe that's us.'

'Churchill did once say that you can always rely on Americans to do the right thing – after they've tried everything else.'

'Don't you make me beat you with my pillow again!'

'OK, OK, I'll stop.'

'You'd better!' she laughed.

In the joy of the moment, and with the partially digested cookie stirring up endless stores of latent caffeine and sugar in my system, I made an uncharacteristically bold move.

'You know, Jak had a different theory about what happened last night.'

'Oh, really?' she replied with intrigue. 'What did *he* think happened then?'

'He thought that maybe...maybe you were a bit jealous.'

Would I touch on a nerve? I held my breath and awaited her crucial judgement.

'Oh...' she responded, a little uneasily, 'well that's Jak for you.'

It was an ambiguous response, but one I was happy with for the time being. It was better to have a flicker of hope than to dash my dreams forever, there and then.

'Yes, that certainly *is* Jak. Anyway, we'd better get to bed.'

'Sure,' yawned April as she sat up from her chair. 'Separately, of course. We don't want to give Jak any ideas.'

'Of course,' I agreed, while that flicker of hope began to grow a little stronger.

ELEVEN

'Come on, you can run faster than that!'

Jak's wilting body was trying to keep up with me, but finding it increasingly difficult.

'Dude,' he gasped, 'no more, no more.'

'But we've only been running for a couple of miles. Come on, we're almost there.'

The entrance to Chautauqua Park was just becoming visible as we continued up the steady incline of Baseline Road. Having finally overcome Jak's lack of will to go running with me, I hadn't anticipated his distinct lack of fitness. However, I saw the outdoor bonding session as a necessity – not only to save his relationship with Kristen, but also to save my own sanity.

'Tell me again why you've brought me all this way?' he wheezed.

'Because we both have women troubles and we're not going to leave this park until they're resolved.'

'Bitches...who'd want them?'

'We would.'

'Oh, yeah.'

His tortuous stride stopped on the gravel track just past the main entrance, where he crouched down while panting like a dog and sweating like a pig.

'Well done, Jak, well done,' I congratulated him

while doing some stretches. 'We can walk to the foothills.'

He rose from his stoop with a reddened face of agony. 'Cool, I'm fine now, I'm fine.'

As we began our walk through the meadow, I wasted no time in getting down to business.

'So, what needs to be done to get you and Kristen back on track?'

'Sex, and plenty of it.'

I adopted a doctor's bedside manner. 'OK, good, that's good. Now you've been dating for well over a month, and she's absolutely gagging for it, right?'

'Right.'

'And you're acting like some virginal priest's son who refuses sex when it's handed to you on a silver platter?'

'Well, I wouldn't have put it quite like that,' he protested.

'Look, I didn't want to have to bring this up, Jak, but Kristen told me about last weekend.'

'Shit.'

'How she stripped naked right in front of you and all you could do was say that you needed to go and do your engineering homework?'

'Well, mid-terms are coming up and I really *do* have a lot to do.'

'Jak, Jak, Jak,' I shook my head in dejection. 'You don't need to spin me that bullshit, OK? This is exactly what we're here to resolve. Now what *really* caused you to run out of that room like a thirteen-year-old homosexual when a flaming-hot girl was stripped down to her boobs and muff, literally begging you to make sweet love to her?'

His voice began to crack with the strain as his emotions abruptly poured out. 'The pressure, man, the pressure! It's just too fucking much. I just can't handle the pressure! I've talked about sex since I was ten years old without ever thinking I would actually get the chance to *do* it, and now the time has come, I've just got all this expectation – from Kristen *and* from me. It's just unbearable, man, I can't deal with it.'

'If you'll permit me to summarise then: you can't get it up. Is that about right?'

Jak became unusually riled. 'Aren't you listening to me? It's the pressure, the pressure.'

'OK, OK, I'm sorry, I'm just trying to establish how all this expectation actually prevents you from having sex?'

'Well, it just stops me from...you know...getting excited about things.'

'*So you can't get it up?*'

'Well, yes, if that's how you want to put it, I guess you're right. I can't get it up.'

Perhaps it wasn't the best time to giggle, but I really couldn't stop myself. 'Hey, erectile dysfunction is nothing to be ashamed of. There are plenty of sixty-year-olds in exactly the same position as you.'

Thankfully he looked sideways and gave a little smile. 'How is this helping me, exactly?'

'OK, it's all out in the open now. We're here, communing with nature, and you've just shared your hilarious little secret with the trees and the Flatirons. Once we get into the hills we're gonna resolve all of your problems.'

'How?'

'Leave that to me. Now, let's just enjoy the rest of the walk.'

'OK, but how about we get your shit out of the closet as well?'

'Well, I'm not as screwed up as you, that's obvious. I feel better already, maybe we should concentrate on you?'

'Not so fast, Mr Cooper!' he mimicked my doctor's patter. 'So you've been *friends* with April for how long now?'

'About two months.'

'Two months, hmmmm, interesting. And you're struggling to accept that you'll only ever be friends with this girl?'

'Possibly.'

'Possibly? I didn't want to have to bring this up, Ross, but Kristen did tell me about that little "gift" she helped you with.'

'Shit.'

'How you secretly removed a photo of April's fifteen dogs and twelve cats from her room, and Kristen helped you to find a special frame for it. Only, before you actually sealed the picture in the frame and gave it to April, you wrote a confession of your undying love on the back of it. Now is that the action of a man who is fully comfortable in his relationship with this girl, or is that the action of a coward with gonads the size of peanuts?' I bowed my head in shame. He'd got me, bang to rights. 'So, now that *your* little secret is out there with the trees and all that shit, let's do something about it.'

'What did you have in mind?' I asked fearfully.

'Well, my remedy for your sad illness, Mr Cooper, is some words of advice that you should absorb and act upon.'

'I'm ready, hit me with it.'

'OK. If you really feel so strongly about this girl, then TELL HER TO HER FACE AND STOP BEING SUCH A PUSSY!' Jak's sudden outcry left a ringing in my ear and a queasiness in the pit of my stomach. 'Man, they're not all like Bethan, you know. You've got to trust again – you've got to take a chance.'

'Easier said than done,' I muttered to the rocky path as we neared the tree line.

No further words were spoken until we were in the thick of the hills – I was far too busy considering Jak's advice while he was no doubt pondering exactly what I had in store for him. His plain speaking was understandable, but he wasn't telling me anything I didn't already know. April and I had built up such an amazing friendship over the previous few weeks, but that next step just seemed insurmountable.

It wasn't long before the clearing I had discovered with Kristen all those weeks ago once again presented itself as a haven from the rugged terrain. It wasn't quite as welcoming in October as it had been in the late summer, but the memories still came flooding back.

I welcomed Jak into my reminiscence. 'Here's the spot.'

'Oh, the place where you and Kristen nearly...' The thought clearly caused him some distress.

'Yes, but more importantly this is the place where *you* are going to shag *me* senseless.' He stared at me with a look of frightened bewilderment. I continued, 'Not *actually* shag me, of course.' He let out a sigh of much needed relief. 'No, what you're gonna do is entice me, allow yourself to relax and just enjoy the rewarding pleasures that come forth from your loins.'

'I think that sounds worse,' he fretted.

'Look, we're just gonna do a bit of role-playing, OK? Now, begin seducing me.'

'What?'

'Loosen up, Jak, just imagine that I'm Kristen.' I pouted my lips suggestively.

'But I don't know what to say.'

'Just tell me exactly what you're going to do to me, in every minute, magnificent detail. Tell me how you're going to tenderly undress me until I'm left exposed to the mountain breeze in my bra and panties, which you will then remove using only your teeth. Tell me how your tongue will explore my every inner crevice and taste every last drop of my desire for you.'

'I'm getting worried about you, Ross.'

'Just prove to me that you're hot and ready for action, you Basque stallion, you.'

'Dude, I knew you British were weird, but I really had no idea.'

'OK, OK,' I despaired. 'Well if saying this stuff to my face is too difficult, how about you just imagine what you would say?'

'OK, I can handle that.'

'Good, so just say the things in your head and see where the mood takes you.'

He began to periodically close his eyes and then open them again as we stood together in the middle of the glade. After around half a minute he stopped and looked at me with satisfaction.

'Cool, cool, let's go home now, Ross – I've done it.'

'What, in thirty seconds? My, my, my, we really *do* have a problem. You need to take your time. You can't just say "hop aboard, baby" and leave it at that. The foreplay is as much for you as it is for her. Right, forget the dirty talk for now. Let's just see how you handle a woman. Take me gently by the waist and lower me onto the grass.'

'Are you out of your fucking mind?'

'Just do it, bitch.'

'I thought *you* were the bitch.'

'Just take me down.'

'If you're sure,' he surrendered, before grabbing me by the shoulders and taking my legs from beneath me with a swift sweep of his right foot. I fell in a heap on the wet grass while he laughed riotously.

I looked up at his chuckling figure in despondency.

'Nice. I'm trying to help you and this is the thanks I get?' In a quest to stem his amusement, I swung both my legs at his and brought his body down right on top of me. His head landed only inches from my own, while his torso rested heavily on mine.

'Ouch!' he moaned.

'Not very nice, is it?' I scoffed.

He began to adjust his position but then, all of a sudden, froze still. He then asked in a slow, breathy whisper, 'What's that poking into my thigh?'

'Great, great, you're really getting into this role playing now,' I praised. 'Go with it now, talk dirty some more.'

'No dude, *seriously*, what *is* that poking into my thigh?'

'Oh, sorry,' I apologised while reaching down into my pocket. 'It's my torch,' I explained while brandishing the Maglite in my hand.

At that very moment there was a rustling in the trees as a remarkably large Alsatian dog stumbled upon our little setting and started barking rabidly. In perfect unison our heads looked skywards at the beast that was bearing down on us, while my hand still firmly gripped the phallic torch proudly in the air. Jak clung tightly to my waist, holding our bodies closely together as the fear swelled in his underwear.

'DOWN OLLY, DOWN BOY,' commanded an elderly lady who had joined our little gathering. The barking stopped sharply before the lady then exclaimed, 'Oh, gosh!' at the sight of our twisted, sweating bodies embracing feverishly on the ground.

'Good afternoon,' we greeted her simultaneously, still not wishing to move a single limb for fear of it being sheared off by the numerous razor-sharp teeth on display.

'I think it's disgusting! You two should be thoroughly ashamed of yourselves,' chastised the old dear before dragging herself and her dog back into the hills.

With the passing of the danger, we both sprung to our feet and brushed ourselves down.

'Lesson over?' I asked.

'Let's just go home and never speak of this again,' insisted Jak.

With his dreadlocks bowed in deference to the fizzing glass of Alka-Seltzer in front of him, Kenny cut a desperate figure in my Creative Writing class the following day. As ever, he had a full compliment of students filling the classroom, and the best part of a crate of beer exuding from his every pore.

'Hey guys, how's it goin'?' he croaked sluggishly at nobody in particular, while struggling to raise his head to meet our enthusiastic faces. 'Today you're gonna become poets. We've done all that story writing stuff for the last couple of months, so now it's time for the real deep shit.' He took a generous gulp from his glass and then paused with a strained expression, before letting out a belch of considerable intensity. 'Ah, that shit's working good,' he continued. 'Anyway, poetry, yes, that's what you'll be writing today.

'But first off, I want you to read some poems to each other in pairs, so hook up with someone, pick up a book from my desk, and get going.' Kenny then staggered to his feet and headed for the exit. 'I think another Bud just completed its journey through my system,' he explained, 'so I'm gonna have to go take the snake for a walk.'

Brandon turned to offer me his services.

'Can I read you some love poetry, Ross? You never pair up with me anymore, and I really miss you!'

April and I had been inseparable partners in Kenny's class since we sorted out our post-Spittoon differences, so she instinctively leapt up to collect a book for us to read from.

'Sorry, Brandon – it looks like I've had a better offer.'

'You bitch,' he smirked on his way to the other side of the room.

'What did we get?' I enquired with obvious dread on April's return.

She flashed the cover at me. 'Don't pull any faces, but it's called *Modern Poetry Classics*.'

'You know I hate poetry! This is going to be hell.'

'Don't be like that, Ross! I don't know what you're problem is with poetry, anyway.'

'I just think it's a lazy way to write. Not many words, no real story, and lots of elaborate bullshit that could mean a million and one things, but we're somehow expected to analyse it and figure out what the writer was eating for breakfast that morning.'

'You're such a cynic. Poetry is so powerful and incredibly creative. You're just jealous because you can't write poems like these guys.'

I took the bait. 'No way! The problem is that *anyone* can write that crap and pretend to be all deep and meaningful, when all you actually have to do is string together a random group of words.'

'We'll agree to disagree for now. Here, I'll read one first.'

April proceeded to read a page of flowery drivel that seemed to be heading nowhere fast.

'Stop, please, no more, I can't take it!' I interrupted while feigning a sharp pain in my chest.

'But it was just getting good,' she defended with a smile.

As if to save my ears from being exposed to any more of the pointless nonsense, Kenny returned from his bathroom break and stopped our activity. 'OK guys, enough of that for now, put those books down,' he instructed us in salvation.

April and I exchanged a playful sneer at each other before Kenny spoke once more. 'What I want you to do now is spend the next thirty minutes writing a poem of your own, but that poem can only be a maximum of fifty words in length.' It appeared to be an overly generous allocation of time from the man who once asked us to write a five-hundred-word short story in ten minutes.

He continued, 'I've just had a call from Tonia – that fine piece of ass I was telling you about last week?' Kenny had, indeed, entertained us with tales of a drunken fumble with a poor unsuspecting girl the previous week. 'Anyways, she's waiting for me back in my room, so I gotta go get some cat. Get writing, I'll be back in thirty.'

With that, he bolted out of the door and left us to our own devices. Our nonchalant commencement of the exercise was testament to how accustomed we had become to Kenny's strange behaviour. He had shared many inappropriate details with us over the semester, and news of his late-morning sexual exploits was just another to add to the list.

'Thirty minutes for fifty words?' I clarified with April.

'That's what the man said,' she confirmed. '*Now* you'll see what true poetry is all about – sweating to craft the perfect combination of words to tell your story with style and elegance.'

'Yeah maybe, *or* I'll just jot something down in a couple of minutes and then go for a long walk.'

'We'll see,' she challenged.

A studious silence fell across the classroom as we set about the task. I spent the first five minutes doodling and trying to disrupt April's work with childish nudges from below the table. During one particularly fierce exchange of shin-kicks, however, I had a sudden moment of realisation. It was a realisation that my poem could serve as a veiled declaration of love just as my pet photo frame gift had done earlier. Sure, it was cowardly act, but at least I was beginning to embrace Jak's advice while giving myself an exciting, if slim, chance of revealing my true feelings for April.

After twenty long minutes of sheer concentration, I had finished my masterpiece and I was ready for an audience of one. The noise level in the classroom had slowly risen as others had finished their work, so I keenly added to the chatter.

'Finished!' I proudly told April.

'Well done!' she patronised sarcastically. 'Just give me a minute and I'll be done too.'

Sixty seconds ticked by and, true to her word, April was ready.

'OK Ross, you go first.'

'With pleasure, April, with pleasure.'

There was no time for nerves – I had only my wits and my cowardice to see me through. With my head firmly down, I began reading my sincere words at a measured pace.

'It began as friendship

Locking eyes across the room
Only speaking in smiles
Volatile beginnings
Exploding into more

An amazing woman
Perfect golden skin of seduction
Rippling brown locks of loveliness
Irreplaceably charming dimples of delight
Lusciously fulsome lips of lure.'

I glanced up from my confession to find April with a look of contemplation. For one exquisite moment I wasn't quite sure how she had taken my poem or if she had been able to decipher the message locked within the words.

'Not bad, not bad,' she finally praised, while still maintaining an air of reflection. 'Do you mind if I have a look?' she asked while gesturing towards the paper in my hand.

Regret rapidly washed over me as my quivering hand passed over the sheet of doom. What had I been thinking? This was neither the time nor the place to be dealing with this sort of thing, and I could have just blown my chances. You idiot, Ross, you spineless idiot.

Her eyes danced down the page and her confusion suddenly cleared to reveal a knowing smile.

'Ah, now I get it. The first letters – I.L.O.V.E.A.P.R.I.L., right?' She laughed, loud and hard. 'Very clever, very clever indeed. I guess now you've proved that poetry really *is* bullshit! I presume that's what you were trying to do?'

With the perfect get-out on offer, I snatched at it desperately.

'Well, I had to show you, didn't I?' I agreed in full headlong retreat. My false laugh resounded awkwardly in my ears, but April appeared to be oblivious to my masked anxiety.

'Good one, Ross, good one,' she giggled, while my testicles shrivelled in disgrace.

TWELVE

'Dude, why do you keep doing this to yourself?'

Jak had just asked me the very question I had asked myself a thousand times.

'Because I'm a fool?' I suggested.

'No, because you're a pussy,' he chided. 'Look, if you just took my advice and actually *told* her how you felt, then there would be no need for these pathetic games of yours.'

'Yes, and if *you* took *my* advice you would have got laid by now,' I countered cruelly.

'I'm working on it, don't you worry. But how will playing these pathetic songs actually make a difference?'

'It's just the latest element of my subversive strategy to tell her without actually telling her, if you know what I mean?' I spoke with such genuineness that I almost believed it myself.

'You're out of your tiny mind. But hey, I'll go along with it if that's what you really want to do.'

'It'll only be a couple of tracks anyway – surely our vast band of listeners can survive without your rap shit for five minutes?'

'They can probably handle the lack of rap, but I'm just worried they can't handle mushy love songs.'

'We'll be fine,' I enthused. 'It's not mushy stuff

anyway, you'll see. Don't sweat it!'

With our radio show about to start, we put on our headphones and I cued up the first song. April had promised to listen to the start of the show while studying for her mid-term exams, and so my latest spineless act was about to get underway.

'Welcome, welcome, welcome!' I greeted our listeners.

'Yes, good evening C.U., I'm Jumpin' Jak, and Ross and I will be here with you for the next two hours, taking you through your late night mid-term studying hell.'

'That's right, so let's get started!' I pressed 'play' on the CD machine and the hard drum and xylophone introduction to *A Girl Like You* by Edwyn Collins began. With the first line of "I've never known a girl like you before" it was the perfect opener that even Jak seemed to enjoy.

'Not bad, not bad,' he admitted while the music played. 'I was expecting some Frank Sinatra shit.'

'I told you not to worry. Just another one and it will all be over.'

'What, your relationship with April?'

'If she couldn't figure out that poem then there's no way she'll realise something's going on here.'

'But we always start with gangsta rap – don't you think she'll notice the difference?'

I began doubting myself. 'Shit, do you think it's that obvious?'

'Well, put it this way, we're now two minutes into the first record and we've normally had at least ten swear words by this point.'

'Maybe you're right. I don't want to be too obvious.'

'Too late for that.'

'Maybe not,' I reasoned, rapidly searching through my folder of CDs to find a more suitable song to play next.

As Edwyn reached his conclusion, I faded the music down and began the cover-up operation. 'So that was Edwyn Collins there, dedicated to Kristen from her beloved Jak on this extra special mid-term exam show. We'll be playing dedications and requests throughout the night, so do give us a call on 2-5822 to get involved.'

Jak looked over at me with an incredulous smile while I carried on the pretence. 'So next up we have a song dedicated to April and Laura who are hard at work studying in Cheyenne Arapaho. I hope this doesn't bring up too many painful memories for you both – it's *Cuddly Toy* by Roachford.'

I was rather proud of my song choice at such short notice – the indirect reference to our calamitous pillow fight would keep the mystery alive, while the lyrics still rang true with lines like "What I need is a girl like you, to call my very own".

'Cleverly done,' complimented Jak. 'There's just one problem with this new plan of yours.'

'What's that?'

'Oh, maybe just the fact that April and Kristen are our only listeners. How are we gonna fill the next two hours with dedications and requests when we've just made personalised dedications for our entire audience?'

He had a point, but I wasn't about to be defeated. 'I've got the perfect solution.'

I hurriedly briefed Jak before leaving the studio and picking up the telephone in reception. Just as Roachford was coming to a close, I made the call.

'Hello,' began Jak down the phone, 'this is KVCU and you're live on air!'

'Yes, hello?' I replied in an appalling American accent, trying to sound like an elderly lady with her dentures and hearing aid removed. 'Hello, is anyone there?'

'Yes, this is KVCU and you're live on air!'

'Oh, hello KVCU, it is so nice to be talking to you. I've been such a fan of your show. I tune in every week you know.'

'How lovely of you!' gushed Jak. 'What's your name?'

'Yes, I'm a big fan. My name is Patti Weston.'

'Well, Patti, what is a young lady like yourself doing up at three a.m.?'

'Well,' my voice cackled erratically, 'the nurse has just emptied my colostomy bag so I'm ready for a good shit now.'

'Oh, how nice.' I could tell that Jak's voice was quivering, but he just about managed to maintain his solemnity. 'Well, what music can we play for you, dear?'

'Oh, you're such a nice young gentleman. It's so nice to speak to a young man with manners. And that English co-host of yours is such a charmer too. I've also heard he's quite the man in the bedroom.'

'I'm sure he is, Patti, I'm sure he is.'

'Yes, quite a pile driver by all accounts.'

'So what can we play for you? Maybe something soft to nurse you back to sleep while your bag begins to fill once more?'

'Oh, yes, the record...the musical disc record. Yes, I'm not sure if you'd have this one, as it *is* quite an old tune. But if you have it, and if it isn't too much trouble, I'd be ever so grateful if you could play *Pussy Ain't Shit* by Funkdoobiest?'

'Well, ma'am, I'm sure we can help you out there.'

'Oh, that's wonderful, young man. And please could I dedicate it to my boyfriend, Dick?'

'Of course you can, Patti, anything for you.'

'You know he's only five feet tall, and shrinking by the day, but I've started to call him Big Dick again since we discovered that Niagara stuff, if you know what I mean.'

'Alrighty, that's great, Patti. Well, thank you so much for calling!'

'Oh, thank you too KVCU. Say hi to that handsome Ross for me, won't you?'

'I certainly will, Patti. Goodbye!'

'Goodbye, sugar cheeks!'

'OK then listeners,' concluded Jak, 'especially for Patti and all the other senior bitches out there, here's a little Funkdoobiest.'

'Ross, Ross.'

I became vaguely aware of my name being whispered and my arm being shaken, but was too tired to respond.

'Ross, Ross,' persisted the voice as I rolled over underneath the sheets and moved my head closer to the source of the greeting. April's heavenly scent revived me in an instant and my eyes opened widely.

'Oh...April...hi,' I replied throatily at the sight of her smiling face hunched over me.

She continued to whisper so as not to wake my roommates. 'Tennis, eight a.m., don't you remember?'

'Shit,' I said in acknowledgment of my tardiness. If April had asked me to castrate myself with some rusty scissors I would have, so when she asked if I'd play a very early tennis match the morning after my extremely late radio show, I naturally said yes.

'Don't worry,' she calmed me, 'we've got ten minutes before our court booking starts.'

'Cool, just give me five and I'll be ready.'

'OK, I'll wait out here.' She signalled towards the study room and closed the door behind her.

With barely a couple of hours' sleep under my belt, the world seemed like a strange place and I could sense that my judgment was severely compromised. I had a history of odd behaviour when I was sleep-deprived – I had once shaven my legs instead of my face, and hadn't even realised until the following day when the itching started. In the drunk-like fog that clouded my every action that morning, anything was possible.

I miraculously managed to dress myself in proper sports attire, and then stumble out to join April in the study room.

'Wow, that was quick,' she said cheerfully.

'I'm always quick to come in a woman...I mean, for a woman...I mean...shit, I don't know what I mean.' There was no stopping the flow of idiocy.

'I wouldn't go advertising that one, Ross.'

'Let's just go play tennis.'

We made it outside without any further words as April allowed me the time to adjust to the living world. It was a crisp morning, barely above freezing, and the shock of the cold sobered me up to the point where I could string together a semi-rational sentence.

'Why did I agree to this?' I asked as we headed across campus to the sports centre.

'Because you promised you'd play me some time!'

'But why today, why so early?'

'Hey, I haven't had all that much sleep either, you know. I was studying until two-thirty, listening to your show actually. All those calls you made up were great! Thank you for the dedication too – Laura was very amused.'

'Glad to be of service. But you still haven't answered my question: why today?'

'This is a stressful week with all our exams, so I just thought it was a good way to start the day!' Her enthusiasm was unending.

'I suppose it *did* seem like a good idea at the time.'

'Cheer up, grumpy, you'll enjoy it!'

There was a really excitable edge to April that morning, but I couldn't quite put my finger on where it was coming from. After all, we were in the middle of a week of academic hell, so what was there to be so goddamn happy about?

We were soon on the outdoor court, having collected our rackets and balls from the sports centre reception. I kept my tracksuit on to shield me from the cold, while April keenly stripped down to her polo shirt and Lycra shorts. It was almost too much to take at that early hour, but I somehow managed to contain myself.

'Won't you be cold?' I wondered aloud while we prepared ourselves at the side of the net.

'Not me, I'm hot stuff!'

'Of course you are,' I cautiously agreed.

We parted in order to retreat to our own side of the net, each carrying a racket and a couple of balls.

'Hey, look at these!' called April from the baseline.

I turned around to see her with a ball in each of the breast pockets on her shirt, with her hands squeezing them playfully. It was the sort of joke I would have expected of Jak, Brandon or myself, but never April. Despite not being in the best of fettle myself, it was still staggeringly clear to me that she wasn't being her usual self. Sure, she was a lively, witty and fun girl, but I had never seen this level of bubbliness before. Something was definitely going on.

'Very nice,' I shouted back at her.

'I've never had them this big!'

I was beginning to feel a little uncomfortable with this new April. It was as if she was in the midst of some drug-induced euphoria that just wouldn't end.

'Do you want to serve first?' I offered.

'No, you go ahead. I want to keep my new boobs

for as long as possible!'

I threw a ball into the air and followed its path intently. As its trajectory crossed the early morning sun I was temporarily dazzled by the light and completely lost track of where I was. In that moment of blindness my mind suddenly had the spare capacity to figure out what was going on with April, and the conclusion it drew was one of epic proportions. My face remained pointed skywards while my vision fruitlessly tried to find the bright green fluffy ball. An unexpected bounce on my head confirmed that the ball had already returned to earth.

'You're such a dork!' laughed April coarsely.

'I know, I know,' I conceded, with a nervous excitement at the revelation that April had truly understood the significance of her radio dedication. It was suddenly all so clear – the song had finally cast aside any doubt that she may have had about my feelings. Once she had the full picture of how I felt, she could barely conceal her delight. She wasn't high on any kind of drugs – she was high on love.

'Here, let me serve,' she said while beginning to remove one of the balls from her shirt.

With my mind still too sleep-starved to restrain my bravery, I decided to end her charade there and then.

'So what *has* got into you today then?'

'How do you mean?' she smiled exquisitely.

'You know what I mean – you're just so happy.'

'Well,' she spoke bashfully, 'I did get some pretty awesome news last night.' This is it, Ross, this is it. Enjoy the moment, savour every last drop. Remember every single detail so you can tell the story to your grand kids.

'Oh yeah, what was that then?' I barely needed to ask the question, but felt it only polite. She was practically bursting to get the words out. Her body swung mischievously from side to side as she, too, took great pleasure in the moment. Her faultless lips then opened to speak the words that would change my life forever.

'Shawn, my boyfriend, just got a transfer to C.U.! Isn't that amazing!'

Without pause, she served. I was too stunned to breathe, let alone move my body, and the fiercely struck ball bounced swiftly from the hard surface before nestling itself firmly in my groin.

'Oh, god, are you all right?' came the call from across the net.

'No, I don't think I am,' I replied with complete honesty as I fell to my knees.

I made it through our sixty-minute court booking with a superhuman effort of emotional suppression and tolerance to groinal agony. My tired mind had played the cruellest of tricks on me, while April had compounded the error with a bombshell I had never expected. Since our ice-skating date that never was, she had barely mentioned the homosexual figure skating champion she believed to be her boyfriend, and I didn't even know his name. While that may have been her compassionate way of sparing my feelings any further hurt, there had still been a part of me that optimistically hoped she was forgetting all about him and falling for me. My stupidity had clearly reached new depths.

On our return to Cheyenne Arapaho, April insisted on re-introducing me to her trusty ice pack before I could finally make my excuses and get back to safe ground. I arrived back at my room to find Jak collecting his books together.

'Hey Jak,' I said in a slightly higher pitch than I had possessed before the tennis match.

'Dude, what happened to you?' As well as my voice, Jak was also referring to the ice pack I was tenderly clutching to my groin.

'You don't want to know,' I replied dejectedly.

Jak's face broke out into a glowing smile. 'You told her, didn't you? You finally fucking told her! Dude, that's awesome. Shit though, I guess she didn't take it so well if she ended up kicking you in the 'nads.'

'Believe me, it's worse than that, *much* worse.' I had neither the energy nor inclination to try and explain. 'I'm going to bed, I need sleep.' I made my way to the bedroom.

'OK dude, but before you go I've got some hot gossip for you.'

With the slim hope that Jak's news could perk up my day, I stopped in the doorway and turned back to hear his revelations.

'Go on.'

'You remember Chad from down the hall? Well it turns out he quit last week – something about making so much money selling weed he didn't need a degree anymore.'

Jak had clearly failed me in the exciting news department.

'Cool. Right, well I'm going to bed.'

'Hang on, there's more. He finally moved out last night and Brandon reckons we're gonna be getting someone new on our hall today. Apparently some Californian guy called Shawn.'

Without further words being exchanged, I turned back around and went straight for my bed. The ice pack had done a thoroughly good job of numbing my testicles, so I clutched it to my chest while trying to sleep in the vain hope that it might numb my heart.

THIRTEEN

The emotional and physical exhaustion afforded me an unexpectedly sound sleep on that Tuesday morning. I had no classes at all during the day, as my physics lecturers preferred that we spend our time preparing for the mid-term exams that came later in the week. While the studious future Nobel Prize winners were no doubt following that advice to a tee, I had just endured a tortuous early morning of pain and duly slept through the remainder of the daylight.

I woke just after six p.m. to the sound of Jak and Kristen arguing loudly in the adjacent room. My mind briefly recollected the events of the morning, but the psychological pain seemed to have miraculously subsided. Perhaps it had been absorbed into the moist gel pack I was still holding to my chest, I really didn't know, but I was certainly feeling far more positive than I had been.

I bounded up out of bed and, realising I was still wearing my full tracksuit, strode confidently out into the study room just in time to catch Kristen's parting shot.

'JUST GO TO HELL!' she angrily bellowed at Jak before slamming the door violently in her wake.

'Baby! Baby, please...' called Jak in a futile

attempt at reconciliation, before sinking down into the chair at his desk and acknowledging my emergence with a gruff, 'Morning.'

I sought an explanation for the outburst. 'What was all that about?'

'Bitches, dude, bitches. I should have let you ass-rape me out in the hills and got rid of this damned virginity that's screwing up my life.'

'Has she still not popped your cherry? Crikey, what's your problem now?'

'Same thing.'

'What, the old...' I made an insensitive flopping motion with my arm.

'Yes,' he confirmed, rather sheepishly.

Before I could make my mind up whether to console or mock him, there was a firm knocking sound. Jak rushed to his feet and hopefully opened the door.

'Hi,' came the deep male voice from the corridor.

'Yes?' enquired Jak abruptly.

The door was blocking my view of our visitor so I moved around to join Jak in the doorway. I was faced with a muscular figure and some innocent good looks, wearing a pair of cream Chinos with a blue Oxford shirt tucked neatly in. His greased back dark hair was only marginally slimier than his smile – this guy looked like the stereotypical clean-cut high school quarterback who had all the girls eating out of his oversized palms whilst also scoring straight A's in all his classes.

'My name's Shawn Mentis. I've just joined your hall today so I thought I'd introduce myself to everyone. Pleased to meet you.'

Or, maybe he just looked like a gay ice skater.

Jak took the offered hand and shook it in salutation. 'Pleased to me you too, I'm Jak.'

I fought through the glint from Shawn's toothy

smile to make my own greeting. 'Hi, I'm Ross.' He stepped forward to grasp my hand, which he squeezed with considerable force while looking me straight in the eye.

'Hey, cool accent. Where are you from?'

'I'm from England.'

'England? Wow, that's great.'

He had maintained eye contact and sincerity throughout our brief exchange, which led me to believe that April had told him absolutely nothing of me or our growing friendship.

Jak began the questioning. 'So, whereabouts are you from then, Shawn?'

'California originally, but I *was* studying political science at Ohio State.'

'Cool, cool.'

I then took over, wondering if Jak and I could somehow work a good cop-bad cop routine.

'So why did you transfer here?' I probed.

His smile broadened arrogantly. 'Just a little misunderstanding, that's all.'

Before I could get my nipple clamps out and proceed with further questioning, Jak rudely interrupted.

'So what made you come to C.U. then?'

His grin widened to near lip-splitting levels.

'Shawn heard it was a pretty good party school!'

Did he really just refer to himself in the third person?

'You got that right, man,' agreed Jak. 'Ross here has already spent a night in the slammer.'

'No shit?'

A simple, modest nod acknowledged my experience, while Jak keenly elaborated.

'Yeah, the police busted this party over on the Hill and toasted his nuts. He was bailed out in the end by this chick...'

I swiftly butted in before Jak ruined my tactical advantage.

'Yeah, it was a whole big mess. I'm just waiting for the court date to come through now.'

'Awesome, man, awesome!' enthused Shawn.

I brought us back to the matter at hand – discrediting this prancing ice dancer good and proper.

'So, what was this misunderstanding in Ohio then?'

With gross self-importance, he leant in closer to give his explanation in a lowered tone.

'They said Shawn cheated in some stupid test, that's all.'

His nipples were becoming red-raw as I tightened the screws.

'And did you?'

Jak elbowed me in the side and shot me a look that said I had overstepped the mark. If only he knew who this guy really was.

'Well, yeah, but not actually *in* the test. You see, after they'd returned the tests with our scores on them, the teacher lost our grades so she asked for the papers back. I just changed my percentage slightly, that's all.' The boastful little shit threw us a wink as he finished his explanation. With no further torture necessary, I was ready to begin bashing his head with a blunt instrument until the arrogance oozed messily from his ears.

'Nice,' cooed an impressed Jak. 'So how did they catch you?'

'The bitch found our original grades.'

'Bummer,' consoled Jak.

I took my opportunity to take a veiled swipe at his manhood.

'Yeah, what a bummer indeed.'

'Anyway, guys,' concluded Shawn, 'it was good

meeting you. I'm sure I'll see you around some more.'

'You too, man, see you later,' Jak bid him farewell.

'Bye,' I tersely added.

Shawn went back to schmoozing with the rest of the corridor and I closed the door firmly behind him.

'He seems like a nice guy,' commented Jak.

'He seems like a complete arsehole,' I disagreed.

'What's your problem, man?'

It was time to bring him up to speed.

'April told me this morning that her boyfriend was transferring to C.U.'

'Yeah, so what?'

I was clearly going to have to spell it out for him.

'April also told me this morning that her boyfriend was called Shawn.'

'HOLY FUCK!' he exclaimed as the bulb glowed brightly above his head.

'Yes, holy fuck indeed. What on earth does she see in *that* arrogant bastard?'

'Good looks and biceps?'

'I thought she was a bit deeper than that. I mean, this Shawn is a total wanker.'

'I'm sensing a bit of a feud brewing here, Ross.'

With ample sleep and this new shock to my system, I could see the way forward clearer than ever. I may not have played the gutsiest of games up to that point, but it was clearly time to stop pussyfooting around.

'Do we have a feud?' repeated Jak with excitement.

'April just needs to realise that she's with the wrong guy.'

'Awesome! Fucking awesome!' gushed Jak.

With a stack of textbooks laid out on my table, I had a fair amount of lost time to make up for. I was in The Chessman Lounge – a sizeable, quiet study room within Cheyenne Arapaho that was open twenty-four hours a day as a refuge from annoying or annoyed roommates. To the best of my knowledge I was neither annoying nor annoyed, but I just preferred the atmosphere of twenty sweating students over the two I had left behind in my room. There was something about the plentiful odour of fear that I found inspiring.

My first exam was to be on Wednesday morning. It was Quantum Mechanics – possibly the most impenetrable subject I was taking that semester. My homework assignments had barely scraped a "C" average, so I wasn't approaching the test with the greatest of confidence. However, American exams had an intriguing twist that gave me a glimmer of hope: the crib sheet. We were permitted to take a single sheet of paper into the exam onto which we could write whatever we wanted. Physics exams were essentially a game of picking the right equations to solve the problems, so with my best pencil sharpened to a needle-like point, I had been writing every single equation I had ever encountered onto that sheet of paper.

It was approaching midnight when my masterpiece was complete. From a distance it was just a sheet of grey paper, but on closer inspection it was an entire textbook of information in writing smaller than at the bottom of a vasectomy waiver form. I leant back in my chair, affording myself a brief break to admire my work before getting stuck into some practice questions.

The creak of my chair echoed emptily around the silent room, while the other students continued their work in peace. It was at that moment that the most almighty scream came from one of my fellow students in The Chessman Lounge. It was as if he could no longer handle the pressure and just totally freaked out. He jumped up onto his table and continued to yell manically like a crazed orang-utan. I looked anxiously around the room, hoping to find someone who looked capable of taking him on, perhaps with a tranquilliser gun or a baseball bat.

I was shocked to see a score of students looking unconcerned as they matter-of-factly checked their watches. One by one they then rose out of their seats and joined in with wild screams, while waving their arms madly in the air. Before long, I was the only sane person left in the room as I frantically scoured my surroundings for improvised weaponry. I decided that a sizeable steel plant pot was my best choice, but before I could contemplate making a dive for it, I picked up my priceless crib sheet and hurriedly stuffed it down my shirt. Just as I was about to make my move for the pot and wield it fiercely while making my escape, the door opened and in walked April.

For a moment she seemed to be as dumbfounded as me, but after a brief glance at her watch she appeared calm once more and began walking around the room. It wasn't long before she spotted me – I probably stood out somewhat as I was the only person still at my seat and looking longingly at a plant pot.

'HEY ROSS,' she shouted above the mayhem.

'HI APRIL. DO *YOU* KNOW WHAT'S GOING ON?'

'IT'S MIDNIGHT.'

I checked my watch, and sure enough it was midnight.

'SO, IS THE WORLD ABOUT TO END OR SOMETHING?'

'IT'S A CAMPUS TRADITION DURING EXAM WEEK – EVERYONE SCREAMS AT MIDNIGHT. STRESS RELIEF, I GUESS.'

'WELL,' I continued, just as the screaming abruptly ended but without the ability to adjust my own tone in time, 'THEY LOOK LIKE A BUNCH OF DRIBBLING IDIOTS TO ME.'

The silence intensified, as countless shocked faces stared questioningly at me.

April giggled before jumping to my defence. 'Don't worry, everyone, he's British.'

While the room erupted in laughter at my expense, I pondered how I could still inflict a fair amount of pain with that plant pot. The laughter eventually subsided, along with my evil urges, and April and I had to resort to whispering.

'Sorry about that, Ross, but it looked like they were about to lynch you!'

'I was about to do worse to them, believe me.'

'So how's the studying going, anyway?'

'Oh, not bad. I just finished my first crib-sheet – what do you think?'

I removed the partially crumpled page from my shirt and showed it to her.

'Very, er, comprehensive.'

'*I* thought so. So what have you been doing since this morning?' I asked with instant regret.

'Showing Shawn around campus – he arrived at lunchtime.' Her face lit up vibrantly. It was excruciating to watch. 'It's so great to have him here!' she effervesced, now a little louder than a whisper.

'SH!' reprimanded an anonymous shusher who had been screaming like a chimpanzee only a few moments earlier.

April lowered her tone again. 'Yeah, I'm just so lucky he decided to transfer.'

April's comment immediately triggered the memory of my meeting with Shawn. 'He *decided* to transfer?' I stressed the word 'decided' rather zealously.

'SH!' flew in yet more castigation. I ignored it, sensing I was onto something significant.

'Sure. He said he couldn't bear to be apart from me any more...oh, sorry, this is a bit too mushy for you, isn't it?' She chuckled like a schoolgirl.

'SH!' I looked around to see who dare interrupt us when I was so close to the breakthrough I was looking for. Not able to target the culprit, I reasoned that vengeance would wait.

'No, carry on, please,' I assured her, in the hope that the short-term torture would be worth it.

'Yeah, well he just missed me so much that he decided to transfer here. It was incredible how quickly it all happened too – he must have really pushed them to get things happening so quickly.'

'Yes, I'm sure he must have.'

My delight at uncovering Shawn's web of deceit was instantly replaced with pity and anger. I was upset for April as she quite clearly loved the guy, but at the same time I was completely enraged that Shawn could treat her so dreadfully. The feud that Jak had been baying for was on. It was most definitely on.

'So what did *you* do today?' asked April, snapping me back to reality.

'Oh, not much. I just slept really. Oh yeah, by the way, thanks for the ice pack. It really did the trick.' Indeed it did, in more ways than she would ever know.

'No problem.'

'SH!' chastised a hideous looking girl across the table from us, with such venom that her spittle landed on my books. I was in no mood to apologise, so I looked her square in the eye with an intense look that said, "Don't mess with me, love, OK? Not tonight."

She cowered back to her books as April gave me a congratulatory nudge on the shoulder.

'Why don't we take a quick break?' I suggested.

'But I've only just got here.'

'Don't worry about that, come on.'

I got up from my seat and headed for the exit. April followed, but I stalled just as we reached the door and then turned around to address the peaceful crowd.

'I'm just popping upstairs for my AK47,' I announced with deadpan sincerity. 'It's been a while since I went on a decent killing spree.'

April hurried me outside and delicately closed the doors behind us. She made sure we were a suitable distance away before laughing with me.

'You can't say that!' she protested at my outburst. 'They were only trying to study.'

'I know, I know. Anyway, come upstairs and I can give you back your ice pack.'

We crossed reception and passed through the doors to my corridor, where all was quiet. We entered my room to find Jak asleep at his desk while Kazuki was studying and still wearing the cowboy hat he had brought home as a souvenir from his night at The Spittoon.

'Hey Kaz,' greeted April, quietly.

'Hello April!' he beamed. 'You like my hat?'

Everyone had been asked at least five times over the last few weeks, and April was no exception.

'Yes, it's great,' she answered with well-practiced enthusiasm.

'It from Mary-Lou, we fucked!'

April was slightly taken aback by the additional information that she had previously been spared.

'Really? Well, good for you!' was all that she could muster in response.

'Yes, she dirty whore!' confirmed Kazuki with a

glow in his cheeks.

I picked up the ice pack from my desk and handed it to April.

'Thanks again.'

'My pleasure. Should we go so we don't wake Jak?'

'Nah, don't worry about him, he's dead to the world.'

With the door still ajar there was a light tapping before it opened wide to reveal Shawn's still immaculately dressed presence.

'Hey Ross,' he opened smarmily.

'Oh, hi,' I lukewarmly returned.

'April! What are you doing here?'

'Oh, just picking up something that Ross borrowed,' she explained. 'I didn't know you two had met already?'

'Sure, Shawn and Ross are good friends, aren't we, buddy?'

Where was that plant pot when I needed it? Or the AK47.

'Yes, good friends indeed. Anyway, I've got to get back to my studying.'

'Yes, me too,' joined in April. 'Sorry, baby,' she apologised to Shawn. 'I'll see you later?'

'Sure, babe.'

She gave him a peck on the cheek and accompanied me back down to The Chessman Lounge.

It was four a.m. when I finally called it a day. April had retired an hour or so earlier, and only one other hardy soul had remained with me until the bitter end. Cheyenne Arapaho was completely deserted at that hour, and I didn't pass another soul as I walked back to my room with a stack of textbooks balanced precariously in my arms.

As soon as I opened the door into my corridor, I became aware of some hurried movement further down the hall. I looked up to see Shawn slumped on the floor outside his room. He jumped to his feet and began walking purposefully towards me, displaying none of the toothy friendliness he had afforded me earlier in the day.

We closed rapidly on each other until he was practically on top of me. Without warning, he took a juvenile swipe at the books in my hands and sent them cascading to the ground. I was taken aback by the sudden turn of events, and simply stared down at the textbooks whilst wondering what was to come next.

'Have you got a problem?' he vehemently demanded.

There was a hint of spiced chicken in the flavour of his breath. Or maybe it was raw human flesh, I couldn't be absolutely sure. Despite the unfamiliarly hostile situation, I felt no anxiety. I knew that this guy was scum, and I couldn't wait until April knew as well. I raised my head to look him in the eyes, and tried to rile him further with some misplaced humour.

'Yes, as a matter of a fact, I *do* have a problem.' I pointed to a book that had opened wide on the floor. 'Do you know how to solve Schrödinger's equation?'

'Listen, Ross, let's cut the crap. Shawn is here to tell you to back off from April, OK?'

I couldn't believe the arrogance of the man. 'Hold on, hold on, let me get this right. You waited up until four a.m. to slap away my books like some sissy and tell me, in the third person, to stay away from your girlfriend – is that right?'

His brow furrowed and his hands began to twitch erratically. 'Don't push me, man, don't push me.'

I had no fear. All I knew was that I wouldn't allow

this brute to ruin my relationship with April, whatever that relationship actually was.

'What are you so afraid of, Shawn? April and I are only friends. *You've* still got a chance with me too, if that's what you're worried about. I know how jealous you ice dancers can be.'

A protruding blood vessel on his forehead was throbbing to the point of explosion, as his face reddened deeper. 'Your friendship with April ends right here, right now. No more cosy study sessions, no more tennis matches, no more country dancing. Got it?'

Shawn had certainly been doing his homework in the previous few hours. I tried to push him further.

'So, could we maybe see a movie together? Perhaps have some dinner afterwards? You'd be more than welcome to join us, you know. We could share stories of how you try to run her life behind her back. We'd have a great time!'

'Just remember that Shawn is in town now, and Shawn *will* stop you seeing April.'

With that veiled threat, he turned around and stormed back to his room. I was left to wonder what had got him so wound up and exactly how he had discovered so much about me and April in such a short space of time. I stood surrounded by books full of questions, but with a head completely devoid of answers.

FOURTEEN

'Dude, how did it go?'

I had left for my first exam before Jak had even surfaced, so on my return he was eager to catch up.

'Not too bad. That crib sheet really paid off.'

'Nice. So what time did you get back from Cheeseman last night?'

'From *Chessman*? Around four I think.'

'No, man, it's *Cheeseman*!' he laughed. 'That's what Dip-Shit Shawn called it last night, anyway.'

'"Dip-Shit Shawn?" What happened to "he seems like a nice guy"?'

'Dude, you wouldn't believe what went on here last night.'

'Neither would you,' I retorted. 'You go first.'

'Well, I was studying, right? And I must have fallen asleep for a while or something, then I woke with my head in my books and heard Shawn talking to Kaz. I pretended I was still asleep and heard the whole thing. You know Kaz – he really didn't understand what was going on – but I could tell clear as day that Shawn was totally playing him. He was saying how he'd take Kaz to all these parties with loads of chicks and they'd have a great time together. By the end Kaz would probably have given him a blowjob if he'd asked. Anyway, then Shawn starts asking him all these questions about you – how you knew April, how long you'd been friends, what sort of stuff you guys did together. He's one jealous bastard.'

'You're telling me! He waited up for me last night and made a few threats. He said I should stay away from her.'

'What a prick. I mean, it's not like you're madly in love with her or anything, is it?' Jak's ironic tone highlighted the flaw in my defence.

'Well *he* doesn't know that, does he?' I had a sudden panic. '*Does he?*'

'No, I didn't hear Kaz say anything about that. I think he had enough sense to keep that much to himself.'

I began to lose my composure a little. 'Good, fine. So as far as this guy knows we're just friends and there's nothing more to it. So what's his problem?'

'I'd be careful if I were you. He's not exactly a lightweight and his mental stability is questionable.'

'Listen, we're grown adults now. There's no way I'm going to be bullied.'

'Fair enough, man,' Jak reasoned. 'But I'm just saying that if he's threatening you, I wouldn't be so sure he won't follow those threats with actions.'

'I might not be able to match him in a fight, but knowledge is power too. He'll find that out soon enough.'

Kazuki then bounded into the room.

'I kick exam's ass!' he exclaimed with pride.

'Well done, Kaz,' congratulated Jak.

'Yeah, nice one,' I concurred.

'Now me and Shawn gonna get drunk and get laid! Shawn my new best friend!'

'You might wanna be careful, there,' advised Jak.

'Yeah, Kaz,' I added, 'please don't say anything to Shawn about me liking April, OK?'

Kazuki appeared confused. 'Jak, you not like Shawn? Ross, you not like April?'

I tried to clarify as best as I could. 'Shawn and April are boyfriend and girlfriend, you know?' He nodded. 'So, if Shawn thought I liked April then...' Jak helpfully intervened with the swipe of an imaginary knife across my throat. '...so you see, Shawn cannot find out, OK?'

'Ahhh! No, no, no, I not say anything about you marrying April, OK? My lip is sealed. What the saying? Your safe is secret with me!'

It was reassurance, of sorts, and the best I could hope for in the circumstances. My thoughts then went back to Kazuki's earlier comment. 'So, Kaz, what exactly *are* you going to do with Shawn?'

'Well, he told me not tell you.' Kazuki's brief look of seriousness rapidly collapsed. 'But you my friend, you my roommate, so of course I tell you! He got party on Hill tonight. Lots of pussy, he say, lots of pussy!'

'Interesting,' I pondered, 'very interesting.'

My afternoon was spent in the room that was, from that day forward, known as The Cheeseman Lounge. My schedule showed that I had three more exams to endure – two on Thursday and then my final one on Friday morning – so I set about crafting my crib-sheets amongst a handful of other Cheyenne Arapaho students. In complete contrast to the evening crowd, this bunch didn't mind a bit of chatter and I happily overheard conversations on a range of topics from philosophy to bestiality. It certainly passed the time, and almost prevented my brain from completely overloading on electromagnetic theory.

Just as I had begun to reach my threshold of studying pain, the door swung open and there was

April's smiling face answering my prayers yet again. She had no books or papers with her, just a small carton of juice and a chocolate bar.

'Jak told me you were down here,' she explained while sitting down next to me. 'I thought you could maybe use a drink and a snack?'

She passed me the juice and Milky Way bar. It was the sort of generous and thoughtful gesture that April made all the time.

'Thank you,' I said appreciatively.

'So, how's it going? More crib-sheets?'

'Yeah, well my first one did a fairly good job this morning, so I figured I may as well carry on.'

'Oh, so it went well then?'

'I think so. How are yours going?'

'Well I only have a couple of mid-terms – all my other classes are based on coursework. It's English Lit. that I need to study, but with Shawn here I'm finding it difficult to concentrate! He promised he'd give me some space tonight, though, so I can focus.'

'Oh, right. So what's he doing then?'

'He's gonna spend the night in the library while I study down here.'

It was becoming increasingly apparent that Shawn wasn't the sharpest skate on the rink. While he had been hurriedly buddying up with Kazuki, it had never crossed his mind that roommate loyalties overruled all other friendships. There was clearly no end to his arrogant stupidity.

'So,' she continued, 'what do you think of my Shawn, anyway? You haven't really said much about him since he arrived.'

I could have told her there and then. I could have said what a two-faced liar her boyfriend was, and how he didn't even deserve to be with someone who was a fraction of the girl that she was. I could have told her to get rid of the jerk and spend the rest of her life in blissful happiness with me, because I loved her with all of my heart and would be faithful and truthful to her until the day I died. I *could* have said all of that and so much more, but I didn't.

'He seems...nice.'

'*Nice?*' My artificiality must have been a little too obvious. 'Is there something going on between you two? I mean, I sort of sensed from Shawn earlier that he'd rather I didn't spend so much time with you.'

'Maybe he's feeling a little jealous?' I suggested tentatively.

'Jealous?' she laughed. 'What would he have to be jealous about? We're only friends, after all.'

It pained me to hear her speak those words so casually.

'*We* know that, but you know what guys can be like.'

'You're probably right. Shawn *is* a very sensitive guy.'

I resisted the urge to laugh riotously in April's pretty face. Instead I managed to utter, 'I'm sure he is,' with an insincerity that was positively drooling out of my every orifice.

'He really is,' she smiled. 'Oh, speak of the devil!'

April was looking towards the doorway where her beloved, sensitive Shawn had appeared, resplendent in his fake smile. He gestured for her to join him outside The Cheeseman Lounge. No doubt he had just witnessed a group of thoughtless children cruelly taunting a defenceless little kitten, and he needed the reassuring smile of a loved one to reaffirm his faith in human nature. Or perhaps he just wanted April out of the way so he could tear me limb from limb.

'I'd better go,' said April. 'I'll see you down here later, no doubt?'

'No doubt you will. See you later!'

Shawn stepped aside to let April exit the room, before giving me the deadliest of looks and following her out of the door.

'It's over!' I triumphantly proclaimed to Jak as I returned to our room that Friday lunchtime.

'Me too, dude! That was a complete week of hell.'

'And what's our reward for getting through it? Seven more weeks of studying then another week of hell.'

'Who gives a shit, let's just enjoy the moment.'

I threw my pencil case onto my desk, along with a piece of mail I had picked up from reception. I was so excited at completing my exams that I hadn't paid any attention to the marking on the envelope, which now cruelly revealed itself to say "Boulder County Police Department". In that brief moment I had journeyed from ecstasy to anguish.

'Oh, shit,' I uttered while picking the envelope back up.

'What's up?'

'It's from the police – probably my court date.'

'Bummer.'

I gingerly tore open the seal and removed the letter. I carefully unfolded the sheet of paper as if kindness now would correct all my wrongdoings of that evening. My eyes worked their terrified way down the page until they hit on a paragraph that merited an audience.

I began reading: 'We must apologise to you for this gross lack of conduct by our officer. We hereby notify you that no further action will be taken against you, and the Boulder County Police Department considers your case closed.'

'*What?*' asked a stupefied Jak.

I was just as bewildered. 'I think they let me off!'

'Are you shittin' me?'

I read through the letter again, and its words didn't change. 'No, some technicality apparently. The guy that busted me was under suspension. Holy shit, I'm free!'

'That's awesome, man, awesome! I wonder why he was suspended?'

'His moustache was probably over the legal limit of bushiness or something.'

'Dude, exams are over and you're not going to court. The world is a place of beauty right now. I think this merits a par-tay!'

'Let's do it, let's do it!' I agreed excitedly.

That afternoon we made the necessary preparations. There wasn't really much to do, other than gathering food and drink and inviting a select crowd to share the evening's festivities in our room. For a bunch of underage students we managed to pull together a pretty impressive array of alcohol, due in no small part to some of Jak's Spanish contacts who were over twenty-one.

We weren't naive enough to wheel in a keg of beer through reception, so we had planned a cocktail night instead. Our bedroom turned into the drinks preparation area, with Jak's bed tipped up against the wall and my desk moved in as the bar. Its surface was covered with spirits, fruit juices, and a large blender we had borrowed from Brandon. In the corner we had a plastic barrel with several bags worth of ice cubes gently melting away.

It was early evening when we kicked off the party. With everyone inside, we barricaded ourselves in by placing a couple of mattresses against the door. It was a campus-wide urban myth that this prevented any noise from escaping, thereby stopping any suspicious hall monitors from catching us drinking. With some of Jak's best tunes beating out from his stereo, there were around fifteen of us crammed into the two rooms, all noisily chatting and drinking.

'What'll it be?' I asked Kristen during my first stint behind the bar.

'Oooh, what would you recommend?'

I looked through the cocktail guide we had bought for the occasion.

'Well, mademoiselle, for you I would recommend Ross' Rusty Nail, or maybe Kristen's Kamikaze.'

'The Kamikaze sounds good – hit me!' she smiled.

I deftly poured a generous measure of vodka over a glass of ice, and added the merest splash of lime.

'There you go, enjoy!'

'Thanks...I think,' she replied with a quizzical look at her glass. 'Great news about the court case, by the way. Jak told me.'

'Yeah, I can hardly believe it. It's also great news that you and Jak are talking again.'

'Well, I figured it's not really his fault so I can't punish him forever. I just wish we could say goodbye to Mr Floppy.'

'Mr Floppy?' I sniggered.

'Oh shit, don't say anything to him, will you? I swore I wouldn't tell anyone what I've been calling it.'

'Hey, your secret's safe with me!'

'Moving swiftly on, where's April?'

'Oh, I think she was going to the movies with Laura.'

'Jak's told me about this Shawn guy. He sounds like a real jerk.'

'You're not wrong there. He's been a bit quiet for the last couple of days though, so maybe I've got through to him.'

Kazuki joined us at the bar.

'What you drinking, Kristen?' he enquired.

'A Kamikaze,' she answered.

It probably wasn't the most politically sensitive drink for an American to be discussing with a Japanese guy, but he didn't seem to mind.

'Bartender!' he chimed with his finger raised skywards. 'I drink Kazuki Kamikaze please!'

'Coming right up, Kaz.'

Kristen retired to the study room while I mixed Kazuki's drink.

'Shawn a jerk!' said Kazuki, repeating Kristen's earlier sentiments.

'Oh, you overheard that?'

'Yes, but he *is* jerk! He promised pussy but never took me to party.'

'I know, I know,' I consoled him. 'But you've got to let it go, Kaz. Maybe we can go to The Spittoon again?'

'Dirty whores? Cool!' he responded positively.

I poured the vodka even more liberally than before and passed Kazuki his drink. Within a few moments he had thirstily guzzled it down.

'Slow down!' I urged.

'Kazuki want another!'

As the evening passed, the drinks continued to flow freely and the tipsiness levels steadily rose. Kazuki was inevitably the first to succumb, and he was curled up on his bottom bunk well before ten o'clock. We soldiered on around him though, as the bar continued its brisk business. Jak's Spanish friends were as resilient as ever, but Brandon soon became the hot favourite to be next to call it a night. His speech began to slur heavily under the weight of an unadvisable mixture of spirits he had christened the Brandon Blow Job.

'Ross, Ross,' he slobbered while draped over Kazuki's desk in the study room. 'Let's go shove some batteries up Kaz's asshole. Yeah, that would be *awesome!*'

'Where *do* you get these ideas from?'

'Or maybe sausages, have you got any sausages?'

'I think you might be ready for beddy-byes, Brandon.'

'I need more boooooze! Is there more booze there?'

'Yes, lots and lots of the stuff,' I encouraged him.

'OK, take me to beddy-booze! I want to go to beddy-booze!'

'OK, OK, I'll take you. Let's go.'

I took him by the arm and helped him down from the table. Jak was chatting with Kristen next to us, so I asked for his assistance. 'Jak, could you give me a hand with the door?'

'Sure thing,' he obliged. 'I'll put the mattresses back after you've left. Give us three knocks when you get back so we know it's you.'

'No problem.'

Jak moved the mattresses aside and opened the door. We were suddenly faced with two imposing figures clad in black jackets with the words "Hall Monitor" emblazoned on them. One was staring Jak straight in the eye with look of a self-satisfaction, while the other had his head to the ground with only the top of his baseball cap visible.

'Evening gentlemen!' greeted Jak, while the chatter behind him died and the music stopped dead. I forged in front of Jak with Brandon on my arm, irrationally believing that he was my ticket out.

'I was just taking my friend back to his room,' I explained. 'It must have been something he ate.'

'Oh, really?' came the smug retort from the baseball cap, which slowly moved upwards to reveal the wearer.

'Shawn?' I shrieked in disbelief.

'Hi Ross. Didn't I tell you I got a job as a hall monitor?' The smarminess oozed so much that I could barely stay on my feet. 'RIGHT THEN' he shouted into the room, 'YOU'RE ALL BEING REPORTED FOR UNDERAGE DRINKING.'

The loudness of his announcement briefly sobered Brandon. 'Shit, shit,' he muttered, 'I've gotta go, gotta go.' He broke from my grasp and went headlong for the partially open window at the back of the room. He dived into the gap and the window duly swung wider and threatened to swallow him. It was then that his open fly hole caught on the window handle and his head was left suspended a metre from the safety of the outdoors, while his feet flailed violently around our room.

'Where does *he* think he's going?' asked black-jacketed Nazi Shawn.

'Maybe he was just popping out to get you one of his special cocktails?' I thought out loud. 'You look like you could use a Brandon Blow Job.' The room erupted in drunken laughter while the vein on Shawn's forehead threatened its own eruption.

Black jacket number two then joined the fun. 'Is that Brandon Thomas?' he wondered while pointing to the legs in the window. 'Sweet! That's the third time we've caught his ass. You know what that means?'

I didn't have a clue, but Shawn felt it his duty to tell me.

'What it means, ass-wipe, is that your buddy is getting kicked out of the dorm.' He couldn't contain his jubilation. 'That makes the hours we stood out there all the more worthwhile.'

'You mean you've been standing out there all night?' I asked him in disbelief.

'Nobody fucks with Shawn and gets away with it, Ross – maybe you'll remember that the next time you think about speaking to April. You've just cost your buddy a roof over his head.'

FIFTEEN

'Right, close the door behind you,' commanded the sour-faced Hall Director of Cheyenne Arapaho. Jak, Brandon, Kazuki and I, shuffled in to the stuffy office where Jess Pullitt sat self-righteously behind her oversized desk. We formed an orderly line in front of her and awaited the sermon.

She looked through her half-glasses towards some papers on her desk. 'It has been reported to me that you were involved in an incident yesterday concerning late night noise and the consumption of alcoholic beverages.' She languidly raised her gaze over her glasses and down her nose as she continued. 'This behaviour is in violation of rules one and four of the residence halls rules and policies, and therefore I must reprimand you accordingly.'

She now afforded particular attention to me and Kazuki. 'The legal age for consumption of alcohol in *this* country is twenty-one, and the presence of alcoholic beverages in halls of residence is strictly prohibited for all ages. Do I make myself clear?'

Our four voices mumbled a variety of acknowledgments.

'This incident will be noted on your hall records, and any repetition will *not* be tolerated. The others who were present at your little gathering will be dealt with accordingly by their own Hall Directors.

'Now then, Mr Thomas,' she added with intent focus on Brandon, 'this isn't the first time we've met under such circumstances, is it?'

Brandon sighed deeply.

'During your last student conduct meeting it was made abundantly clear to you that any further violation of hall rules would result in the termination of your residence here. I must therefore inform you that I have no choice but to terminate your residence accordingly. You have seven days to vacate your room.'

'But...' Brandon was only able to extract one word from his mouth before the witch cut him down.

'*No* discussion will be entered into on this matter. You're all dismissed.'

Brandon stood open-mouthed while she rudely continued about her business.

'Let's go, Brandon,' consoled Jak with an arm around his shoulder. We duly trudged out of the office and into the hall reception area, closing the door firmly behind us.

'Bitch,' summed up Brandon while still aghast.

'I'm really sorry,' I apologised, still feeling guilty that my conflict with Shawn had been ultimately to blame.

'It's not your fault, it's that bastard Shawn,' he responded angrily.

'You've got that right,' agreed Jak.

'I know she old and mean,' contributed Kazuki, 'but you think Hall Director Pullitt got tight pussy?'

'Always looking for your next girlfriend, eh Kaz?' chuckled Brandon, briefly relieved from the gravity of his situation.

'I put smile on that bitch's ugly face!' he added with a crude thrust to ram home his point.

As we stood there in shock and without a clue of

what to do next, I heard the sound of a bouncing table tennis ball from across reception. I seized the chance to shield Brandon from the harsh realities for a little longer.

'Hey, why don't we go play table tennis in the games room? We could show Jak and Kaz how good I am.'

'Ping-pong? Sure, why not.' His enthusiasm was well concealed.

We walked across to the games room, whose double doors were only slightly ajar. I apologetically squeezed my head through the gap to make the necessary arrangements, but then briefly glimpsed April and Shawn hitting across the table to each other. I rapidly extracted my head from the room and looked back at the others who were about to wade in.

'Looks like they're in a serious game, guys,' I warned. 'Let's come back later.'

'Nah,' insisted Brandon. 'I've only got seven days left so let's go in now.'

He placed his hand against the door to make his entry, at which point I swiftly grabbed his arm.

'Let's just leave it for now,' I pleaded.

'What's going on?' he challenged, breaking free from my grasp and shoving one of the doors wide open. It revealed half of the table and a smiling April, who looked over at the four of us while the ball bounced right past her.

'Who's that?' came a voice from the background, at which point Brandon propelled the second door open to expose Shawn's joyful face at the other side of the table. 'Oh, hi guys,' he greeted us. 'How are you doing?'

Brandon's face bubbled in anger while Jak, Kazuki and I exchanged worried glances. Without warning, Brandon then charged across the room and collided heavily with Shawn's muscular chest, which deflected him decisively to the ground. Jak and I leapt in to hold him back from any further futile stampedes while Shawn put on a display of ignorance for his watching girlfriend.

'Hey, what was that for?' he appealed with calm.

'You *know* what,' frothed Brandon as we struggled to restrain him, 'you *know* what. I've just got kicked out because of you, you bastard.'

April looked across in shock at the news while Shawn maintained his caring pretence.

'I'm so sorry if you got kicked out, Brandon, I truly am. I was only doing my job, I feel terrible. April, could you maybe get Brandon a cool drink, to calm him down?'

She dutifully left the room, presumably heading for the drinks machine in Cheeseman. After a delay sufficient for her to get out of earshot, Shawn quickly shrugged off his halo.

'I hope you've learned your lesson now, Ross.'

As Brandon strained at the leash, I decided to lead a more civil response.

'I knew that steroids would eventually make you paranoid and infertile,' I began, 'but I never imagined they could cause such a huge dick to grow out of your head. Maybe we should just tell April what you're really like?'

'Tell her what? You've got nothing on me!'

'Oh, there's just the little matter of *why* you transferred here. Oh yeah, and the little parties you've been going to without telling her. God knows what you've been getting up to behind her back.'

'Hey, Shawn has done nothing wrong, and you can't prove a thing. Face it, Ross – Shawn wins. You can't beat him.'

'Oh yeah?' joined in Brandon. 'Well I bet he could beat you at ping-pong.'

Jak and I looked at him in bewilderment.

'What?' asked Shawn with similar confusion.

'I bet Ross could beat you at ping-pong,' Brandon repeated.

'Well, Shawn *could* beat Ross at ping-pong too, if that's what you want, but it wouldn't change a thing.'

'Maybe it would wipe that smug look off your face, for starters,' reasoned Brandon. 'And maybe stop you referring to yourself in the third person like an asshole.'

His words struck a delightful chord. I dearly wanted to put Shawn in his place, and maybe an epic duel across the table tennis table was just the ticket.

'Yeah,' I added, 'let's do it.'

'Fine, seven p.m. tonight then,' agreed Shawn. 'I'll look forward to beating your ass.'

'Hey, I only agreed to table tennis,' I goaded. 'You ice skaters won't give up, will you? No means no, OK?'

With the battle lines drawn, we relaxed our grip on Brandon and he obligingly led our withdrawal from the games room. The grudge match was on.

'Hi Ross! What are you doing here?'

Provoking Shawn was half of the truth.

'I just wanted to see you, April!' was the other half.

She glanced suspiciously at her watch. 'I thought you were supposed to be playing ping-pong now?'

'*Table tennis*, yes. Shawn said he'd meet me in your room, so here I am!'

'Ah, now it makes sense. Come in.'

I made myself comfortable on the edge of Laura's bed while April curled up on her own.

'What are you doing tonight then?' I asked.

'Oh, nothing too exciting. I might get my laundry done and do a little reading.'

'So you're not gonna watch our game?'

'I'm not *that* bored,' she giggled. 'It's good to see you and Shawn getting on, anyway. He feels really awful about Brandon, you know. He *was* only doing his job though – he really didn't have any choice.'

If only she had known the reality of the situation.

'Brandon's pretty distraught.'

'I'm sure he is. Where do you think he'll go?'

'He's not sure yet. He knows a couple of guys in a house down in town though, so maybe he'll see if he can stay with them for a while.'

'Well, that's something.'

I was about to continue our conversation when my eyes made a startling discovery as they skirted around April's room. The special 'secret message' picture frame I had given her was still resting soundly on the shelf above her desk, but it was no longer displaying the photo of her pets. That photograph, on the back of which I had openly declared my love for her, was nowhere to be seen. As if this revelation wasn't unnerving enough, the frame was now proudly showing off a photo of her and Shawn riding together on the back of a horse. No doubt some deaf and blind horse that sensitive Shawn had saved from the knacker's yard and nursed back to life in the horse sanctuary he had set up after many hard years of fundraising.

'Are you OK?' asked April at my unexpected loss of attention.

I decided it would be relationship suicide to mention the photo. After all, if she had seen my declaration and not said anything about it, then it was a pretty strong indication that my feelings weren't being reciprocated. I preferred, however, to live in the world where April had definitely not seen my message, and so her deeply repressed feelings for me were still very much latent.

'Er, yes, yes, I'm fine,' I said while clinging onto

the latter version of events. 'Just focussing on the game, that's all.'

'All this over ping-pong?' she laughed.

Without so much as a knock, Shawn barged into the room and interrupted our exchange.

'Ross, there you are,' he accused, while straining desperately to withhold his anger.

'Oh, Shawn, hi! You're late,' I cheerfully replied.

'No, *you're* late.' The vein began throbbing.

'I thought we arranged to meet in April's room? We've just been chatting while I waited for you.'

'Let's go then,' he spat through gritted teeth.

'Sure, I'll just pop back to my room to get my bat, and I'll meet you downstairs. I'll see you later, April. Have a good night washing your knickers!'

She blushed at my English phraseology, as I made my escape past an undoubtedly seething Shawn.

I jogged down the stairs to my room and picked up my sword of war. Earlier that evening I had performed the same bat-cleaning ritual that had served me so well before all of my other great victories. After squirting a ball of specialist foam on the rubber surface, I had worked it in delicately with the professional-grade bat sponge, moving outwards in ever-increasing circles. Each precision rubber was then pristinely protected behind a sheet of clear vinyl, shielding the surfaces from any contamination that could reduce the all-important tackiness. With my weapon further sheltered inside a padded case, it was this case that I carried proudly to the battlefield.

I entered the gladiatorial arena to rapturous applause from Jak, Brandon and Kazuki. Memories of past glories in division seven of the Lancaster Thursday night league came flooding back, as I wallowed in the majesty of the occasion. Stood at the edge of the table was a rabid Shawn, just about ready to dispense with use of balls so he could begin exchanging flying bats with me.

'Shall we play by traditional Queen of England rules?' I offered. I didn't know what the hell that meant, but I had always been keen to grasp any opportunity to unsettle an opponent.

'First to twenty-one points, five points per service, two clear points to win, right?'

My confidence took a sudden blow.

'Er, right.'

My supporters retreated to their seats at the side of the table, while Shawn and I took to our own ends and prepared for combat. My confidence then took its second knock as Shawn proceeded to take his bat from its tailor-made case and remove his own vinyl sheets from the rubbers, revealing surfaces that were positively glistening with violent intent. I readied my own bat while pondering that I might have to fight hard for this particular victory.

'Warm-up?' I asked, with a ball readied in my hand.

'No,' Shawn tersely replied.

'Play for serve, then?' I suggested, referring to the age-old tradition of playing an initial exchange to decide who should have the advantage of serving the first five points.

'No, you serve,' he scowled.

Cocky bastard, I thought to myself.

So the initiative was with me. Until, that is, my first three serves dribbled pathetically into the net like diarrhoea through a soup strainer. My fan club looked on nervously, while Shawn swaggered about the table. I kept my cool, taking a more cautious approach to my subsequent two serves. They both successfully reached Shawn, who returned them timidly into the net to highlight his own match-rustiness.

At 3-2 down I resolved to make a statement with

my return from Shawn's first serve, and duly smashed the thing at great velocity and without particular accuracy. Jak was sent diving for cover as the ball bore down on him, barely missing his cheek and only just avoiding what would have been an impressive battle scar.

'Sorry!' I apologised in the direction of his cowering figure, but he doggedly got back to his feet and sat back in his chair to continue enjoying the spectacle.

It was fair to say that, thus far, neither of us had demonstrated table tennis prowess at its finest. The quality did pick up, however, as we both began to reach our stride and start hitting the ball with increasing poise. The match progressed on a fairly even footing, with clever topspin lobs, deft backhand slices, and dirty looks being freely exchanged until we reached a score of 10-10.

'I'll stop going easy on you now,' panted Shawn on the exchange of serve.

Having heard all manner of trash talk back in England, I took no notice of his pathetic mind games and didn't dignify it with a response. Instead, I replied with my best service of the night – a low, fast topspin delivery that hugged the left sideline to perfection. Shawn casually leant across to impossibly scoop the ball up and across to the opposite corner of the table, out of my range. It was truly a shot of the highest calibre, and I began to wonder whether he had, indeed, been toying with me for those first twenty points.

From that moment, no matter how speedy my serves, Shawn would return them faster. No matter how well placed my shots, he would land his own out of arm's reach. Within a few short minutes my game was in tatters and the score was 20-10. He was a mere point from victory, while I was a mere point from humiliation. I was about to taste a bitter defeat.

'Time to put you out of your misery,' he gloated. 'Shawn is about to end this thing.'

It was then that the meaning of our titanic encounter finally hit home. I wasn't playing for fun, nor was I playing for simple bragging rights. This match was all about pride, about rising up and taking a stand against a bully, about saving my friendship with April, about retribution for the cruel punishment of a close friend, and, most importantly, about wiping the smile from the smarmy git's face. I looked to the crowd for further encouragement.

'You can take him, you can take him,' insisted Jak with steely determination.

'Never give up,' urged Brandon with a look of shear concentration.

'Shawn kicking your ass!' chirped Kazuki, helpfully.

I closed my eyes, took a deep breath, and visualised the vintage performances I had produced only months earlier to seal ninth place in Lancaster's division seven. Yes, that was the stuff. I knew I had more in me, and I was about to unleash the fury. Shawn wouldn't know what had hit him.

I concentrated on the accuracy of my serves and made a superhuman effort to return every shot he could fire at me. Several times he came at me with a smash that would have normally gone sailing over my head, but my eagerness paid dividends as I chased the ball to the rear of the room and gave a solid return. My confidence was so high that I even managed to return a smash with one of my own that had Shawn staring in disbelief as the ball flew back off the table and narrowly missed his face.

My supporters murmured excitedly as I gradually narrowed the gap and refused to allow Shawn the final point he needed for victory. At 20-19 I had made a comeback of epic proportions. My opponent was rattled, my dander was up, and wild orgies of celebration were only moments away.

Shawn stepped back from the table, pausing briefly in an attempt to regain confidence and instil a sense of doubt in me. It would not work, it *could* not work: I was unstoppable. He returned for his final serve before we were to enter a sudden-death showdown. He threw the ball into the air and warily served against his side of the table and safely over the net, without a great deal of speed or spin. I watchfully followed the path of the ball as it sailed lazily towards my baseline, from where it was about to be smashed back down his throat.

Time passed slowly as the ball fell closer to its bounce. It eventually reached the table, but only made contact with the very edge. The wretched edge then callously sent the ball spinning into my groin and down on to the floor. The game was over. I had lost. Shawn had won. On a fluke.

While my fans winced in anguish, I awaited the outpouring of joy from my opponent. Shawn didn't even crack a smile.

He reached into his bat case and brought out a photograph, which he slammed down on the table with such force that one of the legs gave way. As the picture slid down the leaning table, I immediately recognised it as the one that was missing from April's frame.

'You're just lucky I found it before she did. Now Shawn will tell you one last time – stay the fuck away, got it?'

I couldn't mount any kind of response before he had brushed past me and out of the room. All I had left was my shattered confidence and a shattered table, both of which were in need of urgent attention.

SIXTEEN

A morning run would have ordinarily blown away the cobwebs, but not on that particular Sunday morning. With the wound of my crushing table tennis defeat still raw, I had set out on a lengthy route in an attempt to prevent infection from taking hold. But no matter how many miles I consumed or how hard I pushed myself, the malaise was unshakable.

I returned to campus after a couple of hours spent aimlessly pounding Boulder's streets and parkland. I arrived at the front of Cheyenne Arapaho to find Brandon loading up his car with various boxes and suitcases.

'What's going on?' I enquired while resting on the bodywork to catch my breath.

'Hey Ross. My buddies said I could move in with them, so I figured no time like the present.'

'Wow, that was quick. Do you need a hand?'

'Nah, don't worry. Jak's just coming down with the last box while I try and squeeze everything in. Good run?'

'Not really, but it passed a couple of hours I suppose.'

'You should enter some races, you know. I bet you'd do pretty well with all the training you do.'

'Yeah, right!'

'No, seriously man. There's a 10K on campus in December – the Winter Warmer. I reckon you'd have a pretty good chance.'

'I've never had the urge to run a race before and I'm not about to start. I just to do it for a bit of fun and to stay healthy, that's all.'

'Fair enough...oh, here's Jak.'

Jak was ambling down the stone steps and peering over the top of a cardboard box.

'Hey Ross,' he said on his arrival. 'Well, Brandon, that's the last one.'

'Thanks for all your help, man. I'll just stuff this one in and get going.'

The quiet morning air was then rudely disturbed by a deep roaring that intensified until we could finally see its source emerging from behind the building. It was a beast of a black pick-up truck, with obscenely large wheels and insidiously tinted side windows. As it rumbled round to the front of our dorm, you could practically see the polar ice caps melting before your eyes. It thundered alongside us, and the driver's window moved down to reveal our nemesis.

'Hello, girls!' growled Shawn as he cruised past us. 'Bye bye, Brandon!' With that, the window slimily moved upwards and Shawn sped off.

'I *hate* that guy,' grimaced Brandon, echoing the sentiments of us all.

He continued to rearrange his belongings while we watched on in silence. He eventually solved the jigsaw puzzle and closed the boot on his time in Cheyenne Arapaho.

'Well then, guys, that's me done.'

'Don't be a stranger,' said Jak while shaking his hand.

'No way, man. Hey, Ross, I'll be seeing you in

Creative Writing on Wednesday?'

'Sure, Brandon, take care.'

Jak and I waved him off and then sat down on the steps together.

'Fucking Shawn,' cursed Jak resentfully.

'It's funny how thing change,' I mused. 'I mean, I was on top of the world on Friday. My exams had finished, and I was a free man. Then in the space of a couple of days everything has turned to rat shit. And to top it all off, we've got classes again tomorrow.'

'I know what you mean, dude, but we're a resilient breed and life goes on. We've just got to learn to take the rough with the smooth, that's all. Hey, why don't we go to the shopping mall and take our minds off things?'

I looked at him in shame. 'Jak, we're not women you know.'

'I know, I know, but in times like these there are two words guaranteed to cheer a man up – "Nursing Lounge".'

'What on earth's that? The place in the mall where they administer first aid?'

'Dude, you'll want to bend me over and give it to me hard in thanks when I reveal the secrets of the nursing lounge, trust me. I won't take no for an answer. Get showered and then we'll go.'

With no better plans for the rest of that Sunday, I joined Jak in his mysterious quest. He drove us to the FlatIron Crossing mall, where lunchtime business was brisk. Jak refused to reveal any further details of his secret until we were sat down in the food court eating Subway sandwiches.

'OK, Ross, are you ready?'

'Just tell me what this "Nursing Lounge" is – I'm getting bored now.'

'OK, OK. Well, the mall has a place where women

can go to feed their babies.'

'The "Nursing Lounge"!'

'Right.'

'Awesome, simply awesome!' I enthused.

'I said you'd thank me.'

'So let me get this right. There's a room in this very mall, where scores of women are just sitting around topless?'

'Yup.'

'And what, is there a viewing gallery behind one way glass or something, like in those fancy operating theatres I've seen on TV?'

'Not quite, Ross, but it's not like there's a lock on the door or anything.'

'So what, they allow visitors to just wander in and watch topless women lactate? Is Sunday some kind of open day in the nursing lounge?'

'Well, it *is* women-only in there, naturally, but there are ways to get in, believe me.'

I was captivated. 'So you've actually been in one of these places before?'

'Sure.'

'Do the women ever rub each other a little, you know, like they normally do in communal showers?'

'All the time.'

Yes, it was childish; yes, it was idiotic; and yes, it was bound to get us into trouble. But it was precisely the kind of diversion we needed from our woes that day. Jak shared his grand plan with me over our sandwiches and Cokes before we stepped forth into the heaving masses and headed towards our destiny.

The door was there, just as he had described. On closer examination, a great deal of thought had gone into its location. Slotted in between a lingerie shop and a chemist, it seemed appropriate that mothers could stock up on sexy bras and nipple pads before venturing in for their afternoon feed. The inconspicuous white door had a small, understated sign that simply read "Nursing Lounge – Women Only". I could barely contain my excitement.

'It's here, just like you said, it's here!'

'Right then, remember the plan, Ross. Give it at least twenty seconds so I get a good look, right?'

'Whatever you say, boss.'

'Cool.'

Jak donned his mirrored sunglasses, straightened his back, and fixed his gaze forwards. After a few intentionally bumbling bangs on the door with his hands, he pushed the door open and ventured in while holding both arms stiffly outwards.

I listened intently until the door closed behind him, but couldn't hear the slightest sound. I had at least expected a scream from a baby or a mother, depending on where Jak's wandering hands had ended up first. After his allotted twenty seconds, I followed Jak's path into the forbidden land.

I was faced with something quite dissimilar to the salubrious lounge I had been imagining so vividly. There were no leather sofas in sight, and no wide-screen TVs showing tasteful pornography either. Instead, there were a handful of bolted-down tables and seats like you would see in a fast food restaurant, and only three women spread thinly amongst them.

'I'm terribly sorry,' I began as I entered. 'Russell, Russell!' I shouted over to Jak as he blindly approached one lady. 'You're in the wrong room, you're in the wrong room!' The women all looked up at me while their children thirstily drank on. I took the opportunity to look around while apologising further. 'He's blind, I'm so sorry. A lady outside thought she saw him wandering in, and here he is. I'll take him out.' I couldn't see anything worthwhile as the children's heads were all blocking my view.

'Oh, Simon, there you are,' said Jak as I reached

him and took him by the arm. 'I thought this was the chemist? Ass cream – I need to get my ass cream.'

'Sure you do. Come on, let's get you out of here.'

We sauntered slowly back to the door while Jak's eyes were no doubt rapidly scanning the room behind his shades. Just as we were passing the final table, the reward for our bravery sprang forth. A rather attractive mother was seated there, and she briefly moved her child away to reveal the most humungous left breast I had ever witnessed, either on screen or in print. It was truly a wonder of the modern world, and it took all of my self-control to allow myself only the briefest of glances as we walked past. Jak, on the other hand, had no such restraint.

'Holy shit!' he blurted out, while the gravitational pull of the boob caused his head to turn in its direction.

'Hey, *he's* not blind!' came the cry from the breast's owner, as we quickened our pace and ran out of the room in hysterics.

'Dude, how good was that?' asked Jak as we walked swiftly to the mall's exit.

'I had my doubts, I must admit, but you certainly delivered.'

'That thing was gigantic!'

While we made our getaway in Jak's Mustang, our women troubles inevitably bubbled to the surface once more.

'So, Jak, are you going to tell Kristen of our little escapade?'

'She'd kill me if she knew I'd just done that.'

'Don't worry, I'm sure she'd be happy that you had done it for a good cause.'

'What, getting to see some young mom's titties?'

'No, cheering up your friend, of course.'

'I'm just happy to help,' he smiled wryly. 'Actually,

there was one good thing to come out of our party on Friday night, you know. I haven't had the chance to tell you.'

'Go on, I'm intrigued.'

'Well, you know Kristen and I have been...well...we've been having problems?'

'Yes, Mr Floppy and all that. Continue...'

'Mr Floppy? Bitch, she swore she wouldn't say anything...'

'Don't worry, it's only me. I already knew you couldn't get it up anyway. Carry on.'

He shook his head to dispel his annoyance. 'Yeah, so, anyway, we've come up with a solution.'

'Porn?'

'No.'

'Hiring a prostitute to assist?'

'Don't be sick, dude. No, we've decided *not* to have sex.'

'Oh, right.' I was unimpressed. 'Isn't that exactly what you've been doing for the last few months?'

'You're missing the subtlety here, Ross. Before, there was always this expectation that it was going to happen, but now we've put all that to one side and said that it definitely *won't* happen. Suddenly the pressure's off and we can both relax again.'

'Oh. Well, whatever works for you both, I suppose.'

'Trust me, it's like a huge weight has been lifted, it really is.'

'And how does Kristen feel about it?'

'She's happy too, I think.'

'You think?'

'Well, *she* suggested it.'

'Jak, Jak, Jak. You can be so naive at times, you really can.'

'What?'

'Well, she clearly suggested it in the hope that you

would relax a little. Then when you're next making out and getting all hot and heavy, she'll pounce on that erection of yours and try to screw your brains out.'

'No, man, you've got it all wrong. There'll be none of that.'

'Whatever you say, but just you watch out, OK?'

'As you're so wise then, what's your plan with April from here?'

'You know what, earlier today I was ready to throw in the towel and call it a day, I really was. But suddenly I'm feeling bright again, I'm feeling alive, and I'm feeling like finishing off Shawn properly this time.'

'Yeah, baby. I'm liking the sound of that!'

'I think I might pay April another visit when we get back, and sort this thing out once and for all.'

'So you're gonna tell her how you feel?'

'One step at a time,' I retreated, hastily. 'No, first things first, I need her to realise who Shawn *really* is. I need to tell her the truth.'

'Hi Laura! Do you know where April is?'

'No.' It was an unusually pointed response from a girl I had previously found to be quite friendly.

'Oh. Well, has she been gone from your room for very long?'

'No.' There was a slightly angry expression in her face that I couldn't quite fathom.

'Right, well did she say when she'd be back?'

'No.' Was she incapable of saying anything else?

'OK then, we'll I'll call back later then.'

'No.'

'What do you mean, "No"?'

'I mean you *shouldn't* call back later.'

I started to get a little irritated by Laura's unusual display of disdain. 'Well, is there any particular reason *why* I shouldn't call back later?'

'Yes – because you're a jerk.'

'Sorry? Do you mind telling me what's going on here?'

'Look, just leave us all alone, OK?'

'I apologised about your teddy bear, and that was ages ago anyway. I thought we'd got over it?'

'It's not the teddy bear, now just get out!'

At a complete loss as to what was happening, my only remaining option was to about-face and leave April's room. I walked down the corridor in a daze, almost colliding with Doggy Style who had a laundry basket under her arm.

'Hey Ross!'

'Oh, hi, er...' I still didn't know her real name.

'Are you looking for April?'

'As a matter of fact, yes I am.'

'I just left her down in the laundry room. She's pretty upset about something, so you might wanna go cheer her up.'

'Oh, right...thanks.'

The plot was thickening. I walked onwards to the stairs and then headed down two flights into the basement of the building. That was where the laundry room was situated, along with my answer to the growing conundrum. The room was narrow, with a row of eight washing machines on one side and a matching number of tumble dryers opposite. In the middle was a long wooden bench, where I found April sat alone, reading a book.

'Hi April!'

She looked up for only an instant before burying her head back in the novel.

'April? Is everything all right?'

She looked up again, this time long enough for her glare to send me out its message of hatred, loud and clear.

'What's wrong? I just went to your room and Laura was acting all weird.'

She continued to read.

'Am I supposed to have done something wrong here?'

There wasn't even a flicker of a response.

'I've got something really important to talk to you about. It's about Shawn.'

With the mention of his name she cast aside her book and rose to her feet. Finally, things were about to become clearer.

'He said you'd do this,' she snarled with increasing anger.

'Do what? What am I doing?'

'Covering your tracks, that's what.'

'Please, April, I really don't understand what's going on here.'

'After what you've been saying about me, you're lucky I'm still here talking to you. I don't know how you've got the nerve.'

I had never seen this feisty side of her before, and it hurt greatly to see it directed squarely at me. In a complete state of confusion and with April baying for my blood, it seemed as good a time as any to lay my cards on the table.

'Look, I don't have a clue what I'm supposed to have said or done, but I need to tell you about Shawn. You can't trust him, April – he's been lying to you. He's been lying to you since he arrived here, and he's probably been lying to you before he arrived here too. He got kicked out of Ohio State for starters.'

'This is *exactly* how he said it would happen. Look, Ross, just walk away from this right now before you make things any worse.'

'Aren't you listening to me, April? It's *Shawn* who you need to be angry with, not me.'

'Just leave me alone.'

'Doesn't our friendship mean anything at all to you?'

'What friendship? You've thrown all that away and there's no going back. Goodbye, Ross.'

'But...'

'Goodbye,' she insisted, before sitting back down on the bench and picking up her book.

Words escaped me as my mind struggled to grasp the events that had just transpired. I could only leave the scene and groggily walk back to my room to regroup, and possibly figure out the answers to my questions. I made it to the stairwell and then slowly climbed to the ground floor, at which point I encountered Shawn on his way down, looking even smugger than usual.

'Hi Ross!' he beamed. 'It's absolutely horrible what's happened, isn't it?'

I wasn't ready for more mind games, so I ignored his cryptic comments and carried on my way.

He continued, 'I'm just gonna see how she's bearing up. It must be a very difficult time for her. Just as well she has someone she can trust to help her through.'

With his final comment, I snapped.

'Trust, TRUST! What would *you* know about trust, Shawn?'

'Hey, calm down there, Ross! You don't wanna go making things any worse after what you've said already.'

'What I've said already? What's that supposed to mean?'

'Hadn't you heard? Rumours have been flying around that you've slept with April. Apparently you've been bragging about it to a few people and word has got around. Poor April is the victim of your cruel hoax, while Shawn is the doting boyfriend here to help her through the difficult times and kick your sorry ass as soon as she says the word.'

'You son of a bitch.'

His snarl then dropped for one uncharacteristic moment, as his voice slightly softened. 'Just trust me on this, Ross – you've got to let it go. Believe it or not, Shawn used to be a little bit like you. Not physically, of course – I've never been such a scrawny little shit – but I did once have a schoolboy crush that was going nowhere. You'll be a stronger person when you've let go of it, trust me.'

He slapped my back like an old friend, before reverting to type.

'But don't forget that Shawn *will* happily fuck things up for you again if he ever has to.'

He continued to the basement and undoubtedly into the arms of my beloved April. I slumped down on the cold stone steps and cradled my head between my knees. I hadn't thought the weekend could get any worse, but with my true love conned into hating me and Shawn gleefully picking up the pieces, it clearly just had.

SEVENTEEN

As the weeks rolled by, the pain slowly weakened. It hadn't been easy to let go of the love of my life, but I knew when I was beaten. Despite sharing a writing class with April and bathroom facilities with Shawn, the cut-off in communications had been near total. As the Colorado autumn finally started to cool as we journeyed into November, I channelled all efforts into my Physics classes once again. It was a valiant, if futile, attempt to raise my grades from their mid-term mediocrity, and a reason not to think about the hurt.

I took to the Farrand Hall coffee lounge on a frosty Friday night with my backpack brimming with books. Jak had reluctantly joined me.

'Do you realise how sad it is that we're studying on a Friday night?' he protested.

I sipped my coffee and looked around the room. 'There's lots of other people studying too.'

'Yeah, but they're all sad geeks without social lives.'

'And who are we? A physicist and an engineer who can't get laid, that's who.'

'Fair point.'

We both reached into our bags and began extracting our books.

'This is where I first met Kristen, you know,' I mused.

'How could I forget? She loves to tell the story of how you complimented her buns.'

'Ah yes, life was so much simpler back then. Before I fell for April, before Shawn showed up and ruined my life.'

'Yes, and before stupid pacts not to have sex.'

'Ah, so all is not well with the pact? I told you, Jak, I told you it would end in trouble.'

'It pains me to say it, but you were right. We were making out this afternoon in her room and I think she probably felt a bit of something prodding her, you know, and then all hell broke loose. She just pounced on me and started ripping my clothes off. By the time she'd got down to my pants it was all over.'

'Mr Floppy?'

'I wish you'd stop saying that.'

'Sorry.'

'I think we need to reaffirm the pact so she doesn't get any more ideas.' He opened his notebook. 'Right, I may as well get started with my engineering project then.'

'Oh yeah, what is it?'

'Well, I've got to come up with some clever new innovation for motorcycle helmets.'

'You engineers certainly know how to have fun, don't you?'

'Hey, I bet it's a damn sight more interesting than that crap you're studying.' He leant over to pick up my book. 'Thermodynamics? Yeah, that sounds like *real* fun!'

'So, do you have any ideas for your helmet then? How about painting it purple?'

My juvenility was ignored. 'I thought about adapting one of those flip-up helmets. You know, the ones where the front comes up so you can talk to people without taking the whole thing off?'

'Oh, right. So what are you going to do with it?'

'I'm not sure yet, but I thought maybe something to do with safety. Making it more accessible for medical treatment after a crash or something like that.'

'Fascinating, I'm sure.'

My sarcasm was roundly shunned as Jak went about his work. Seated on the comfortable sofa, and with a hot cup of coffee and muffin in hand, I didn't particularly feel like starting my own work.

'Brandon keeps bugging me about this race next month.'

Jak looked up in annoyance. 'I thought we were here to work?'

'I know, but I can't be bothered.'

He sighed and put his notes to one side. 'So, what's this about the race?'

'Oh, he keeps going on at me to enter that Winter Warmer 10K. He reckons I might have a chance of winning it. He's out of his mind.'

'It's a stupid idea if you ask me, having a race in December when it's probably snowing.'

'I know, exactly. There's no way I'm gonna do it. I just enjoy running on my own, and there's no chance in hell I'm gonna enter some silly race. Brandon just won't let up though.'

'Well, just stick to your guns then – you do what you want. Now, can we get back to work?'

'Sure.'

While Jak sketched out ideas for his project, I read my thermodynamics text and tried to solve some homework problems. After a few, painfully long, minutes of concentration, we were interrupted by a resounding voice that suddenly soared above the background chatter.

'...boom, boom...I licked yo' grandma's pussy...boom, boom...'

We both snapped our heads upright, just in time to see a colossal, ghostly figure making his way swiftly to the exit.

'That was him!' I said excitedly. 'That was the Hall Rapper!'

'Dude, who *is* that guy?'

'So you finally believe me now?'

'Man, does he screw everyone's family or just yours?'

'I have no idea.'

We carried on our work as if nothing had happened, putting in a fairly solid hour of study amid the odd bit of banter and the occasional coffee refill. Jak was then the first to crack.

'I've had enough of this shit.'

'Problems with your helmet?' I sniggered.

'Yeah, I can't come up with anything. Do you have any ideas?'

'Well, I might have come up with something.'

'Go on, I'm all ears.'

'Cool, well, you know you wanted something safety related, right?'

'Yeah.'

'Well I figure these flip-up helmets are good after a crash for giving mouth-to-mouth without taking someone's helmet off and breaking their neck.'

'Yeah, I guess so.'

'Right, so maybe you should approach it from the view of the lifesaver, not the dumb motorcyclist who's got himself killed. Put yourself in the position of the paramedic – you're at the scene, and you flip up the helmet to reveal an ugly guy with a big bushy moustache and half his teeth missing.'

'There's no fucking way I'm giving *him* mouth-to-mouth,' grimaced Jak, getting into the role.

'Exactly. But what if, as you flipped up the helmet, a pair of fake breasts suddenly inflated under his jacket? You could grab them with one hand while holding his nose with the other. It'd take the edge off quite nicely.'

'Somehow I don't think that's quite what they're looking for,' he laughed.

'It'd work for me.'

'Come on, let's go.'

'Where to?'

'I don't give a shit, I just need to get out of here.'

We hurriedly packed away our things and headed for the exit. We emerged to find snow falling on our heads and a considerable covering on the ground. It was the first snowfall since my arrival.

'Wow, this is great!' I enthused.

'Hey, look at Farrand Field!'

I looked down towards our dorm and the white field in front of it. It was littered with excitable students throwing snowballs and building snowmen. We took one look at each other and then ran like children to join in the mayhem.

We perched our bags on the surrounding chain link fence and set to work. I was hardly dressed for the occasion in my light jacket and trainers, but it was of no great concern as we started pelting each other with snowballs and getting involved in pitch battles with a variety of strangers.

While wiping the snow from my face after one particularly brutish encounter, I noticed Kazuki and Brandon in one corner of the field making a strange looking snowman.

'Hey, it's Kaz and Brandon,' I gestured to Jak, and we duly wandered over to see the fruits of their labour. As we approached, the snowman appeared even more unusual than it had done from a distance.

'Hi guys!' we greeted them in unison.

'Ah, hello!' replied Kazuki. 'Snow great, yeah?'

'It sure is,' smiled Jak.

'Hey, what's wrong with your snowman?' I asked. 'He's leaning to one side.'

'He not leaning,' Kazuki explained, 'he limp!'

'Limp? And why does he have such big feet?'

'Dude,' explained Brandon, 'those ain't feet – they're balls!'

'We build penis!' added Kazuki.

We paced around the work of art and, sure enough, it really *was* a snow penis.

'That's quite impressive,' complimented Jak while stroking the sides. 'Hey, let's make some boobs!'

'Yeah!' chimed Kazuki as they scrambled to begin the next masterpiece.

Just as I was contemplating whether to work on the left or the right breast, I caught sight of April walking down the steps of Cheyenne Arapaho. I froze still while following her path down onto the field. She was even less adequately dressed than me – wearing only jeans and a jumper – and she seemed totally disinterested in the madness around her as she sat down on a snow-covered bench. She hadn't even cleared the snow before taking her seat, and she proceeded to bury her head down into her knees and clutch it with her hands. It was odd behaviour, no question, and my instincts told me she was in some kind of trouble.

I looked back towards my friends, who were happily sculpting their mammary mounds, and contemplated what I should do next. April and I hadn't even spoken for weeks, and I was only just becoming able to think about her without feeling a sharp pain in the pit of my stomach. But seeing her there on that bench, lost and alone, I couldn't bare to watch her suffer. I made the decision to go over and see her, just to make sure that she was OK. I started walking away from the erotica and headed straight for her bench. Jak must have finally realised what was going on, and shouted over at me.

'ROSS, ROSS! DON'T DO IT, MAN, COME BACK, COME BACK!'

There was no stopping me. As I neared the seat I could see April's arched back bobbing up and down while the tears were streaming from her eyes. I couldn't hold back any more, and I ran the final few metres before sitting by her side.

I wanted to hug her, to hold her, to cradle her in my arms and tell her everything was going to be all right. But, for all I knew, her anger at me was still strong and any such move could have been unwelcome. I took a more delicate approach – removing my jacket and placing it carefully around her shoulders.

'April,' I uttered softly. 'April, what's wrong?'

She brought her head upwards, took one look at me and then fell against my chest. The tears ran down my T-shirt as she wrapped her arms around me.

'You were right, you were so right,' she sobbed uncontrollably.

'It's going to be all right, I'm here now,' I comforted while stroking her hair.

We held that position for a good five minutes, during which time my bare arms collected a centimetre of snow and the seat of my jeans readily absorbed the slush from the bench. I could barely move from the cold, but there was nowhere else I wanted to be.

'Why did he lie to me?' she blubbered into my chest. '*How* could he lie to me?'

'What happened, April?'

'I found a letter from Ohio State.' She held me tighter while the tears continued to flow. 'It said he'd been kicked out for cheating. He made me believe he came here to be with me.'

Finally, she had seen the real Shawn, but it brought me no satisfaction when the result was such complete devastation.

'We had this big argument and I thought back to you warning me in the laundry room that day. I asked him outright if you'd really said those things, and he just wouldn't answer me. He wouldn't answer me. I'm so sorry, Ross, I'm so sorry.'

'Sh, don't worry,' I shivered. 'Everything's going to be all right.'

We held the embrace for another few minutes until the tears finally abated. April emerged from my sodden T-shirt to see a neat pile of snow on my every extremity.

'You look like a winter scarecrow!' she smiled.

'Well I'm glad that's cheered you up!'

She held my gaze with her reddened eyes. 'I must look a mess,' she coyly remarked.

'You look beautiful.'

April's face twinkled sweetly and I was truly lost in the moment. This was my perfect opportunity – the stage was finally set for my honest admission of love. There would be no more hiding behind framed photographs or stupid poems. I was going to tell her to her face, and say the only three words that could adequately describe how I truly felt.

My lips opened. A cloudy breath exited my mouth but it didn't carry a single word. I took a large gulp of the bitter air and tried again.

'I'm really glad that we're friends again.' Where the fuck had that come from? That wasn't what I meant to say. That wasn't what I *needed* to say.

She smiled awkwardly, and my one golden chance had passed as suddenly as it had arrived.

'Gosh, you must be so cold!' she said while rising

to her feet. 'Here, take your jacket back.'

'No, you keep it on.'

'No, I'd better get back inside and warm up. I'll see you later, Ross. Thank you.'

She passed me the jacket and ran back to the warmth of our residence hall without looking back. I sat with the jacket on my lap and the snow piling higher all around me, but unable to move. Jak must have been keeping an eye on the situation and soon came over.

'Dude, what's up, what's happened?'

'Just take me into the mountains and shoot me in the head.'

'You're shivering, put your coat on.'

He kindly brushed the snow from my shoulders and arms, and I wrapped myself up in the warm jacket.

'I'm such a fucking idiot. She was there, in my arms, literally *begging* for me to tell her. And what do I come out with? "I'm glad we're friends". IDIOT!'

'What happened?'

'Shawn's web of lies finally fell apart, that's what happened.'

'My god! So what did she say?'

'Just that Shawn was a liar and she was sorry.'

'Holy shit, this is huge! How do you feel?'

'Stupid, weak, pathetic...'

'Dude, the floor is open, don't you see?'

'The floor *was* open, but I just slipped on it and fell on my arse.'

'Why didn't you just tell her?'

'That bitch Bethan has so much to answer for – *she's* the one who's screwed me up.' I let out a scream of despair into the bleak sky.

'Just forget about her, man.'

'I wish I could, I really wish I could.' After a

considered pause, I jumped to my feet. 'Let's go see this snow sculpture of yours, then.'

'Sure, buddy,' replied Jak, knowing when to leave well alone. 'You can help us finish the nipples.'

My arse cheeks had finally thawed by the following morning, but my head was still hurting from my stupidity. I tiptoed out of the bedroom so as not to wake the breast sculptors, and headed down the corridor to the bathroom for a shower.

I still found the whole American shower experience to be a little unsettling. Privacy was at an absolute minimum, just as it was in the toilet stalls with their huge gaps down the side of the doors that gave an unsavoury view to anyone who wanted it. Full height curtains shielded the entrances to the two side-by-side shower cubicles – which was perfectly acceptable – and at the back was a full height solid tiled wall – again completely normal. The sides, however, started at the knees and only came up to shoulder height. Maybe I was just a reserved Brit, but it really did feel like you were showering in front of another naked man, and it was definitely not an experience I enjoyed. You spent the whole ordeal trying not to make eye contact with the guy next to you, but all the while feeling the need to make painful small talk.

That morning I started off showering alone. In the midst of my lather, rinse, repeat cycle, I heard the bathroom door creak open, but I couldn't open my eyes to see who had entered. I massaged my skull while the footsteps approached, and it wasn't long before the swoosh of the curtain to the adjacent cubicle could be heard.

'Hey,' came the greeting from my naked colleague.

At the sound of that voice my eyes instinctively opened wide, and were instantly pained by the stinging of shampoo and the sight of Shawn. Either by some miracle of scheduling or, more probably, his questionable hygiene, Shawn and I hadn't previously had the pleasure of showering together. I frantically rinsed my eyes, but Shawn's hairy back was still there when I could finally open them again.

'Hey,' I replied in a mumble, so as not to reveal my identity.

We continued our routines in absolute silence, while I struggled to find the words that could adequately capture my feelings toward him. I didn't feel any kind of smug satisfaction that his relationship with April had fallen apart – only a fierce anger that he had caused her such hurt. I decided to remain silent for the time being, although it took all of my strength to resist offering my shampoo when he started washing his back.

With my shower soon complete, I turned off the water and reached for my towel. I bent down to dry my legs and couldn't avoid seeing his feet at the side of me. Just at that very instant, the water around his toes stopped running clear as it turned an acrid yellow. I was fortunately outside the splash zone, but I nevertheless quickly wrapped the towel around my waist and made a swift exit. Not before making a parting shot, however.

'I know how you feel, Shawn – I nearly pissed myself too when April told me about your lies. Just remember that the plug hole isn't big enough for number twos, OK?'

'What the...?' he replied in surprise at my voice, as I calmly left the bathroom before he could complete his sentence.

With one hand holding my pyjamas, and the other holding up my towel, I walked soggily back down the corridor. With my head bowed low, I swung open the door to my study room. As it closed behind me I released my grip from the towel and began drying myself properly. It was then that a wolf whistle suddenly rang out. I bolted upright and saw her sitting at my desk.

'Looking good, Ross!'

I quickly covered myself back up while staring at her in utter shock.

'Well aren't you even going to say hello?' she continued. 'It's been a bloody nightmare getting here with all that snow!'

It was bizarre to hear an English accent again after three months surrounded by Americans. And I never thought I'd be hearing *that* particular accent ever again, let alone several thousand miles from home.

'Ross, are you surprised or something?'

'Bethan? How...what...'

'Just thought I'd pop in and say hello!'

EIGHTEEN

'So what exactly *are* you doing here, Bethan?'

'Long time no see!'

'Yeah, but you still haven't answered my question.'

'I'd hoped for a slightly warmer reception, you know.'

'A warmer reception? *A warmer reception?* You come to Colorado in mid-November and you visit your ex-boyfriend, who you dumped rather abruptly eighteen months ago and haven't seen since, and you expected a warmer reception? What the *fuck* are you doing here?'

'OK, OK, chill out! Christ, I thought you might be just a *little* pleased to see me, at least.'

'Well clearly I'm not, am I? Clearly the last year and a half I've spent trying to rid my mind of all memories of you has just been wasted, and maybe I'm struggling to cope with that, just a *little* bit.'

'Listen, why don't you get dressed then we can talk properly?'

I stormed through to the bedroom where Kazuki was still snoring but Jak had been woken.

'Dude, what's going on out there?' he croaked. 'It sounded like you were giving someone abuse.'

'Jak,' I whispered heatedly, 'you would not *believe* who is out there right now. You simply wouldn't believe it.'

'Woa, calm down, man. It can't be that bad.'

'It's Bethan.'

'Holy shit, I guess it *is* that bad.'

'How can she just stroll in like this? *Why* would she do that? Why now?'

'Shit.'

'I mean, after all this time without any contact whatsoever, then she flies halfway around the world and just waltzes into my room as if nothing has happened. Just who does she think she is?'

'Fuck me.'

'Just as things are getting on track, as well. Just as I'm *finally* moving on.'

'Shit.'

'Just as things are starting to fall in place for me and April. Just as I'm on the edge of something amazing...'

'Yeah...but *also* just as you failed to tell April you loved her, right? And wasn't that because of this Bethan chick?'

Jak wasn't supposed to be so insightful that early in the morning. He was just supposed to listen and agree with everything I said.

'What?'

'I'm just saying, yesterday you were cursing this chick so maybe now you can finally resolve things, once and for all?'

I flopped down onto my bed and buried my head in the pillow.

Jak continued to reason with me. 'Look, I know it's probably painful seeing her again, and she's a bitch and you hate her, etcetera, etcetera. But don't you see? You've got the chance to wipe the slate clean here, to put those demons behind you and get on with your life. Whether that be with April or someone else, you need to do this. You've *got* to do this.'

'Why does life have to be so complicated?'

'It just is, dude, it just is.'

I rested for another few moments, enjoying the warmth of the sheets against my skin, enjoying Kazuki's rhythmic snoring, enjoying being there with my friends, enjoying not being out there with her. For all his perceptive comment and compassion, Jak quickly fell back to sleep and left me alone with my thoughts. I eventually hauled myself up and began to dress for whatever it was I was about to face.

With every item of clothing came a memory. It started with the first time Bethan and I met as I put on my right sock, and then the first time we kissed with the left one. My boxer shorts appropriately marked our first excited fumblings, and then my long-sleeved shirt signified the first time we slept together. As I completed my ensemble with a pair of harsh, scratchy jeans, her departure from my life replayed through my head. I tied my shoelaces tightly, like the noose around her neck, and then I was ready.

I re-entered the study room and she hadn't moved an inch.

'Have you settled down now?' she asked.

'Just a bit.'

'Well that's a relief. You look really well, by the way. And not just without your towel on!'

Through the fog of anger that had filled the room earlier, I hadn't really given Bethan proper consideration. But then, with the mist clearing, it was soon apparent that she had lost none of the qualities that made me fall so heavily for her in the first place. It was her cute smile I had first noticed when we initially met, and it felt like that day all over again. I had to tell myself that times had changed and life had moved on. It was time for some answers.

'So, for fear of repeating myself, *why* are you here, Bethan?'

'I'm on my way to a climbing expedition in Alaska, so I thought I'd plan a little layover on the way. I should have got here last night, but with all the snow everything was delayed. I've hardly slept!'

The way she giggled at the end of her sentences when she was excited was another endearing feature.

'So when do you leave for Alaska?'

'Ready to get rid of me already, eh?' She checked her watch. 'My flight's in about five hours.'

'So why here? Why me?'

She unfastened her winter jacket as she made herself comfortable. The svelte figure she revealed was another attribute I had long admired.

'I don't know, to be honest. Maybe I've been thinking about you a lot recently, and I just made the decision on an impulse. That's just the way I am – you know me!'

'Well I *thought* I knew you. So what *have* you been doing for the last eighteen months?'

'OK, maybe I deserve that. I've just been travelling around England really, working in bars and saving money for this expedition. I'm so excited to be over here, you know.'

'I'm sure you are.'

She tossed her short black hair to the side as if to strengthen the spell she was casting over me.

'So how are you getting on over here?'

'Not too bad. It beats being in Lancaster. How did you find me, anyway?'

'I just heard that you were in Boulder, and thought I'd get here and look around for you. Yours was only the third hall I tried, so I suppose I was pretty lucky! Anyway, I've got to get the bus back to the airport in a couple of hours, so are you going to show me around this campus of yours or what? It looks amazing from what I've seen so far, and it's so pretty with the all snow.'

'OK, let me get my coat.'

I gave her the tour while the snow sparkled on every roof and treetop. As the sun cut down through the icy air, it weakened my resistance and gradually warmed me to her presence. For the three months of our relationship Bethan had been my closest friend, and that familiarity soon flooded back as we caught up on each other's recent history.

'So this is where the physics happens, then? I'm so proud that you're making your dreams come true, Ross, I really am.'

'Didn't you ever want to go to university?'

'For a while, maybe, but there was just so much other stuff I wanted to do first. I doubt I'll ever get there now, especially as I'm getting old.'

'Twenty-one is hardly old.'

'Perhaps, but it does feel like I need to get on with things – maybe start settling down.'

'Settling down? My god, you really *have* changed!'

'Hey, don't laugh! I know I've moved around a bit over the last few years, but maybe I just needed to see what was out there before I could decide what I *really* wanted in life.'

'So have you decided then?'

She avoided my question by pointing to the dome atop the Duane Physics building. 'Wow, what's that thing?'

'It's the observatory.'

'Cool.' She frantically looked for another diversion. 'Hey, are you hungry? I haven't eaten since this really nasty sandwich they gave me on the plane last night.'

'Sure. I'll take you to the UMC – we can get something to eat there.'

We made the brief journey amidst an unspoken tension. It was as if she wanted to tell me something, something of great importance, but she was waiting for the right moment.

'What do you feel like eating?' I asked as we arrived at the food court.

'Oooh, I'd love one of those bagel things that Americans always talk about.'

'OK, let's go to Baby Doe's.'

I directed us towards the counter where we were cheerfully greeted by a nametag called Bob. I gestured for Bethan to order first.

'Hi,' she began, 'please can I have a bagel with butter?'

Bob strained his ear closer. 'You wanna bagel with what?'

'With butter.'

'What?' He was clearly struggling with the accent.

'Butt-er,' she repeated, loud and slow.

'I'm sorry?'

She turned to me for help. 'Ross?'

'God, I hate doing this,' I muttered before looking up at Bob. 'Budder, with *budder*!'

'Oh, why didn't you say?'

Bob scurried away to toast a bagel while Bethan despaired. 'My god, is it always like this?'

'Not always, it's just a few words they seem to have a problem with. For god's sake please don't ask me to get you some water.'

'It's the bloody Queen's English. I mean, what else could I have possibly been asking for on my bagel?'

'I know, believe me, I know.'

Bob soon returned and obligingly fetched a Danish pastry and a couple of coffees before we sat down to eat. After a few hungry bites, Bethan looked up from her buttered bagel.

'This is a bit like the first time we went out. Do

you remember?'

'Yes,' I smiled. 'I waited 'til midnight for you to finish work at that bar.'

'And then you took me to the kebab shop – how romantic!'

'Well I didn't know any better, did I! I was only a seventeen-year-old school kid.'

'And *I* was the corrupting older woman?'

'I would never have had the courage to ask you out.'

'You just needed a little help, that's all.' She looked deep into my eyes, almost dreamily, before looking at her watch. 'Oh god, my bus is in half an hour. We'd better get cracking.'

The reminiscing stopped dead and we finished off our breakfast in quiet contemplation. With my last mouthful of the Danish, it was time we were going.

If she had wanted to tell me something, then her window of opportunity was rapidly closing. We got to our feet and made our way outside the UMC and back onto the white walkways that would lead us to the bus stop on Broadway. It was then that she made her move.

She was walking on my left and gradually gravitating closer towards me until her hand brushed mine and then, finally, held it tight. I was taken aback and wracked by indecision, so I took the easy option and did nothing. We just continued walking while our joined hands swung gaily in the breeze. The unspoken bond between us strengthened with every footprint we left in the snow, as I was catapulted back to some of the happiest times of my life.

For that moment we were together, I had forgotten Bethan's cruelty and the callousness with which she walked out of my life all that time ago. But my memory lapse was only for that briefest of moments.

For it was then that I saw April heading towards us. I suddenly forgot where I was. I forgot who I was with. I could only see the most beautiful woman in my world walking towards me and filling my life with joy. Her figure gracefully approached us and then she smiled her wonderful smile.

'Hey Ross!'

'April, hi! It's beautiful out here, isn't it.'

'Yeah, it sure is.' She looked to my left at the something that stood next to me, and then worked her eyes downwards to my hand. As well as forgetting what I was standing next to, I had also forgotten that I was holding its hand. I urgently turned to see the horrible truth there beside me, and was sent crashing back into the real world.

'Oh, April, sorry...' I stumbled while gruffly releasing my hand from the devil's grasp, '...how rude of me. This is Bethan – she's...well...a friend from back home. Bethan, this is April.'

'Oh, hi Bethan.'

'Hi April, pleased to meet you.'

'So what brings you to Colorado then?'

Bethan looked bashfully towards me. 'Unfinished business, I suppose.'

'Really? Well, you picked a *great* time to visit!' I almost detected a double meaning to the comment, but couldn't quite be sure.

'Yes, this snow is amazing! It's such a beautiful campus here.'

'Yes, it certainly is. Well, I'd better let you two get on your way then.'

'OK,' I interjected. 'I'll see you later, April, OK?'

'Sure Ross. Bye, Bethan. It was nice meeting you.'

'Yes, you too. Bye!'

We carried on our way and I tried not to dwell on any false impressions that may have been given to April. There were far more pressing concerns that had to be dealt with before that bus left for the airport.

First things first. 'So what was all that handholding about?'

'Do you like that girl?'

'Bethan, I asked you a question.'

'It seemed to me that maybe you liked her.'

'*Why* did you hold my hand?'

'I suppose she is *fairly* attractive, if you like that sort of thing. A bit plain for you though I would have thought.'

'Stop, just STOP!' She obeyed my demand and we faced-off in the middle of the path. '*Why did you hold my hand*?' I repeated.

'I just wanted to show you a little affection, is that so wrong?'

'Affection? *Affection*? A letter or a phone call would have shown me some kind of affection. Was that too much to ask?'

'I want us to be close again, don't you get it? Don't you understand what all of this is about? Why I've come all this bloody way to see you?'

'Clearly I don't, so you're going to have to spell it out for me.'

'I miss you.'

I shook my head in disbelief. '*I told you that I loved you*. Do you know how hard that was for me? I'd never said it to anyone before, and I've never said it to anyone since. I told you that I loved you. I gave you my heart, I gave you everything.'

'I was confused, I didn't know what I wanted...'

'So what, you just walk away, break things off and leave town?'

'It really frightened me, I couldn't deal with it.'

'*You* couldn't deal with it? How do you think *I* coped? You were everything to me. You were my best friend. We barely spent a moment apart for those three months. And then to have you just leave like that – vanishing into the night without even a hint of an explanation. My world was over, my *life* was over. I was completely lost without you.'

'But I'm more settled now, I know what I want.'

'Do you really? So you decide you can just fly over here and wrap me around your little finger again, and it will be as if the last eighteen months had never happened. Is that what you honestly thought?'

'I want *you*, Ross. I want *us*. I want us to be together again, I want to share my life with you. I'm ready now.'

'You know, I spent endless nights dreaming about this day. I hoped…I wished…I prayed that you would realise what a huge mistake you'd made and come back to me. I had it all planned out – I'd make you sweat for a while, but eventually I'd tell you how much I still loved you, and how I couldn't live without you. And then you'd say exactly the same thing back to me. And then I'd get down on one knee and give you the ring I'd been carrying ever since you left…'

'Ring? You mean…'

'…and then we would kiss, and it would be magical.'

'Well kiss me then. We can do *all* that, just kiss me now.'

'But now that day is here, now that day has finally arrived, I don't want *any* of it to happen. It's taken me so long to get you out of my mind. So long before I could wake up in the morning and realise that I'd gone a whole twenty-four hours without aching for you. And then I came here, to America, and left your memory well and truly behind. Now I've fallen in love again, and with someone far more deserving of my affection.'

'April?'

'Yes, April. I'm in love with April. I *love* April.'

It felt incredible to finally say those words out loud after hiding them away for so long. My anger and aggression suddenly fell away. It was as if all of the troubles of the world had just evaporated into the air, and nothing else truly mattered other than those words. I turned away from Bethan and shouted it to the world.

'I LOVE APRIL! I LOVE APRIL! I LOVE APRIL!'

I returned to find Bethan wearing the look of gallant defeat.

'I'm...I'm pleased for you,' she said graciously.

'I'm sorry, Bethan. I know this isn't what you expected.'

'It's fine, it's OK. I had to come and try, otherwise I would never have known. For what it's worth, I'm sorry for the hurt I caused you.'

'Come on, your bus will be here soon.'

With everything said that needed to be, we silently carried on our way and reached the stop just as the express for Denver International Airport was pulling in. The doors hissed open and Bethan stepped aboard, pausing to give me her parting thoughts.

'April seems nice. I hope you're happy together.'

On her final word, the doors folded shut and took her away. I was left with only one pressing purpose in life – to find the one person in the whole world who I *really* needed to be telling that I was in love.

NINETEEN

I was gasping for air after my frantic battle through the snow, but I had made it back and I was more than ready to face my destiny. It was time to cast aside the clouds that had been stalking me. It was time to start living my life again. I didn't have a single doubt in my mind when that door opened before me.

'Hey Ross, what's wrong? You look terrible.'

'Oh, Laura, hi. Just a bit out of breath, that's all. Do you know where April is?'

'Listen, I just wanted to apologise for, you know...calling you a jerk and everything. I feel really bad.'

'Don't worry; it's water under the bridge. Just tell me where April is, please?'

'I don't know where she is. She *was* here about five minutes ago. She looked a bit upset or something, actually, but she wouldn't tell me what was wrong.'

'Damn,' I muttered to the floor, half-wondering if it had been the handholding that had caused her such anguish. Perhaps she *had* been harbouring some feelings towards me? 'So, did she go back out or something?'

'Well I'm not sure. That jerk came around then.'

'What, there's *another* jerk?'

'The jerk of all jerks,' she smiled. 'Shawn.'

'Oh, *that* jerk. So did they go somewhere together, do you think?'

'I don't know. I gave him the evil eyes so they went in the hall to talk, but she never came back in.'

'You do the evil eyes very well, trust me. He's probably on a flight to Brazil by now.'

'God, I wish. You know she swore she wouldn't ever speak to him again, but as soon as he came knocking it was a completely different story. What do you want to see her for, anyway?'

'Oh, nothing much. I just wanted to see how she was.'

'Aw, you're so sweet, Ross. Why can't she go out with a nice guy like you?'

I laughed clumsily. 'OK, I'd better be going then. I'll see you later.'

My mind worked quickly to figure out where I should look next. It decided on the car park behind Cheyenne Arapaho. If Shawn was still on campus then his beastly machine would be out there, just waiting for its next opportunity to deplete the ozone layer. At least then I would know how widespread my search would have to be. I raced to reception and then out of the building. I charged down the main steps, with flagrant disregard for the icy conditions, and duly slipped on the final step and wound up in a graceless heap with a face full of snow.

I quickly wriggled my extremities to make sure nothing was broken, and then raised my head from the snow. I wiped the flakes from my eyes just in time to see the underside of Shawn's global warming wagon as it accelerated away. I jumped to my feet and caught the silhouette of a longhaired passenger through the back window – it could only have been April.

I scrambled back up the steps and went straight for my room. I started calling for Jak before I even got through the front door.

'Jak, Jak, we need to go, we need to go *now*!'

I looked around the study room and saw that he wasn't there. I desperately needed his car and his help – where could he have been at noon on Saturday? I opened the door to the bedroom and heard Kazuki's snoring still going strong, while Jak wriggled uncomfortably in his bed. I went over and pulled his blanket away.

'Jak, Jak.'

'Woa, what are you doing?' he replied with his eyes still firmly shut.

'Come on, get up, we've got to go. We need to go, *now*!'

'Man, what time is it?'

'It's noon. Come on, let's go.'

'Dude, I had the weirdest dream. You know your ex, Bethan? Well she turned up in our room. How fucking funny would that be!'

'Hilarious, absolutely hilarious. Now get some clothes on.'

He sleepily sat up and swivelled around to put his feet on the floor. 'So what exactly are we doing?'

'We need to find Shawn and April – they've just gone off in his pick-up. I need you to drive.'

'Where've they gone?'

'I'm not sure.'

'You're not sure? Well where the hell are we driving to then?'

'I don't know.'

'Screw that!' He moved his feet back on the bed and lay down again. 'Come back when you know where they're going, and *then* I'll drive you. And give me back my blanket.'

'Shit.'

He was right, of course – they could have been going anywhere. I needed some more information to work from – I needed some intelligence. It wasn't a word I had previously associated with Shawn's roommate, particularly after witnessing a rather intimate discussion he'd had with the paper towel dispenser late one evening while I was on the toilet. Regardless, he was my only hope, so I rushed down to his room.

'Ross! Whassup?' he answered at the door with fully dilated pupils, while a thick haze swirled around his braided goatee beard and began to spill out into the corridor.

'Hi, Brad.'

'It's Chad.'

'Sorry, I thought that was your roommate.'

'Yeah, it was. But I'm now Chad for...er...legacy trading purposes.'

'Right, whatever, anyway, do you know where Shawn is?'

'Dude, who's Shawn?'

'Your roommate, Shawn?'

'No, my roommate was Chad. He left.'

'Yes, I know he left. But then *after* he left, you got a new roommate, didn't you?'

'Oh, yeah.'

'And he's called Shawn.'

'Right, I'm with you now. So what was it that you wanted?'

'*Where* is Shawn?' He looked at me dimly, clearly in need of some further clarification. '*Your roommate.*'

'Right, right, my roommate Shawn. Yeah, well he was here, like just five minutes ago. You must have missed him or something.'

'I know I missed him. I saw him driving off in his pick-up. Do you know where he went?'

'Yeah, man, he went out in his pick-up.'
'For the love of god, *where* did he go?'
'Denver.'
'He went to Denver?'
'Did he?'
'That's what you just said.'
'Did I? Yeah, Chad's gone to Denver, dude, that's where you'll find him.'
'No, not Chad, *Shawn*.'
'Yeah, Shawn's my new roomy. That's the guy that's just cruised to Denver.'
'So *Shawn* has gone to *Denver*, yes?'
'If you say so man. Are you going there too?'
'Yes, yes, I am.'
'Sweet. Well, can I hook you up with some weed for the road?'
'As much as you're clearly a glowing endorsement for your products, I think I'll pass.'
'What?'
'*No*, thanks.'
'No problem, man, I'm always here if you need, just remember.'
'Sure.'
'Later man, say hi to Chad for me.'

He closed the door and the search was back on. I sprinted back to Jak.

'Jak, we're going to Denver, come on.'

He sighed deeply and then laboured out of bed before starting to look through his wardrobe.

'We don't have time for clothes selection, Jak. We're not going to a fashion show.'

'All right, all right. Just give me a minute.' He picked up a pile of yesterday's clothes from the floor and started to dress. 'Why are we going to Denver, anyway?'

'Because that's where Shawn's going.'

'What's he doing in Denver?'

'I'm not sure, but something tells me he's not going to a counselling session for gay ice skaters who piss in the shower.'

'He pisses in the shower? That's disgusting.'

'I know.'

'I'd never do that...well, not when anyone could see me, anyway.'

'*You're* disgusting.'

'So what's so urgent that you have to see him now? Are you gonna have a throw-down with him or something?'

'No, April's with him. I'm going to tell her that I love her.'

'Yeah, right. I've heard that one before.'

'No, seriously. Trust me, Jak, the whole world has changed while you were asleep. I'll tell you everything on the way.'

The roads were mercifully well cleared of snow, allowing Jak's Mustang an untroubled journey out of Boulder. I had been filling him in on the morning's momentous events as we sped down US-36.

'So you have *me* to thank for all of that?' said Jak. '*I* actually advised you to sort things out with Bethan?'

'I know it's hard to believe. You told me that I had the chance to wipe the slate clean, and it was the only way I'd be able to move on with April.'

'*I* said all that?'

'Yes, you did. And then you fell back to sleep.'

'Shit, I can't remember a word of it. I suppose it explains my dream, though.'

'I thought you were speaking too much sense to actually be awake.'

'That's awesome though, Ross. I can't believe you're gonna do this, this is so huge!'

'I know, but I'm ready.'

'What about Shawn though?'

'That might be a complication.'

'Would you still tell her if they were back together?'

'I don't know. Let's just hope they aren't.'

'So, as we're heading for this city of half a million people, where do you propose we start looking?'

'Well, he's probably just gonna take her out for a posh meal or something, don't you think? He'll be apologising and saying how it will never happen again and how he's learned his lesson...'

'...and he promises never to piss in the shower again...'

'...yeah, and he promises to stop looking at the other male ice skaters in the changing rooms. So maybe we could look for his truck in the car parks, or just check out all the restaurants near the 16th Street Mall? They're bound to be there somewhere.'

'Sounds like a plan.'

We parked at Larimer Square – a small district of fancy shops in the heart of downtown Denver. The parking garage was practically teeming with behemoths identical to Shawn's, so our restaurant search soon became the only sensible option. We moved on to the 16th Street Mall's pedestrianised strip that runs the entire length of the city centre. We took it in turns to venture inside the various eateries and play the "I'm just looking for my friends, don't mind me" line while scouring every single table. On a Saturday lunchtime that was no easy task, and after a solid hour of searching we were losing faith.

Jak emerged from the final place we could find on 16th Street – a pretentious-looking Mediterranean restaurant.

'I'm sorry, Ross, they weren't in that one either. Is it worth carrying on? I mean, we must have tried more than fifty places.'

'Maybe you're right,' I sighed.

'If they *are* here, then I just don't think we're gonna find them. I'm sorry, man.'

'OK, let's call off the search. Maybe we should get some lunch ourselves?'

'Well, considering I haven't had a thing all day I'm glad you finally got around to offering! So then, do you think we can find anywhere to eat in this town?'

We laughed together and the frustration subsided. At the very least, it had felt good to be doing something positive rather than just sitting around and waiting back in Boulder. I treated Jak to a burger at the Rock Bottom Brewery – chosen because it had the hottest waitresses of all the places he had visited that day. The impressive range of beers was sadly out of reach for our underage hands, but the Coke flowed freely and we enjoyed the break. As we left with satisfied stomachs and bulging bladders, I was feeling distinctively unhealthy.

'I think I'll need to run ten miles to get rid of that burger.'

'Hey dude, that reminds me. I've been thinking about your running.'

'Is this another dream of yours, Jak?'

'No, dude. I've been looking into that Winter Warmer 10K race – the one that Brandon wants you to do?'

'Not you as well. Listen, I'll say to you what I keep saying to Brandon – *no bloody way*! Never.'

'You know, professional athletes from all over the world come to take part. It's normally some Ethiopian or Kenyan who wins it. But imagine this – there you are, a complete unknown, starting off in the middle of all the idiots wearing animal costumes and shit, and then you just sail through the field, overtake all the Africans and win the damn thing.

Completely out of the blue, completely unexpected. You'd be in all the newspapers – it would be awesome!'

'You talk so much more sense when you're asleep, Jak. There's no way on earth I'm gonna be entering that race. End of story.'

'It was just an idea.'

'OK then, back to the matter at hand. Let's reassess our options.' I checked my watch. 'It's past three now, so they're not likely to be eating anymore. Maybe we should just head home?'

'We *could* head home, but how about we just look round some of the shops first?'

'Jak, there's about ten times as many shops as restaurants. Our odds aren't good.'

'I didn't mean to look for April. There's a...well...a "specialist" item I need to look for. I can't find it in Boulder and I haven't had the chance to come out here for a while.'

'A "specialist" item?'

'Just something to keep Kristen happy, you know.'

I feigned ignorance. 'What, like perfume?'

'No, not perfume, you know...'

I wasn't going to ease up until I made him blush. 'Chocolates?'

'No, women things.'

I raised my voice so as to be heard clearly above the din of the hundred people walking by. 'Oh, you mean a VIBRATOR?'

'Sh, you idiot. Everyone's looking now!'

'Don't be so shy. I think it's nice that you're taking care of her needs. Come on then, where do we go for this stuff?'

'I think I saw a place down one of the side streets.'

We ventured back along 16th until Jak found what he was looking for.

'It's here,' he said. 'Look, down there.'

I glanced down the street to see a huge neon sign that read "GIRLS, GIRLS, GIRLS".

'Isn't that a strip club?'

'No, not "GIRLS, GIRLS, GIRLS". There's a smaller sign, closer to us.'

'Oh, I see! "Sam's Adult Emporium"? Right then, let's go.'

Neither of us had ever frequented such an establishment before and Jak was particularly nervous. As we approached the entrance he started to have second thoughts.

'I'm not sure I can do this.'

'Come on, a quick "in and out", that's all it takes!'

'Shut up,' he giggled. 'Oh, shit. Come on then.'

We opened the door and passed through some heavy black curtains to reveal the other world. Everywhere we looked there were inordinately lengthy plastic objects sticking out from display cases, some of them buzzing ferociously and rotating in all manner of directions. It appeared that the ground floor was completed dedicated to this particular type of equipment, and god only knew what filth lay in the floors above.

Jak hurriedly picked up the first box he could get his hands on and headed for the till.

'Woa, Jak, woa! Let me look at that first.' I took the box from his hands and read the essential details. 'This is nine inches, Jak – *nine fucking inches*! Now I don't know what you're packing down there, but you might want to pick something a little smaller. There's no point giving yourself impossible standards to live up to now is there?'

'Fair point, Ross. What do you recommend?'

'How would I know? Let's ask the expert.'

'No, no, don't, please don't,' he begged me with decreasing volume as we reached the cashier.

'Can I help you?' asked the short, plump, balding

man we were naively about to trust for sexual advice.

'Yes,' I began. 'My friend here...' Jak smiled sheepishly, '...is looking for something to pleasure his lady friend, but perhaps something a little smaller in size than most of what you seem to have on display.'

Without saying a word, he reached under the counter and brought out a more modestly sized box which he proudly placed down in front of us.

'This is just what you need, sir – "Four Inch Freddy".'

'I'll take it!' said Jak, eagerly.

'OK then. And would you like any batteries with that?'

'Sure.'

'OK, and any lube?'

Jak's eyes asked me for advice and I nodded confidently.

'Er, yes please.'

'Good. And will that be anal or vaginal?'

The tension of the moment suddenly got to Jak. 'I'm not fucking sick, you know. Standard, regular, normal, will be just fine.'

'OK, OK! Freddy's forty dollars, so with the extras and the tax, your total is $49.56.'

Jak looked at me as if to say "Holy shit, ten dollars an inch?" but he was already committed to the sale and dutifully handed over the money. We escaped to the street with our ears still humming and our eyes still wide open.

'Money well spent, Jak,' I reassured him. 'Ten dollars an inch isn't too bad.'

'I'm just glad you made me put back that nine-incher – it would've cleared out my bank account!'

We returned to Boulder fully refreshed after our afternoon in the city. As Jak parked his car we could see that Shawn's pick-up truck had returned, and my heart beat faster at the thought of confessing all to April. There were no nerves though, only excitement.

Having shaken the urgency of the task from my mind, I decided to return to my room first so that I could freshen up before seeing her. My plans were thrown out of the window, however, when we wandered into our room to find April chatting away with Kazuki. She stood up from my desk chair at our arrival.

'Hey, Ross! I've been waiting for you.'

'Well that's nice to hear,' I replied while taking off my coat.

'So where have you two been?'

'Oh, just to Denver.'

'Really? Me too!'

'Oh, what a coincidence.'

'Yeah, Shawn took me to the zoo.'

Jak and I looked at each other in astonishment at the obviousness of the answer to our problem. How could we have overlooked Denver Zoo? Where better for sensitive Shawn to work his magic than surrounded by cuddly animals? I could have kicked myself.

'That sounds nice. Were there many animals out in the snow?'

'Quite a few, surprisingly. But the snow leopards were a little tricky to spot!'

'Yes, I bet they were.'

'So what did you two do in the city?'

'Oh just a bit of shopping really.' I nodded towards the brown paper bag Jak was about to hide away in his desk drawer.

'Oh, nice. What did you buy, Jak?'

'Yeah,' I added, 'show her what you bought, Jak.'

He fumbled the bag onto the floor, only just

preventing its contents from escaping. 'Oh, nothing really,' he nervously mumbled while picking up the bag. 'Just a little toy for Kristen.'

'Aw, how sweet,' said April.

'Yes, it's called Freddy,' I added.

With the pleasantries over, it was time to get down to business.

'Jak, Kaz, do you mind just giving me and April a couple of minutes alone? Hey, Jak, maybe you could show Kaz what you bought?'

'Yeah!' beamed Kazuki with enthusiasm. 'I want play with Freddy! I want play with Freddy!'

'OK, Kaz,' agreed Jak, 'if you insist. Let's go into the bedroom then.'

April and I waited for the door to close and then both started talking at the same time.

'I'm sorry, you go first,' I insisted.

'Well, I just wanted to thank you for being so kind last night.'

'Really, it's not a problem. I was just glad I could be there for you.'

'And sorry again for believing those stupid things you were supposed to have said. It was so dumb of me to think that you'd ever do that. I'm really, really sorry.'

'Honestly, it's fine. Apology accepted.'

'Good, good. Anyway, Shawn and I are back together now. We had a good talk today and he's promised that things are going to be different from now on. He really loves me, you know.'

'Oh.' Things were definitely not going to plan.

'And you've got Bethan now, so everything's just worked out perfectly really, hasn't it?' I couldn't make out if she was asking me the question or telling me the answer.

'Well actually, Bethan's gone.'

'Bethan's gone?' She sounded somewhat surprised

by the news.

'Yes, she was only on a layover on her way to Alaska.'

'But I thought the two of you...you were holding hands.'

'We just sorted out some unfinished business, like she said, that's all. There's nothing more to it than that. There never was.'

'Oh, I see. Well...'

'It's good to hear that you and Shawn are back together though. I'm happy for you.'

'Thanks.'

It almost seemed as if she was a little dazed by our conversation, but I didn't know where to take things next. I had wanted so badly to tell her, but it was no longer the ghost of Bethan that was preventing me from doing so. It just suddenly didn't feel right with her and Shawn back together. There was no way that he really *had* turned over a new leaf, but I just wasn't comfortable in creating more hurt and confusion for April, no matter how right it may have been to get rid of that smarmy bastard.

'So where *is* Shawn then?'

'You don't need to worry, if that's what you're thinking. He's accepted that we're friends and promised not to interfere with that.'

'Oh, well that's something.'

'He's out running actually. He's training for that 10K race in December – the Winter Warmer? I reckon he's got a pretty good chance of winning it, you know.'

'Oh, really?'

'Hey, *you* should enter, you know! I mean, you go running all the time, don't you?'

'Yes. I've already entered, actually.' The words just blurted out before I could stop them. 'I entered weeks ago. I'm really looking forward to it...I'm really looking forward to the race.'

'Oh, cool. Maybe you and Shawn could go training together?'

'Yes, maybe we could.' The lies were positively gushing.

'OK, well I'd better be going, anyway. I'm glad we had this little chat.'

As soon as the door clicked shut behind her, Jak rushed out of the bedroom.

'Dude, that was brutal.'

'I should have known you'd be listening.'

'You did the right thing, man. It just wasn't the right way to tell her.'

'I know, I know, that's what I thought.'

'So what's next then?'

'Well, I suppose I'd better get training for the Winter Warmer. Especially if I'm gonna beat *that* smarmy tosser.'

'And the Africans, dude, don't forget the Africans. This is gonna be awesome!'

TWENTY

We were poised for action. Our Sunday schedules had been completely cleared in preparation for the day's critical events, as we sat in a circle of silent and bloodthirsty contemplation. Finally, the knock came. It was the three-two-one combination we had been waiting for, and I rushed to the door to reply with a two-three-four sequence just as I had been instructed. The following five slow and deliberate death knells indicated that the hostilities were about to commence. I unlocked the door and opened it just wide enough for him to slide through, before I shut it securely once more. As I sat back down, he entered our circle and spoke.

'Gentlemen, the British runner Roger Bannister achieved the impossible in 1954 when he broke the four-minute mile barrier. We're here today to continue that great British running tradition of achieving the unachievable. I must warn you, all of you, that it will not be easy. Sir Roger himself once said that; "The man who can drive himself further, once the effort gets painful, is the man who will win". If *we* are to win then we must show this drive. We must show this determination. We must strive to our thresholds of pain and beyond. We must...'

'I'm dying for a piss here,' interrupted Jak, 'do you

mind getting a move on?'

'I spent all night writing this!' protested Brandon.

'And it's great, truly it is,' I assured him, 'but maybe you could wrap it up?'

'Yeah!' added Kazuki. 'Finish so we can start kick ass!'

'OK, OK,' conceded Brandon. 'Let me just conclude then by saying that it will be hard work, for sure, and some innocent men *will* undoubtedly be lost on the way. But this time the good guys *will* prevail, and Shawn Fucking Mentis will get the ass kicking of his life. Now put your hands in and say "Winter Warmer" on three.' Our hands joined dutifully in the centre of our circle. 'One, two...'

'WINTER WARMER!'

'Now then,' he continued. 'I've made a few preparations.' He picked up his backpack, pulled out a lever arch file and opened it before us.

'Holy shit,' exclaimed Jak as the thick wad of paper, newspaper cuttings, and foldouts presented themselves before us. 'Did you do all *that* last night, too?'

'No,' replied Brandon while proudly stroking his creation. 'I've built this up over the last few months. I knew it was only a matter of time before Ross caved in and decided to race, so I put together a dossier for victory.'

'Wow,' I joined in, 'it looks...comprehensive.'

'You betcha,' explained Brandon as he flicked through the pages. 'We've got classified results for the last five years of the Winter Warmer, plus profiles and form guides for the leading contenders for this year's race. There's also a map of the route, together with detailed terrain analysis for each of the ten kilometres, including photographs of major potholes and road obstructions. And finally, we have weather data for every December of the last decade, including temperature, humidity, wind speed, precipitation and visibility.'

I was stunned. 'And to think, we always wondered why you never had a girlfriend.'

Jak studied the folder in more detail. 'I'm a bit concerned about all the carefully cut out colour photos of these skinny African men. Is there something you want to tell us?'

Brandon smiled. 'Yes, there is actually. I'm really into athletics and I subscribe to all the magazines. *But*, I'm also really into women, and I subscribe to all *those* magazines too!'

'Fair enough,' replied Jak. 'So where do we all fit in to your grand plan then?'

'I'm glad you asked. I'll be coordinating Ross' training and race strategy, and I want you, Jak, to monitor his diet in the canteen and ensure he's getting the right vitamins and minerals.'

'I'm on it,' promised Jak. 'You can rely on me.'

'Good, good. And you, Kaz...'

'Yes?' Kazuki beamed with expectation.

'You are in charge of opponent intelligence. I didn't have the hindsight to prepare a report on Shawn, so I need you to watch him, see how he's performing, time his training runs, let us know about any injuries he's got, that sort of thing. Can you do that for us, Kaz?'

'I your man!'

'Good, that's great.'

'Erm,' I cut in, 'how about me?'

'You've got the easiest job of them all – you've just got to run.' He took the folder back from Jak and unfurled a poster-sized map of the route. 'If you look here, it's a full ten kilometre road route. That's good, because it means if there *was* any snow, then the roads would be cleared anyway so it shouldn't affect your performance. It starts off on 30th Street, winds its way around downtown Boulder, and then finishes up in Folsom Field stadium right here on campus where you run a lap and cross the finishing line.'

'OK, cool.'

'Now then, there *are* a few potential problems in our way.'

'Go on.'

'Well first of all, there'll be about twenty or so professional runners who'll have a reserved spot at the front of the field, whereas you'll be in with all the public-entry runners. That could cost you a little time working through the pack, but the good news is that Shawn will have the same problem. Now, on to pace. The pro-guys who win these races can run 10K in about thirty minutes, and those who win the public-entry race can do it in about thirty-two minutes. Unfortunately, when I've timed you, you're running at around thirty-six minutes for the distance which would put you *way* out of contention.'

'You've been following me?'

Jak interjected. 'I'm more concerned that he's been going round taking photos of potholes.'

'I only timed you once,' defended Brandon. 'Well, maybe twice. Three times at the most. I needed a few to get a decent average. It was hard to keep up with you on my bike, though, believe me.'

'Well, you've certainly been thorough, I'll give you that.'

Jak joined in once more. 'So, Ross, are you sure you're ready for all this? I mean, yeah, it'll be sweet as hell to see you beat Shawn, and maybe even the Africans, but I don't think it's gonna make April dump him.'

'I know, believe me, I know. But for now I'll settle for some revenge. Revenge for his lies, revenge for my table tennis defeat, revenge for Brandon getting kicked out – take your pick.'

Kazuki could hold back no longer. 'And revenge for him not getting me pussy!'

'That's right, Kaz,' I agreed. 'We'll show him exactly who he's dealing with. April will come to her senses eventually, but for now we've got work to do.'

'That's right gentlemen,' said Brandon, taking control of proceedings once more. 'We've got only four weeks before the race, so if there are no further questions, then I suggest we get to work. Let's get to it!'

The master plan took shape over the weeks that followed. While Brandon took to the streets on his bike and accompanied my every run, Jak filled me with nutritional drinks and vitamin supplements. Even Kazuki played his role perfectly, feeding us vital details of Shawn's fitness levels and training regime.

Brandon particularly took to his coach's role with gusto, and I had never seen a man so happy to be wearing a stopwatch around his neck. He interspersed my road runs with indoor speed sessions, assuring me that the variation in pace was good for my leg muscles. I hated the indoor running with a passion, but with only a couple of weeks to go before the race, I found myself at the sports centre with Brandon on yet another Sunday afternoon.

'Ross, I'm gonna be timing you for a mile, OK? Just to get you warmed up.'

'But if I'm only warming up, why do you need to time me?'

He glared at me with irritation. 'Look, do we have to go through this every time? *I'm* the coach and timing's what I do. *You're* the runner, and running's what you do, so get to it.'

'I think you're loving the power of that stopwatch a little too much, Brandon.'

'Run, run, *RUN!*' he barked.

'OK, OK! Chill out!'

I set off on my first mile around the indoor running track. It was an unusual circuit, suspended high around the edges of a basketball gym and being incredibly short with very tight, banked corners. Brandon followed my ten laps intently while stooped over his stopwatch in the middle of the starting straight. I detested running round and round when I was so used to roaming wild and free in the open air, and so I eased the boredom by venting my unhappiness to him, one word per lap.

'WHY...DO...I...HAVE...TO...RUN...AROUND... THIS...STUPID...TRACK?'

With my last word, the mile was over and I stepped off the track for my next instruction.

'Less of the disrespect for your coach, OK?' demanded Brandon with absolute sincerity.

'Yes, coach,' I replied, as my face cracked into a thoroughly disrespectful giggle at his expense.

His expression then loosened as he pleaded, 'Please, Ross, *please* let me do the coach bit. I've wanted to do this all my life, and I really think I could be good at it. Just give me a chance, please!'

'OK, I'm sorry. You're the coach, and I'm putty in your stopwatch-cradling hands. *Mould me!*'

'Great, thanks,' he smiled, before assuming grave seriousness once more. 'Now, we need to get you doing some sprinting again, OK? I want you to run down the straights and then walk around the bends. Do it for a mile.'

'A mile?'

'Who's the coach?'

'You.'

'Right, now go!'

'OK, coach.'

I dutifully followed orders, alleviating the tedium as I usually did by watching the basketball game that was being played below me. It was a 'pick-up game' being played by a fairly random bunch of students where, as one guy left the court, another would join in to take his place. Just as when I had played lunchtime football at school many years earlier, teams were distinguished by those wearing shirts and those not. I mused on the severe lack of women in the game as I watched the five topless men jumping around and dripping in sweat.

I further regressed to my primary school sports activities where we played in nothing but our underwear, dwelling on the thought in the context of an all-female five-on-five game of breast bouncing basketball. Just as my wayward reflections were about to cause severe embarrassment in my thin and uncompromising shorts, a new entrant to the 'skins' team revealed his thick and bushy back. I instantly recognised it as the gruesome sight I had encountered in the shower all those weeks ago. I sprinted down the final straight while keeping one eye on Gay Wolf-Man Shawn and almost colliding with a more sedate runner on the inside lane. I reached Brandon for some more chastising.

'Focus man, focus. You've got to pay attention.'

'But I was just...'

'You need to keep your eye on the prize, keep your mind on the task.'

'Yeah, but on the...'

'Enough of the bellyaching, just do as I say. Now give me three miles at your best pace. Go!'

I set off while still keeping watch over the game below. Shawn appeared to be a fairly average player, and the time passed rather uneventfully for my first few laps. Just as I entered my second mile, however, I noticed Shawn's attention being dragged towards one corner of the gym. He would pass the ball and then look over to the same corner, time and again.

After shooting a basket he would send a little grin to the corner, which turned into a sly smile when he knocked an opponent to the ground. On each circuit I strained to look into that crevice, but the object of his attention was too deeply embedded for me to see through the overhanging track. Just as my third mile was drawing to a close, he appeared to wave goodbye to the mystery fan and then continued about his game without further distraction. I completed my run and returned to Brandon.

'Well done, Ross, great work.'

'Thanks,' I gasped while he passed me a bottle of water.

'Here, drink this. We need to keep you hydrated. And do some stretching too, we don't want you pulling a muscle on the way home.'

'So we're done?' I asked hopefully.

'For today.'

I guzzled the water and stretched out my muscles before we left the track. As we walked down the stairs, I finally told him of my discovery on the basketball court.

'Silly bastard,' judged Brandon. 'Only an idiot would play basketball so close to such an important race. Do you know how many injuries you can pick up playing basketball? Kaz never reported on it before though, so I need to have a word with our Japanese friend. We've all got to be on the ball if we're gonna win this thing.'

'Maybe it was the first time he's played?'

'I don't give a shit. If he'd ever even *thought* of playing basketball, Kaz should have been reporting it back to us.'

'Shawn seemed a little distracted, anyway. As if someone was watching him.'

'What, like a friend?'

'I don't know. It seemed like it must have been a

girl – he was being really smarmy.'

'Probably April then?'

'Maybe. I don't know though, I had this feeling it wasn't her.'

We emerged from the stairwell into the corridor leading out to the main foyer. As if to answer our question, we were then faced with April walking straight towards us. My relationship with her had continued to strengthen in the weeks since she had patched things up with Shawn. For his part, he had kept true to his word of not interfering, while only giving me the occasional dirty look.

Upon our eyes meeting, I greeted her. 'Hi April, fancy meeting you here!'

'Hey Ross, hey Brandon! So you guys have been training for the big race then?'

Brandon assumed the role of team spokesman. 'Yeah, we've just been doing some speed sessions. How's Shawn's training coming along? What pace do you reckon he'll run the race in?' He was never one to miss an opportunity.

'I don't have a clue – I'm staying well away from all that running stuff. He's out a lot at the moment though, I know that much. I hardly see him.'

'Interesting,' Brandon pondered.

I brought us back to the matter at hand. 'So, what are you doing here?'

'Oh, I just called in to see Shawn playing basketball.'

'Ah, right.' The mystery was solved.

'Yeah, do you know how I get into the basketball gym?' Or maybe not.

'What?'

'The basketball gym, where Shawn's playing. Do you know how I get there?'

'But, haven't you just come from there?'

'No, I'm just on my way. He told me not to get

here 'til three o'clock, so here I am.'

'Oh, well I think it's just down the corridor there.'

'Thanks, I'll see you guys later.'

April cheerfully stepped off to the gym, while we were left with the conundrum.

'So if that wasn't April in the gym,' I pondered, 'who the hell was it?'

'Good question, Ross. I think we need to have a word with Kaz.'

We returned to my room where Kazuki was studying at his desk. Brandon wasted no time laying into him.

'Hey, Kaz. I thought you were supposed to be in charge of intelligence gathering?'

'Intelligence, ah, yes!' smiled Kazuki.

'Well then, where is Shawn right now then?'

He looked confused. 'I not know.'

'Too right, you not know. He's at the gym, playing basketball. Why are you sat here?'

'I studying. I have test tomorrow.'

'Screw your test, man, this is *way* more important.'

'Calm down, Brandon,' I stepped in. 'Don't you think maybe you're taking this a bit too far? We've all got other things to be doing, other lives to lead. You can't blame Kaz. He can't be expected to watch Shawn day and night.'

'Maybe,' he began to soften. 'This just means so much to me though. I just want everything to go smoothly.'

'And it will, trust me, it will. You just need to relax a little.'

He soon snapped out of his rage. 'You're right, Ross. I'm sorry, Kaz, I don't know what came over me.'

'Ah, that OK!' replied Kazuki, ever quick to forgive. 'I don't want you to think I not doing job though.'

'I'm sure you're doing a great job. Forget what I said.'

'I been studying Shawn lots!'

'I know, I know, just forget it. I'm sorry.'

Kazuki reached into his desk drawer and pulled out a neat tray of clear plastic jars.

'Look, I been studying Shawn lots!' he repeated, pointing to the jars.

'I know, I'm sorry. What *are* they?'

'I have stool samples, see?'

Sure enough, sat in each jar was a festering heap of brown sludge.

'Ugh, Kaz!' grimaced Brandon while staring at the evidence in disgust. 'You sick bastard!'

'I working hard for team, Ross!' he replied with pride.

'Thanks, Kaz, I think,' I said. 'That's definitely above and beyond the call of duty.'

'For you, Ross, I happy to help! I analyse stools to study diet, digestion.'

'It looks like he eats a lot of shit, if you ask me,' I suggested. 'Anyway, tell us your findings later. We've got a new assignment for you.'

'Oh, goody!' he twinkled.

'Yes, we need you to pay a little more attention to what Shawn does when he's *not* running. There might be another girl on the scene.'

'Shawn cheating slut?'

'We don't know for sure, but we need you to dig a little deeper.'

'OK. I happy to dig through toilet, so I happy to dig anywhere!'

'Thanks Kaz.'

'You sick son of a bitch,' added Brandon.

I glanced across at my clock, whose digits told me it was almost three a.m. I had been woken by some excited muttering from Kazuki, who had also been shaking me rather violently.

'Get up, Ross, get up! I need to tell you!'

'But it's three a.m.!' I whispered while Jak slept.

'Come to study room, I got to tell you!'

'OK, OK,' I grudgingly agreed before accompanying Kazuki out of the bedroom and delicately closing the door behind us. 'Now, what's so important that it couldn't wait until morning?'

'I watching Shawn's room, right?'

'*At three a.m.*? Don't you have a test tomorrow?'

'It OK, I study while watching.'

'Whatever you say, Kaz. So, what happened then?'

His face glistened with excitement. 'I saw pussy leaving room, just now.'

'You saw a girl, leaving his room?'

'Yeah, I saw Doggy Style, I saw Doggy Style!'

'Doggy Style? Are you sure?'

'Yeah!' He arched his back and started making animal love with an imaginary woman in front of him. 'Doggy Style!'

'And are you sure Shawn was in the room?'

'Yes, yes!'

'How about his roommate, Brad-Chad? Are you sure he wasn't there?'

'No, he gone away, not coming back 'til Tuesday. We shower together Friday, he told me then.'

'So, tell me again, exactly what did you see?'

'Doggy Style walking out of Shawn's room!'

'Was she naked?'

'No, she had clothes on.'

'Was there a boob hanging out, or anything like that?'

'No boobies. But she in his room in middle of night!' Kazuki whipped the imaginary figure still bent over in front of him and grinned exuberantly. 'She definitely getting it doggy style!'

TWENTY-ONE

Sleep was difficult to come by after Kazuki's late night revelations. I had spent most of the morning's remaining hours sat bolt upright in bed while my mind had worked through countless permutations of what action I should take next.

'Morning, Ross,' Jak greeted me from the comfort of his bed, about an hour after Kazuki had left for his exam. 'Why are you sat up?'

'Just been thinking.'

'Oh yeah? About how you're gonna kick those Kenyans' butts?'

'No.'

'About how you're gonna open up a can of whoop ass on those Ethiopians?'

'No.'

'About how you're gonna rub Shawn's face in some shit after you beat him?'

'No. I've been thinking about April.'

'Dude, forget about her until after the race. You don't need the distraction.'

'Shawn might be cheating on her.'

'What?'

'Kaz saw Doggy Style leaving his room in the middle of the night.'

'Holy shit! The dirty, lowlife bastard.'

'Well, we don't know anything's going on for sure.'
'What?'
'I mean there *are* other possible explanations.'
'*Of course* there's something going on! Have you been going to the fucking idiot's convention? Is that where you and Brandon have been going every day, learning your craft?'
'She could have been there for loads of reasons. Maybe she left her keys in his room or something?'
'Yeah, or maybe he left his dick up her ass. Come on, man! He's got to be doing the dirty on April – you know what he's like.'
'Maybe, but I'm not about to rush in without more evidence.'
'What more do you want? A photo of her reddened ass-cheeks?'
'I just don't want to make the same mistake twice. Shawn's a devious bastard, and you can bet he's got a way out of all this.'
The pause highlighted Jak's increasing understanding of my reluctance to rush in.
'You know what, Ross, maybe you're right. I know he's burned us before, so perhaps we *should* tread a bit more cautiously this time.'
'That's what I eventually decided...after three or four hours.'
'So what's the plan?'
'No plan. Let's just be alert and take it as it comes. You know, like you and Kristen are doing?'
'Dude, don't mention me and Kristen. I've got the biggest fucking boner under these sheets right now, and there's nothing I can do about it.'
'I really didn't want to know what was going on under those sheets.'
'Trust me, it's like this every morning. It takes hours to get rid of the thing, but if Kristen got within a metre of it, then it'd be all over. It's like she's got

some kind of force field of shrinkage or something.'

'So is she still enjoying Freddy?'

'Yeah, he's still buying me some time. He's costing a fortune in batteries though, believe me.'

Our laughter was interrupted by a pounding on the door. We both knew it would be Brandon, readying me for our usual morning run.

'Jak, I think *you* should go see who that is!'

'I couldn't get close enough to the door to reach the handle! You just go, and leave me alone.'

'All right, but no funny business under the sheets, OK?' His pillow flew towards me at an impressive pace, but I skilfully caught it while climbing down from my bunk. 'Nice try. Hey, keep this Doggy Style thing to yourself for now, would you?'

'No problem, man. Now get out there and run.'

I closed the bedroom door behind me and opened the door to the hallway. I had fully expected to see Brandon and his stopwatch, but I was instead faced with Shawn and his sliminess.

'Good morning, Ross,' he grinned with piercing intensity.

'Shawn...what do you want?'

It was a fair, if blunt, question, considering we would never even acknowledge each other if we passed in the corridor. He leant against the doorframe, pausing for dramatic effect before he replied.

'Well that's not very polite now, is it? What do *you* think Shawn is here for?'

I looked at his undeniably powerful figure, with his thighs bulging in his running shorts and his biceps rippling beneath the sleeves of his T-shirt.

'Are you going ice-skating? I heard they were auditioning for "Dick Heads On Ice" – is that where you're going?'

The smile vanished. 'I may have put up with your

shit recently, but that's only to keep April sweet, OK?'

'As much as I'm enjoying our little chat here, Shawn, maybe you could get to the point?'

'I just wanted to see if you were man enough to come for a little run with me?' His devilish glare indicated that he didn't exactly have a friendly jog in mind. 'I thought we could head up into the hills and see what happens?'

'Look Shawn, I've told you this a thousand times before – you're not going have your wicked way with me, so don't think I'm gonna fall for that "run in the hills" nonsense and end up with my shorts around my ankles.'

The throbbing vein on his forehead returned like an old friend. It had been a while. 'I'm gonna beat you so badly in that race, and then April will see what a pathetic loser you really are. Shawn will bring you to your knees.'

'Me on my knees – is that another of your perverted little dreams?'

'Laugh all you want. I've been training hard for this race, and the trophy has my name on it.'

'You know, I think you might look a little worried about me beating you. Actually, maybe you just look a little tired. Did you have a late night?'

I almost caught a glimmer of fear in his eyes. His anger bubbled and he turned on me once more.

'Shawn *will* beat you, Ross, and the victory will be sweet. It will be so special to see you cross the finishing line way after me, while I'm already kissing April.'

'Don't you close your eyes?'
'What?'
'When you kiss April, don't you close your eyes?'
'Of course I do.'
'Well then, how are you going to watch me cross

the line when you're kissing her?'

The vein throbbed and swelled like never before.

'I don't have time for this fucking shit. Shawn has a race to win.'

As he left behind his profanities and spittle, I called down to his departing figure.

'Before you go, just a word of advice.' He stopped in his tracks, but didn't turn around. 'Basketball games can get you into all sorts of trouble...with injuries, I mean. You might want to be careful.'

He continued walking without looking back.

It was difficult to tell if I had a struck any sort of nerve during my encounter with Shawn, but my support team and I remained vigilant over the following days nevertheless. Kazuki, in particular, stepped up his surveillance activities, but didn't yield anything of significance other than a few firm stools to add to his collection.

As well as the intense training just over a week before race day, I was also contending with the horror of four Physics classes reaching their deathly climax in the approach to final exams. Creative Writing, however, provided its usual pleasant distraction. Particularly on that Thursday as Kenny had tasked us with writing a story with a partner. April and I had her room to ourselves that evening as we began work.

'So, what do you think we should write about?' she asked from her cross-legged position on her bed.

'I'm not sure,' I replied while making myself comfortable beside her. 'Maybe we could come up with two sides to one story?'

'Hey, I like your thinking! Like a murder scene or something, giving the view of the murderer and the victim?'

'Yeah, or the cheating husband and his wife?'

She didn't even flinch. 'Or the dog and his owner?'

'The dog and his owner? Since when do dogs talk?'

'Hey, I talk to my doggies all the time! They're really smart.'

'If you insist.'

'I'm missing them so much you know. I can't believe I'm gonna get to see them again in just a couple of weeks. Christmas break has come so quickly.'

'I know. I can't believe the semester has gone by so fast. Only one more week of classes before finals, and only nine days 'til the Winter Warmer.'

'Are you ready, then?'

'For finals? Maybe. I feel much better prepared for the race though. Brandon's keeping my training times to himself for now, but we've got a dry-run of the actual course on Saturday then he's going to finally reveal all. I doubt I'll be winning any medals, but it would be nice to at least get in the top hundred.'

'Yeah, I think Shawn's finally realised he can't beat the pros, but he still reckons he can win the public-entry race.'

'So, are you two getting on all right then?' I had to take the chance while it was there.

'Sure,' she hesitated, 'things are good.'

'Good? Shouldn't things be great?'

She looked back towards her notebook so as not to lie to my face.

'Yeah, things *are* great.' With the lie told, she met my eyes once again. 'Hey, have you heard from Bethan since she got to Alaska?'

'No, and I don't expect I will.'

'Oh, I see.'

As the buzzing of the fridge under her bed suddenly appeared louder than a thousand Four

Inch Freddies, we struggled to find the words that would take us away from the uneasiness. I eventually brought us back to our assignment.

'How about a man and a woman who've just found out they're going to have a baby?'

'Hey, that's a great idea!' she smiled in relief. 'We could have them walking home from the doctor's surgery or something...'

'Yeah, and they don't say a word to each other but their minds are just full of torment.'

'Cool, let's go with it, Ross. So if I write what the woman is thinking, and you do the guy?'

'Sure. If we write it paragraph by paragraph, then we could alternate them in the final piece. So what is the woman thinking then, April?'

'Hmm, let me see. Maybe she's wondering who the father is?'

'Nice, very nice! And...now let me think...maybe *he's* thinking about how to break the news to his secret gay lover?'

'Oooh, that's twisted, I like it!'

With the seed sown, we both started our scribbling. My side of the story began to flow nicely, with only a slight setback when I thought it better to retreat and remove all references to the guy being a hairy-backed ice skater.

'How's it going?' I asked, with my first few paragraphs written.

'Not bad,' she replied, without taking her eyes or her pen from her notebook. 'Do you think *you'd* like to have kids someday?'

Her question caught me completely by surprise, and it took all of my strength to avoid an instinctive reply of "With you, of course! Let's get started!"

'Well...er...' I stuttered, 'definitely.'

'Me too! I think I'd like a really big family, you know?' As her head tilted to one side, her emerald eyes twinkled with enchantment. 'At least three, maybe four.'

'How many does Shawn want?'

She briefly froze her pen's movements before ignoring my question. 'How much have you written?'

'Three paragraphs, so far.'

'Come on, we'd better get some more down.'

I laboured over my fourth paragraph while deliberating over her reaction to my comments about Shawn. It was certainly possible that all wasn't well with their relationship, but it could have been equally true that she was just not comfortable discussing it with me. There was also a third possibility, albeit a very remote one. Perhaps she had only got back together with Shawn because she thought I was with Bethan, and she had been cursing her decision ever since? I tried not to dwell on my wishful thinking, but April made it difficult not to with another unexpected question.

'So, what *really* happened with you and Bethan, then?'

This time she rested down her pen and gave me her undivided attention.

'We just...we just resolved things, that's all.'

'Resolved what?'

'I suppose our relationship ended a little abruptly, so we just tied up the loose ends.'

'But you guys *were* pretty close? I mean, I take it that your famous L.O.V.E. paragraph was about how she hurt you, right?'

My mind was cast back to the bitterness and loathing I had still felt for Bethan all those weeks ago.

'Maybe. It's all history now though.' I then looked her straight in the eye with unwavering honesty. 'I've moved on.'

'Come on,' she sharply instructed while turning back to the page in front of her, 'let's get back to it. Enough talk.'

I didn't say a word in reply. I wasn't sure I had the brain capacity to formulate speech anyway, as my grey matter worked overtime to make sense of our conversation. Where April's curiosity had suddenly sprouted from was an absolute mystery. Had it all been related to her uncertainty over Shawn, or was it just April being her usual friendly, talkative self? We completed our assignment without exchanging another single sentence of unrelated chat, and the riddle remained unsolved.

In spite of the December cold I was literally dripping in perspiration as I slumped down before Brandon at the entrance to Folsom Field.

'Was that the best you could do?' he asked without an ounce of sympathy. 'I cycle behind you for ten kilometres and that's all you can manage?'

'What...' I panted, '...what was my time?'

'Do you honestly have nothing left in you? Couldn't you have sprinted that last stretch just a little harder?'

'I'm dying here,' I spluttered, my face firmly planted into the cold concrete slabs. 'Just tell me my time.'

'I want to see you begging me to stop, I want to see you crying in pain, I want to see you vomiting on the sidewalk.'

'You've just had all I've got to give. There's no more in the tank, nothing. Now what was my time?'

Brandon sighed deeply while rustling through the papers on his clipboard. 'Thirty-four minutes. *Thirty-four* minutes. You know, at thirty-four minutes you're barely gonna make it into the top one hundred. *The top one hundred*! Do you know how bad that is? All those professionals, all those Africans, they'll be way in the distance, and you'll be surrounded by Americans. *Americans!* We can't run distance for shit, and yet some of us will be beating your sorry ass.'

'I've cut two minutes off my time over the last few weeks, now that's not bad.'

'Not bad? *Not bad?*' I looked up from my squatted position to see Brandon's schoolteacher face shaking in shame. 'Do you think Bannister settled for "not bad"? Do you think if he'd run the mile in four minutes and one second he would have been happy? Do you think if he'd been beaten by a hundred Americans he would have been happy? And do you think he would have got laid so much if he didn't push himself that little bit further?'

'Sir Roger got laid?'

'How would I know? The point is, you don't get *anything* unless you give *everything*.'

'I've given everything, there's no more left to give. I'm not bothered about winning the thing anyway.'

Brandon made a sharp intake of breath as if he had just found me making love to his mother in the backseat of his car. 'I'm doing this all for you, you know?' he hissed. 'It's not like I haven't got better things to be doing with my time. Finals are only a week away, you know, as well as the race.'

'I know, I know, but I think we need to be realistic here. I'm not going win the pro-race – it's just not physically possible. Those guys train constantly and get paid to do this stuff. We can't compete, let's be honest. And as for the public-entry race, well that's clearly out of reach too. All I really want to do is to beat Shawn, anyway.'

'But doesn't he reckon he's gonna *win* the public race?'

'I really doubt he's *that* fast. Look, I think we've

done as well as we can here, Brandon. You've got to see, this dream of yours is just not going to come true. I'm sorry.' My words may have been harsh, but I spoke the truth. He contemplated them carefully while I rose to my feet.

'It was a wonderful dream though, wasn't it?' he mused while staring wistfully into the sky.

'Of course it was.'

'I thought we could win the thing, I really did.'

'I know you did.'

'It was our one true shot at glory.' He looked back at me. 'But you're not gonna win, are you?'

'No, Brandon. No, I'm not.'

'OK, right, that's fine,' he finally acknowledged, before shaking his head vigorously as if to rattle away the disappointment. 'But you're still gonna beat that bastard Shawn, right?'

'I'm going to do my best, believe me.'

'Well that's fine then, I can live with that. Right, the race is only seven days away, so we need to taper down your training. We've got to protect the progress we've made, OK? So I want you to spend the next week relaxing. We'll just have a couple of gentle runs before the big race on Saturday.'

My old coach had made a welcome return.

'Whatever you say, boss.'

I stared at the pitch-black ceiling, unable to close my eyes.

'Are you asleep, Jak?'

'Nope.'

'Are you asleep, Kaz?'

'No, I awake.'

'I can't sleep.'

'It's a big day tomorrow,' said Jak. 'Are you ready?'

'I couldn't be more ready. It's time to settle a few

scores with Shawn.'

'Too right, dude, too right.'

'April will finally see what a loser *he* really is tomorrow. I'm ready to beat him, Jak, I really am. It's just a shame we couldn't get anything more on him and Doggy Style, though.'

'I know you're Mr Cautious on that whole thing, but they've got to be banging each other, they've *got* to be.'

'But we've only got that one piece of evidence. I just wish we had more ammunition, that's all.'

Kazuki suddenly spoke. 'I got more.'

'What?' Jak and I asked in harmony, as I leant over the edge of my bed to point my ears firmly towards Kazuki's bunk below.

'I got more...how you say...amm-unition.'

I was confused. 'But you said you hadn't seen anything else?'

'I saving it for tonight. I want you angry in morning. I want you ready to kill Shawn!'

'Nice thinking, Kaz,' complimented Jak. 'So, what's the juice?'

'I went undercover, spent time with Doggy Style. She called Kelly. Japanese like small tits and she got real small ones!'

'Hold on, hold on' interrupted Jak. 'You've seen Doggy Style's tits?'

'Yeah, they tiny! She like sex, she like *a lot* sex!'

'You've slept with her?' asked Jak in disbelief.

'Doggy style?' I added.

'Yeah, I fuck Doggy Style doggy style!'

'This is amazing!' exclaimed Jak. 'How did you get her into bed? I mean, no offence Kaz, but you're not quite the kind of guy I thought she'd go with.'

'She like Japanese men. We considerate lovers. Anyway, so I give her third orgasm, then...'

'*Third* orgasm?' I blurted out. 'Shit, you Japanese

are considerate.'

'Yeah, we kind to the pussy! So, third orgasm, then I ask about Shawn. She say she bored with his Four Inch Freddy. She prefer big Japanese sausage!'

'Holy shit!' cried Jak.

I recoiled back to my pillow and closed my eyes. I visualised the devastating defeat I was about to inflict on Shawn, while trying not to visualise the scene Kazuki had just described so vividly.

'That bastard,' I said resolutely to the ceiling. 'That complete and utter bastard. He's going down. Believe me, he's going down.'

TWENTY-TWO

Brandon leant over from the back seat and spoke purposefully.

'Before you get out of this car, I want you to think about Shawn – his lies, his cheating, his treatment of you, his treatment of me. I want you to think about it all. Dwell on it. Hold that anger inside of you and direct it to those legs of yours, because it's those legs that will defeat him. It's those legs that will bring glory to our team. It's those legs that will finally crush the spectre of Shawn Fucking Mentis. Winners are just ordinary people with extraordinary determination. Now go out there and be a winner.'

Jak and Kazuki roared in agreement with Brandon's inspirational words, and I was entirely focussed on the task at hand. I was there to beat Shawn, and it was as simple as that.

I swung open the door of Jak's Mustang and stepped into the atmosphere. The air was filled with the buzzing chatter of thousands of voices, eagerly anticipating the coming event. The mid-morning weather had been kind, with a temperature of around 5°C and a cloudless sky, as I steadfastly walked the couple of blocks to the starting area while my entourage followed in a ferocious silence.

The scene that greeted us was exactly as Brandon

had described. A vast stretch of 30th Street was cordoned off, with the 10,000-plus runners assembling within its confines. Markers at the side of the road directed runners to line up in according to their estimated finishing times, and so we headed straight for the front section designated as "30-35 minutes". Just behind the small group of elite runners, it was a much quieter area than amongst the massed ranks at the rear of the field, albeit still with a few hundred people. Nevertheless, we had plenty of room to prepare on the pavement just outside the string cordon, and I began stripping off my tracksuit.

'Good, this is good,' said Brandon. 'We can slot in at the back of this group and then we'll keep you well away from all the really slow guys. Now, do you remember our race plan?'

'You've got a race plan?' ridiculed Jak. 'Surely he's just got to run as fast as he can for about half an hour?'

'I'll ignore that comment. Remember, Ross, not too fast at first. You're bound to get carried away in the moment and all the others will be going at a hellish pace, but just stick to your own race. Even if Shawn goes flying past you, you mustn't chase after him.'

'I can't make any promises.'

'Look, Shawn's probably got a similar pace to you. If he tears off too quickly then you'll still catch him at the end anyway.'

'Shawn's not getting out of my sight, sorry.'

'Why do I bother?' Brandon asked nobody in particular. 'Just don't do anything silly, OK?'

'OK, boss.'

I was soon ready, with my running number firmly in place on my high wicking T-shirt, and my legs thoroughly exposed by my skimpy running shorts.

For the special occasion I had gone without underpants, in an attempt to reduce my running weight further. I instead trusted the tight inner lining of my shorts to hold things in place.

'FIVE MINUTES, FIVE MINUTES, FIVE MINUTES,' boomed the announcement over the tannoy.

Brandon checked his watch. 'Better do some stretching,' he directed. I followed orders while the others chatted.

'Have any of you seen Kristen?' asked Jak.

'No,' answered Kazuki.

'Not me,' concurred Brandon. 'Have you guys slept together yet, anyway?'

'Don't start,' said Jak.

'I don't know what your problem is. She's a hot chick, man. I'd be in there every night.'

'Hey, that's my girlfriend you're talking about there. Maybe I'm ready now, anyway.'

'You ready for pussy?' said Kazuki. 'Jak ready for pussy, Jak ready for pussy!'

With my legs appropriately spread wide open, I saw Kristen approaching from behind my band of merry men.

'Guys,' I whispered, 'you might want to talk about something else.'

'Why?' replied Jak. 'Kaz is right – I think I *am* ready for the pussy. Bring on the pussy, bring it on!'

'Morning, boys,' greeted Kristen coldly, yielding a collective shriek of horror.

'Kristen, hi,' apologised Jak. 'We were just talking about...er...'

'I *know* what you were just talking about, and I don't appreciate it.' She looked over to my sprawling figure. 'Good luck for the race, Ross. I'll see you at the finish.'

She headed straight back to wherever she had

come from, leaving behind a forlorn Jak.

'You could have warned me, Ross.'

'I tried, I tried.'

Before we could begin to assess the damage to Jak's relationship, another voice then spoke.

'Morning, ladies.'

It was the voice of a closet-homosexual cheating yeti bastard from California. I rose up from my stretching to meet him with the disdain that he so richly deserved.

'You've got a nerve.'

'So what are you girls doing up here?' he continued. 'This is where the *real* runners are supposed to start.'

While my friends glared at Shawn with steely resolve, I preferred to stoke the fires. 'I hope you're not planning to cheat today...in the race, that is.'

'Why would Shawn need to cheat? It's not like you're gonna be able to keep up with me.'

'I just thought it was your style, that's all. Where *is* April, anyway?'

'You might wanna think carefully before making any wild accusations, Ross. We all know where that got you last time.'

'You've had your last chance with April. As soon as I beat you today, she's going to find out exactly what you've been up to.'

'You really need to let go of this crush of yours – it's just not healthy.'

I concentrated hard on Brandon's advice, channelling my anger deep into my legs where it could inflict the most damage. Shawn's eyes looked over my shoulder and, by his changed tune, I could tell that April was on her way.

'Well, good luck in the race, Ross!' he chimed like the choirboy he wasn't. 'Maybe we could run together, if I can keep up with you!' He looked over my shoulder once more. 'Oh, April, thanks for parking the pick-up!'

'No problem,' she replied. 'Hey Ross, are you all ready for the big race?'

'Just about. I was just telling Shawn how I can't wait to cross that finishing line.'

'I'll bet!' She turned to Jak. 'Are you guys gonna be at the stadium for the finish?'

'Sure,' he replied. 'I guess we'll see you in there?'

'I wouldn't miss it for the world.'

'ONE MINUTE, ONE MINUTE, ONE MINUTE.'

We huddled back into our group for some final private words away from Shawn and April.

'You've got the measure of him,' said Brandon. 'No doubt about it. Now, I've bought a little something for you, for the race.'

He pulled an unusual plastic object from beneath his coat and proudly presented it to me. I cautiously took it from his grasp and studied it carefully. It was an elongated donut-like vessel with a thin hole through the middle and a flip-up lid at the top. The sloshing yellow liquid inside told me it was a drinks bottle unlike any other I had ever seen in my life. As I apprehensively slipped my hand through the slit down its centre, I couldn't help but think that it looked a bit like a vagina.

'What's he supposed to do with *that*?' asked Jak. 'Fuck it or drink from it?'

'It's a runner's bottle,' Brandon explained. 'That hole is for your hand, to make it comfortable to hold when you run.'

'So it's not for his dick, then?'

'No, Jak. It's full of sports drink. Ross, you don't want to be wasting time picking up refreshments from the water stations on the way. There's half a litre in there – that's all you need for the ten ks. It should save you a bit of time.'

'Er...thanks,' I said, still looking uneasily at the contraption in my hand.

'THIRTY SECONDS, THIRTY SECONDS, THIRTY SECONDS.'

I ducked under the cordon and into the roadway at the back of the pack. Shawn joined beside me, and I glanced rearward to see a few metres' gap to the "35-40 minutes" group behind us. When my eyes returned to the front, Shawn had already muscled his way deeper into the crowd, but I really didn't care. A few metres wouldn't make much difference over the course, and I was pleased to have some space around me.

Jak, Brandon and Kazuki were still alongside me, and I saw their lips mouth a variety of encouraging speeches although I couldn't hear them above my concentration. My attention moved over to April, who had stayed beside my position despite Shawn's advancement. Our eyes locked together intimately, just as they had that first night I had spent in her room, and just as they had out in the snow on Farrand Field. She smiled her sweet, innocent smile, and then she winked at me with the most delightful flutter of her left eyelid. At that very same instant the starting gun sounded, but I was completely frozen in the moment. Within half a second I was swept up in the sea of runners and involuntarily on my way.

As my feet started moving and I got into my stride, my first thought became, "What was that wink all about?". As my legs began to move faster, my second thought then became, "Crikey, I'm not wearing any underwear here and my balls are swinging all over the place!". It genuinely felt as though I was running bollock-naked through the streets of Boulder, with the crowds on the sidelines all screaming hysterically at my manly display.

I snapped out of the confusing events of the start, and eventually stepped up to my usual pace while passing through the field. I tried to cast aside the wink while concentrating on the race as we hurtled south on 30th Street. My eyes scoured the bobbing heads and I eventually found what I was looking for – the bright reflection from Shawn's oily skull. He was only a matter of metres in front of me, and I briefly quickened my pace to pull level.

We exchanged a fierce glance, but no words, as we continued side by side for the opening kilometres. I spent the time quietly contemplating how the race was about to pan out. Shawn appeared to be a strong and capable runner, and he was gliding along effortlessly at a speed that was soon exceeding my comfort zone by some margin. I knew that it was going to take all of my reserves to realise the victory I had so desperately craved.

By the third kilometre we were heading north, away from the university campus on Folsom Street, and I decided to take my first sip at the sports drink Brandon had given me. I flipped up the cap with my thumb and brought the spout to my mouth, but failed to extract a single drop of the juice. After much grappling I literally had to go at the bottle like a porn star, sucking and squeezing the thing until I was blue in the face. My reward was, rather appropriately, about a teaspoon of fluid that barely wet my throat. I made a mental note to rent more adult movies so I could refine my technique for any future races.

'Having a little trouble there?' jeered Shawn at my efforts.

'I'm sure you've got more experience than me with this sort of thing,' I replied, before wrapping my lips back around the bottle and continuing the lewd act.

'Why don't you just give up following Shawn now? You obviously can't take the pace.'

'I'm doing just fine, Shawn, don't you worry about me. If I were you, I'd concentrate on how you're gonna explain your indiscretions to April after we've finished.'

'What indiscretions?' he laughed. 'You really should stop this pathetic attempt to steal April.'

'*Steal* April? She doesn't belong to you, you know. And neither does Kelly.'

'Kelly? Who...who's Kelly?'

My comment had clearly flustered him.

'You tell me.'

'You've got nothing. You're shooting in the dark.'

'Something you'd know all about.'

With a look of irritation he clammed up and then began to accelerate. He couldn't shrug me off though, as we weaved through a pack of runners.

'Do you know what hurt you're going to cause April?' I persisted. 'Do you even care?'

'*You're* the one who's gonna cause her hurt if you start spreading lies.'

Shawn's words brought home to me the magnitude of what I was proposing to do. If I *did* tell her about his misdeeds, then how would she react? It was undoubtedly going to cause her hurt and upset, and I suddenly began to fret over how I could possibly break the news to her. She needed to be told, no question, and she needed to be rid of Shawn once and for all. But every time I played the scenario through my head I could only see her devastated face in floods of tears, and it pained me to imagine putting her through such torture.

Our route turned left and then left again, and we were soon closing in on the halfway mark as we powered south once more, this time along 19th Street. The crowd was sizeable on both sides of the road as we were cheered towards our final five kilometres. In the midst of my turmoil I hadn't realised it, but the concentration of runners had thinned out considerably as I had been carried along by my duel with Shawn. As we passed the five kilometre marker I saw a huge electronic counter displaying our halfway time of just under sixteen minutes. I then became aware that there was nobody in front of us whatsoever. I glanced behind to see lean scattering of other runners, but it was clear that Shawn and I were now heading the public-entry runners while the twenty or so professional athletes had vanished in the distance.

At the shock of my situation, I sucked feverishly at my bottle to try and give me the strength to maintain my miraculous position. I was a picture of exhausted masculinity, with sweat dripping from my face, my cheeks blowing in and out, and my testicles manfully swaying from side to side without restraint. I tried to resist the urge to daydream about winning the public-entry race, but it was difficult not to. I was sent crashing back down to earth, however, when I glanced over at Shawn, who didn't have a single bead of sweat on his extensive forehead and looked like he was merely out for a casual Saturday morning jog. He looked back at me with a smile as greasy as his hair.

'You look to be struggling, Ross. Is Shawn going too fast for you?'

I just about managed to mask the pain in my voice.

'No problem, I'm doing just fine.'

We forged onwards, and I returned to my deliberations over April in a hopeless attempt to distract myself from the agony my body was experiencing. I knew there must have been a better way to resolve matters – a way in which she still removed Shawn from her life, but felt no heartache in the process. The more I thought about Shawn's actions, however, the angrier I became. It eventually blocked my ability to think of a solution, and finally reached the point where I could control my rage no longer.

'So why exactly *have* you been screwing Kelly when you're supposed to be with most amazing woman in the world?'

'I've told you before...'

'Yeah, yeah, you haven't done anything. Well I've had enough of your bullshit.'

'There's nothing...'

'Just stop lying for one minute and tell me why you did it. Tell me why you've been cheating on April. Tell me why you've been shoving your tiny four-inch dick inside Kelly.'

He was taken aback at my added detail. At last, the sweat appeared on his forehead and trickled down his swelling vein.

'OK, OK, so I've been with Kelly a few times. There, I've said it. So what? So fucking what? April hasn't been putting out since we got back together, so Shawn just had to go elsewhere. It doesn't change a thing – I'm still with April, and *you're* still a sad, lonely loser who needs to get a life. The world goes on. *So fucking what?*'

'I'll tell you what, I'll tell you *exactly* what. "Shawn" has a relationship with *the* most perfect, incredible, intelligent, caring, sexy woman I have ever met, and yet Shawn treats her like a piece of dirt. He lies to her, he cheats on her, he acts completely different to her face than he does behind her back. *Shawn disgusts me.* You don't deserve to be with *anyone*, never mind April. And to top it all off, you're an ice-skating nancy boy who probably prefers men anyway and desperately needs to shave his back. There, now *Ross* has said it.'

There was fire in the eyes that looked back at me, but he didn't have anything to say in his defence. He just turned on the pace again and began to edge away from me. The fury pulsed through my body and didn't let me hold back. I rolled up alongside him once more and we continued to push each other along the route.

Through the sixth and seventh kilometres we were heading closer towards campus, still neck and neck. Shawn was now showing the strain as well, and his broad shoulders began to sag under the weight of the sweat that was being absorbed by his T-shirt. As we ran down Pearl Street, the sight of a water station up ahead reminded me to top up on fluids, so I duly wrestled with my bottle again. My movement sprang Shawn's vocal chords back into action.

'Still struggling, Ross?'

'Not at all,' I lied.

We ran side by side as we approached the table full of water bottles, with my body in between him and the refreshment.

'Maybe it's about time you stopped and left me to win this thing?' he said, while glancing edgily towards the drinks.

'No, I don't think so.'

'Well I do. Actually, are you still a little thirsty?'

Without warning, he thrust himself into my side and sent my body hurtling into the table. The watching crowds gasped as hundreds of bottles sprung up into the air and my torso toppled onto the wooden surface. The legs swiftly gave way under my weight and I was sent crashing to the ground with a jolt, while Evian rained down on me from all directions.

With my head resting groggily against the ground, I opened my eyes to see Shawn's gleeful face moving further and further away. While the crowds rushed over to attend to my injuries, countless legs sprinted past my prone position and my hopes of victory ebbed rapidly away.

TWENTY-THREE

'Oh my gosh, are you all right?'
'Hey, man, can you get up, are you OK?'
'Oh my god, oh my god!'
'Don't move a muscle, let me check you out first.'

Voices swirled around me while thirsty runners flew by. I was dazed, lying flat on the floor, and unable to decide what to do next. Shawn had just cheated, yet again, and it seemed inevitable that he would get away with it.

An unmistakable voice then towered above the din.

'...boom, boom, boom...chicka boom, boom, boom...chicka boom...'

A pair of Herculean arms wrapped their way around my body and roughly pulled me to my feet. I looked upwards to see my saviour – the shadowy figure of the Hall Rapper, fully clad in running gear.

'...boom, boom...if you let the fucker win, then he'll do it again...boom, boom...so go beat that mother fucker, and tell the bitch you love her...boom, boom...'

The man was right. By some miracle of rap, he was right. I began jogging again, tentatively at first, but then gradually building up speed. I turned around to thank him, but he seemed to have vanished into thin air. Had he really helped me out, or had I just imagined his presence in some sort of concussed stupor? There was no time to resolve the mystery, as I looked again to the road in front of me and made out Shawn's distant silhouette through the twenty or so runners who had already sailed past me. Incredibly, I was feeling no pain whatsoever, or at least nothing that registered above the adrenalin that was pumping through my system. I cranked up the pace and began to gain some ground while slowly picking off some of the opposition.

Whether from the Hall Rapper or from my subconscious, the solution to my conundrum with April had now become perfectly clear. I needed to stop concerning myself with Shawn's dastardly deeds and stop worrying about them causing April hurt. *I* was holding the one true key to her lasting happiness, and that was my unending love for her. The time had come to lay myself at her mercy.

I continued towards my destiny without a hint of the fatigue or race-weariness that had enveloped me only minutes earlier. I took encouragement from the supporters on the sidelines who were cheering my progress and even giving me the occasional wolf whistle. At least, that was what I assumed until I overtook a man dressed in a bikini and waving a fairy's wand and realised that he was a more likely target for their affection. Regardless, the applause strengthened my determination and it wasn't long before the opposition were behind me and only Shawn remained in my sights.

The closing kilometre of the race was soon upon us, as we headed up the brutal incline of Folsom towards the stadium. I could see Shawn's stride begin to weaken up the hill, while I continued to power forward with confidence. He hadn't even looked behind to see if he had any approaching rivals, and the sight of my sprightly figure would have been the last thing he had expected. Nevertheless, as we reached the brow of the hill and turned right towards Folsom Field, I cruised past his disbelieving figure and didn't look back. I had no further words for the man, and I didn't wish to listen to any more of his. I simply left him in my wake and sprinted closer to the victory he had never deserved.

As I approached the perimeter of the stadium I began to hear the rumble of the public address system, as the announcer was filling time in between the professionals finishing and our arrival.

'So with thirty-one minutes on the clock, we're expecting the first of our public-entry runners to enter the stadium any moment now. In the meantime, may I remind you that today's event is being sponsored by the kind folks over at Granny's Tarts. Remember, if it's warm and moist, then it's got to be Granny's!'

I made my way through a dark tunnel and emerged into a corner of the football field, where a shield of fencing directed me to run clockwise around its perimeter before I could reach the finishing line.

'And here it is folks, we have our first arrival! It's runner number...number 8362.'

I looked around and saw a generous crowd, easily in the thousands, all heaping their generous applause onto me.

'8362...that's...that's Ross Cooper, a student here at C.U. from Cheyenne Arapaho hall! Give the man a cheer!'

I scoured the stadium, but struggled to distinguish anyone from the sea of faces. I carried on with my powerful sprint as I neared the end of the first straight and made my way around the bend. I rose up from the curve with the finishing line in sight, and then noticed Brandon's crazed figure bent over the front row of the seating, midway down the final straight. He was screaming manically towards me.

'ROSS, ROSS, YOU CRAZY BRITISH BASTARD! GO, GO, GO, GO, GO! YEEEEEEEEHAAAAAA!'

The announcer cut back in. 'And here we have our second runner, that's runner number 1693.'

I quickly scanned around Brandon's location and saw Kazuki's rotund outline jumping up and down with similar delight.

'Runner 1693 is Shawn Mentis, yet another C.U. student from Cheyenne Arapaho! Give him a cheer!'

It was then that I saw her. She was about ten rows above the wild celebrations of my team, stood on her seat next to Laura and clapping enthusiastically. It was time to realise the dream.

I stopped dead alongside Brandon and Kazuki, and jumped upwards into their appreciative arms. Brandon continued his demented ranting.

'WE'VE DONE IT, ROSS, WE'VE DONE IT! YOU'RE GONNA WIN THE RACE! WE'VE DEFEATED HIM, WE'VE BEATEN HIM! THIS IS THE GREATEST MOMENT OF MY LIFE! THIS IS THE GREATEST MOMENT OF MY ENTIRE LIFE!'

I grabbed his arm and hauled myself up onto the concrete barrier he had been stooped over. I stepped up onto the bench and almost fell right back off as my superhuman exertions finally caught up with me. A little queasiness wasn't going to stop me, though.

'HEY, ROSS, YOU'VE STILL GOT TO CROSS THE LINE!'

I ignored Brandon's screaming and began climbing through the rows of seating while thousands of heads followed my unexpected diversion. The nausea worsened the higher I climbed, but I soldiered onwards.

'ROSS, WHAT ARE YOU DOING?' continued the cries from below. 'YOU HAVEN'T FINISHED YET, YOU HAVEN'T WON!'

I cut my way through the crowds until I was finally next to her. While staring at her angelic face, I prayed to god that I wasn't about to throw up all over it.

'Ross, hi,' she opened, rather bashfully.

'Hi, April.'

Please don't vomit, please don't vomit, please don't vomit.

'Shouldn't you be down there, winning the race?'

'Well, I *did* think today was all about winning the race and beating Shawn, but then I finally realised – none of that really matters.'

'COME DOWN, ROSS, COME DOWN! YOU CAN STILL BEAT HIM, JUST COME DOWN, COME DOWN NOW!'

'What *was* it about then?'

'Today was about you, April. It always had been, I just didn't know it.'

'YOU CAN STILL MAKE IT, ROSS! FOR THE LOVE OF GOD, PLEASE GET DOWN HERE NOW AND WIN THIS THING! PLEEEEEEEASE!'

'How do you mean?'

'It was all about you. It was all about *us*.'

The tannoy rang out, 'And the winner of the public-entry race is...Shawn Mentis! Give him a cheer!'

'NO, NO, NO, NO!' came the yell from below. 'WHY, ROSS, WHY? NO, NOOOOOOOOO!'

April hadn't run away from me yet, which was a good sign, and my nausea was passing too, which was another good sign.

I took a deep breath. 'April, do you remember when we first met, and you told me the difference between first floor and ground floor?'

'How could I forget?'

'Well, ever since that day there's something I've needed to say to you. It took me a while to realise, and then it took a while before I could even say it to myself, but now I'm ready to say it to you.'

Her face lit up with anticipation as her body swayed playfully.

'What are you ready to say to me, Ross.'

'April...I love you.'

After a brief pause, she smiled. 'I know.'

'You...you know?'

'Well, there *was* the back of that framed photo you gave me...'

'But how did you...'

'...and there was also that poem you wrote in our writing class...'

'But you said...'

'...oh yeah, and that song you played for me on your radio show.'

'I thought...'

'Ross, I just never said anything because I was confused. I was with Shawn and I didn't know how to handle it, so I tried to run away and ignore it. But then when I found out about Shawn's lies, and you and I spent that time together out in the snow, everything changed. I knew I was only kidding myself by staying with him, but then Bethan goes and shows up.'

'Oh, yeah, sorry about that.'

'So I got angry about *that* whole thing, and had a bit of a weak moment and took Shawn back. Since then, Shawn and I haven't...well, you know...I've never really trusted him since then.'

It wasn't my place to tell her about Shawn's cheating ways and how much of a complete bastard he really was. That would all come out in good time. For now I only had one concern.

'So, what does all this mean?'

'It means, Ross, that I love you too and I have done for a *very* long time.'

It didn't seem real. While my sickness had passed, my world was still spinning. The next thing I knew, April's soft lips were touching mine and we were kissing. The audience erupted in rapturous applause, and we emerged to see our faces on the huge Jumbotron screen at the end of the stadium. The view briefly cut to a dejected Shawn slumped beyond the finishing line, with the inappropriate caption of 'Winner' superimposed across the bottom. The crowd cheered once more as the shot reverted to April and I as we held each other tightly. We gave a joyous wave to the camera before embracing again.

'Here, get your tracksuit back on.' Brandon had made his despairing way up through the terraces with Kazuki. 'You're soaked. What happened out there?'

I suddenly realised that my entire body was still drenched from my unscheduled visit to the water station, and I was beginning to shiver.

'Thanks, Brandon.'

'What happened to your leg, too?'

I looked down to see a deep scratch down the length of my left thigh, oozing blood.

'Oh, it was just Shawn trying to beat me.'

'*Trying* to beat you? I think you'll find that he *did* beat you.'

I duly wrapped myself back up in the extra layers, and then took April into my chest.

'Can you ever forgive me, Brandon? I know you wanted me to beat him so badly.'

'Nah, forget about it, I'm over it. I think you made the right decision.'

I looked down at April and knew that he was right.

'So then, April,' spoke Laura, who had been watching the events unfold silently up to that point. 'I kept telling you that Ross seemed like a really nice guy, but you never said a word. And I thought we were supposed to be friends!'

'Sorry, Laura!' she replied. 'I just didn't know what to do. I didn't tell anyone. I *couldn't* tell anyone.'

'That's all right, you're forgiven! I'm just glad you've ditched that no-good Shawn once and for all.'

'Yeah,' agreed Brandon. 'That Doggy Style cheating bastard never deserved you.'

There was a momentary pause as we all recognised the secret that had just been revealed. April slowly rose from the warmth of my chest.

'I thought as much,' she said matter-of-factly. 'Now I'm *really* glad I didn't trust him after we got back together.'

'Son of a bitch,' muttered Laura to herself.

The awkwardness was broken as Jak and Kristen came bounding down the stairs to join our little gathering.

'Hey, Ross!' said Jak, with lipstick covering almost every inch of his face. 'What did we miss? Did you win, Ross, did you win?'

'I certainly did!'

He finally saw that April and I were holding each other, and let out a huge grin.

'Dude, that's awesome! Congratulations to you both, well done. About time, too!'

'Yeah, that's great!' agreed Kristen, her hair looking like it had lost an argument with a brush.

'So the question is, what have *we* missed?' I asked of the pair.

They looked at each other in panic, and then back at me.

'I don't know what you mean,' said Kristen.

'Yeah,' added Jak. 'We just went...er...we just went to look for some drinks and stuff.'

'Well, it certainly looks like you found the "stuff" all right!'

'You been fucking!' Kazuki bluntly observed. 'You been fucking! Pussy, pussy, pussy, Jak got pussy!'

While Jak and Kristen blushed furiously, Kazuki reminded us of the poignant wisdom he had shared with us all those months ago.

'I told you true love is key to all happiness, I told you both!'

While our friends continued to dissect the morning's events, April and I slipped quietly away and began to head home, hand-in-hand.

'Can you believe this?' she asked.

'Not, not really. Why didn't you tell me sooner?'

'Why didn't *you* tell me sooner?'

'Fair point. You know I actually thought you'd asked me on a date when we went ice-skating that time. I couldn't believe it when fifty of your friends were there too.'

'Well, it kind of *was* supposed to be a date, actually.'

'I knew it!'

'I sort of chickened out at the last minute though and invited all my friends. I had to tell you about Shawn there and then – I didn't want to have any secrets from you. So now I've admitted *that*, maybe you can tell me what you did to that photo in the frame you bought me?'

'I didn't do anything, I swear! How did you find the message, anyway?'

'Oh, you used an old trick I once saw in a movie. Ever since then I always check out the back of any photos I'm given.'

'Damn, we obviously both saw the same film.'

'It still doesn't answer my question though. That photo went missing, and I assumed you'd taken it to destroy the evidence?'

'Well I didn't.'

'Then who did?'

'Shawn. It was Shawn who took it. He'd guessed that I liked you and he kept threatening me, demanding that I stay away from you. Anyway, I guess he found the photo somehow and pretty much shoved it down my throat.'

'God, I'm so sorry, Ross. I had no idea he was doing all that. I'm really going to give him a piece of my mind when I see him.'

'Here's your chance.'

We had arrived at the edge of Farrand Field, on the opposite side to our hall. We found Shawn sat alone at a bench with his despondent head in his hands and his winner's medal dangling lifelessly from his neck. April wasted no time in charging up to him.

'You lowlife bastard!' she snarled, displaying teeth I had never seen before. It was simply marvellous to watch.

His startled head looked upwards to her fast approaching figure. 'April, hi!'

'Don't you "April, hi" me, Shawn.' She slapped him firmly across the cheek. 'Do you take me for some kind of fool?'

'No, you know...'

'I'm not gonna take any more from you, OK? You saw what happened on that screen in the stadium. I'm in love with Ross, and I have been for a long time. So the slut you've been having your wicked way with can keep you, I really don't care.'

'But, baby...'

She slapped him again. I could barely contain my delight.

'Don't you *ever* call me "baby" again, do you hear me? *Do you hear me?*'

'Sure, sure, I hear you.' He looked resigned to his fate as he buried his head once more and the medal swung grimly between his legs. That medal was the only thing he had left, and he knew he hadn't even deserved that.

Carrying onwards across the field, April soon calmed down.

'You were really feisty there, April. I enjoyed that!'

'Sorry, I just couldn't help myself.'

'Trust me, no apologies are necessary. I would have paid to watch that.'

She stopped and took both of my hands into her own.

'So, Ross, where do you think we go from here?'

'I just want to be with you, April – that's all I've ever wanted.'

'Me too,' she smiled, before giving me a delicate peck on the cheek. 'But I think we have some more immediate matters that need to be attended to, don't you think?'

'I don't know what you could *possibly* mean!'

'Well, first of all we need to get you showered, and then I'm going to take you to my room and explain the rest in *great* detail. Possibly with the assistance of some massage oil.'

'Oooh, I like the sound of that.'

'I think we've waited long enough, Ross. Let's go!'

TWENTY-FOUR

I could sense the heat of the sun caressing my face, and the warmth of naked skin pressed tightly against my own. I opened my eyes carefully, so as not to wake me from the dream, and saw April's sweet, soulful lips resting tenderly against my chest while she slept soundly.

I could see one of my arms embracing her close to my body, and I delicately moved the other to discover its location. I was rewarded by the sensation of smooth, supple skin beneath my fingers, which I gently explored before resting on the soft purity of her waist. As dreams went, it was beginning to rank right up there alongside the time I single-handedly repelled Hitler's invasion of Britain.

'Morning, Ross,' whispered a female voice that didn't belong to April. Just as Hitler was finally about to be surpassed atop my list, I then saw Laura's fully clothed body leaning over me and opening the curtains above April's bed.

'Oh, morning...Laura.'

'Sorry, I didn't mean to scare you. As it's nearly midday I thought it was about time you guys got up!'

April began to stir, and looked sleepily into my eyes.

'Morning, handsome!' she purred lovingly.

'Morning, beautiful!' I echoed.

'Eugh!' protested Laura in mock disgust while returning back to her desk. 'I don't need to hear that!'

April and I snuggled together under the sheets, and I finally began to accept that I wasn't in any dream.

'Did yesterday really happen?' I asked while kissing her forehead.

'I think so...I hope so. I love you so much, Ross, I truly do.'

'I love you, April.'

'*Hello*?' objected Laura. 'I'm still here!'

April and I giggled together while continuing our cuddles. There followed a knock at the door, and Laura duly welcomed in our guest.

'Oh, *there* you are,' said Brandon.

'Morning,' I replied, while April clutched the sheets to protect her dignity.

'It's nearly twelve. Come on, let's go.'

'Go? Where?'

'Well, for a run of course.'

'But the training's over, Brandon, the *race* is over.'

'Maybe, but after that heroic performance of yours yesterday you need to get out there right away to keep your muscles loose. We don't want them seizing up, now, do we?'

'Will you *ever* stop being my coach?' I laughed.

'I'm in this for the long haul, buddy. Especially with the Summer Sprint 10K coming up next May.'

'Oh, no. No, no, no! It's not gonna happen, Brandon. No way, never, no way.'

'But I'm already preparing the folder, man! Don't let me down now. I think we've got a real shot at it with five months of training. Now come on, hop to it!'

He stood in the middle of the room, as if I was

about to leap naked out the bed and dress right there in front of him.

'Maybe I could have a little privacy, then?'

'Oh, sure, sure,' he finally realised. 'I'll be right outside, you've got sixty seconds.'

Laura closed the door behind him before I looked at her with similar astonishment.

'Er, Laura? Maybe you could just give me a quick minute here, too? Please?'

'Oh, sure Ross,' she agreed. 'I'll wait outside with Brandon. Don't be too long.'

'Thanks.'

As the door shut again, I pounced on April and kissed her passionately as we rolled around her bed with childish laughter.

'Come on, Ross, enough now! You'd better get going or Brandon won't be happy!'

'OK, OK,' I finally conceded. 'Don't look, though, OK?' I said playfully while stepping out of the bed.

'I wouldn't dream of it!' she replied with a spank on my bottom.

'I thought you were never coming out!' teased Laura.

'Sorry. Thank you for being so understanding.'

'Hey, it's my pleasure. I'm just glad you two finally got it together.'

'Are we ready to run, then?' asked Brandon.

'Almost. I just need to go to my room for my running gear.'

'Come on then, let's get going.'

While Laura returned for the inevitable tell-all chat with April, I went back to my room to face my own board of inquiry.

'Ross, dude!' Jak welcomed me back into the fold. 'Where were *you* last night?'

I simply smiled, before noticing Kazuki's mattress tucked away in the corner of our study room.

'Never mind me, where did *Kaz* sleep?'

'Oh, er...yeah, he was out here last night.'

'Giving you and Kristen a little privacy, eh?'

'Something like that,' he stuttered while his face reddened. 'Holy shit, Ross. Can you believe what happened yesterday? *Can you believe it?*'

'Hardly. Barely. Not really.'

'Me too, me too.'

'Hey!' interrupted Brandon. 'Spare a thought for me and Kaz. We're the only ones who *didn't* get laid last night.'

'Yeah,' said Jak, 'but you got off on that race yesterday. That was almost like sex for you, right?'

'Well, maybe,' admitted Brandon. 'But that's beside the point.'

'You sick bastard.'

'Anyway, Ross was just about to change into his running stuff.'

'You've got him running again, *already*? Shit man, is this like a double orgasm for you or something?'

'Well I need to keep him loose if we're gonna win the Summer Sprint next year.'

'You mean there's another race? Awesome!'

'It's not happening,' I argued. 'Trust me, there is *no way* it's going to happen. Once is more than enough, thank you very much. Never again.'

Jak persisted. 'Hey, maybe you could beat the Africans next time? Brandon, do you reckon he could do it?'

'With five hard months of training ahead of us, anything is possible.'

I shook my head and changed the subject. 'So, Jak, what are you doing the rest of today?'

'Studying, man. I can't believe we've got five days of finals starting tomorrow.'

'Bollocks, I'd almost forgotten about that.'

'I know, me too.'

'Somehow, though, I'm actually quite looking forward to it.'

'Dude, you could be having root canal surgery right now and you'd still be smiling!'

'You're probably right. Women, eh?'

'Yeah, women!'

'Sorry I'm late.'

'No problem, Ross, just sit yourself down.'

I made my way around the room to sit in between Brandon and April. I felt a warm hand on my leg, and duly turned to exchange a loving smile with April. The hand then roughly squeezed my thigh, as Brandon leant in and whispered in my ear, 'Are you still taking care of those running legs?'

As I flinched under the table, he laughed wickedly at my expense.

'So,' Kenny continued, 'I was just saying how I appreciate all of you making it here today. I know most of you are in the middle of a fucked-up week of finals, but it means a lot that you made it here for our final Creative Writing class together.'

He was looking remarkably fresh-faced, without even a hint of a hangover. This wasn't the Kenny we had become accustomed to.

'So, you're probably wondering why I'm not in some screwed-up state right now? Well, *I've* got finals too, you know, so even The Fox has to have the occasional night off.' A look of disgust washed over his face as he shook his head disconsolately. 'Shit, did I just call myself "The Fox"?'

Ten faces nodded.

'Shit, man! This bitch I've been banging calls me that all night long. It's just in my head now – I'm even calling myself "The Fox"! Anyway, enough of my sex life, for now anyway. So what do you guys wanna do today? I mean, you've already submitted your final portfolios, so what shall we do? Any suggestions?'

Ten faces replied blankly.

'I thought as much. Well, what *I* think we should do then is to get creative with each other. Now I'm not talking about any kinky shit here, I just mean telling each other some creative stories. Yeah, I know the class is supposed to be about writing, but telling a good story is a skill with many uses too. So pair up, and spend five minutes spinning each other some stories.'

Before I could turn to April, Brandon had his hand on my shoulder.

'Me and you, Ross?'

'Get your hands off me, you leg squeezer! Find yourself another partner.'

'I feel so cheap and used,' he grinned before turning to partner the guy next to him.

'So, how was your exam this morning?' asked April.

'Surprisingly good, actually. Yet another crib sheet came through for me, I think.'

'Well done, baby, I'm proud of you!'

'Just one more tomorrow and then the last one on Friday. It'll be nice when they're all over.'

'Yeah, and then it'll be Christmas and I'll get to see my family and friends again!'

'Don't forget your dogs and cats.'

'I didn't – they *are* my family! I can't believe you're gonna be left here on your own over the Christmas vacation, though. I'm really going to miss you.'

'I know, and I'll miss you too. But it's only for a few weeks.'

'Maybe we should get on with the assignment, anyway. Tell me a story, Ross!'

'Well, let me think...Once upon a time, there was a beautiful princess called April...'

'Ross?' interrupted Kenny. 'What the fuck's going on here?'

'Well, we're just telling each other a story.'

'Yeah, but what's with all this mushy crap? Please...no...please don't say it.'

'What? I don't understand.'

'Ross, man, please don't tell me you and April are like, dating and stuff. Please don't say it, man, I beg of you.'

April took over. 'Yes, we *are* actually, Kenny. What's wrong with that?'

'OH, FUCK!' he screamed, a little louder than perhaps he had intended. April and I exchanged confused glances while the rest of the class stopped their chatter and looked over at Kenny's little exhibition. He wrestled his dreadlocks in his hands while flailing his head in agony and chanting, 'NO, NO, NO!'

As the hush continued, he snapped out of his bizarre display and returned to his desk at the front of the room.

'Class, I just wanna warn you that what you're about to witness is proof positive that you should stay away from alcohol, OK? Just say no, kids.'

His behaviour was strange, even by his usual standards. While we waited with baited breath to see what would happen next, he turned back to me.

'Ross, could you please take this key and go over and lock the classroom door? Make absolutely sure nobody can get in, OK?'

'OK, Kenny,' I replied hesitantly, before carrying out his request and returning to my seat.

'Now, since the beginning of this semester I've had, shall we say, a few drinks with my good buddy Trent. I tell Trent everything about you guys, and likewise he tells me all about the students he teaches. Anyhow, I kind of told him I had these two students who were obviously madly in love with each other, but I just never thought they would actually get it together. He made a bet with me that they would, and now, Ross, April, he's been proven right.'

Our classmates clapped, as April and I looked uncomfortably around the room.

'So,' he concluded, 'I must now complete my forfeit.'

He clambered up onto his desk and proceeded to remove every single item of his clothing, bar his boxer shorts. While April and the other girls whistled in wild appreciation of his well-defined chest, the men desperately tried not to look, but were somehow unable to turn away.

The door handle suddenly jolted, causing Kenny to look anxiously in its direction. While the lock held firm, Kenny stood upright once more and made his speech.

'I, Kenny Fox, hereby declare that I was wrong, and Trent Collins was right. Trent Collins has the...' he bit his lip with the anguish, '...Trent Collins has the biggest dick in the whole of Colorado.' With that final revelation he jumped back down and hurriedly dressed while the classroom erupted in wild applause.

'Thank you, thank you. Seriously though, guys,' he added while looking at me and April, 'I'm really happy for you both. Reading some of Ross' fucked-up writing at the start of the semester, I never thought he'd get his shit together. But here we are, and I'm so pleased that he finally got his head out of his ass! You look great together, and you've been a pleasure to teach. In fact,' he swept his view around the room, 'you've *all* been a pleasure to teach, and I hope you've enjoyed this semester as much as I have.'

The ovation continued and our final Creative Writing class was soon over.

'I fly tonight, I drink tonight!' It was Friday afternoon and Kazuki had just finished packing his bag in preparation for his flight home. 'You drink too, Ross?'

'No thanks, Kaz,' I politely declined the offer of a swig of his paint stripper. 'We've got our radio show at five, and I probably shouldn't be drunk.'

'No, it OK. Kazuki say it OK!'

'No, really, but thanks.'

Jak burst into the room in jubilation.

'Finally, exams are over! They're over!'

'Ah! You drink, Jak, you drink!'

'Pass me the bottle, Kaz!'

'Er, not just yet Jak,' I stopped him. 'We've got our radio show first, remember?'

'Shit, I'd completely forgotten. I don't know why anyone would want to swap for our two a.m. slot anyway.'

'I guess they wanted to fly home tonight. Anyway, we've got to be going in a few minutes.'

'No problem, man, no problem at all. It really feels like Christmas now with all that shit out of the way, it really does.'

'Yeah,' agreed Kazuki. 'I going to Japan for Christmas. I excited! I taking my bitch too!'

'You're taking who?' asked Jak with surprise.

'I taking Kelly home.'

'Doggy Style?' Jak exclaimed. 'You're taking Doggy Style home to meet your parents? I thought that was just research for Ross' race?'

'I love her cute ass and tiny tits. She love my big dong!'

'Sounds like a match made in heaven,' I added.

'Anyway, I got to go now. She driving airport now.'

'OK, Kaz,' said Jak. 'Well you take care. Have a great Christmas, man, and I'll see you in a few weeks.'

'You too, Jak!' he beamed before catching Jak unawares with a huge bear hug. He then rushed over and squeezed me to within an inch of my life as well. 'Bye, Ross!'

'Bye, Kaz,' I managed through my aching lungs. 'Have fun!'

'I have lots of fun! Bye!'

He wheeled his suitcase out of the door and left for untold adventures with Kelly in Japan.

'I wonder what his parents will make of Doggy Style?' mused Jak.

'I have no idea. I just hope their house has thick walls. Come on, we'd better get down to the station.'

'Good evening C.U., you're listening to KVCU!' Jak gushed cheerily into the microphone.

'Yes, and what a good evening it is indeed, Jumpin' Jak!' I added. 'Our exams are over, Christmas is here, and now our listeners have the wondrous pleasure of listening to us for the next two hours. People, you really don't know how lucky you are!'

'That's right, and we're gonna bring you a whole host of Christmas music to get you into the festive mood. Starting with this old favourite, *Grandma Got Run Over By A Reindeer*.'

The music played while we chatted.

'Hey, Ross, I could get used to being on so early again. I don't know how we've survived a semester of those late-night shows.'

'Yeah, I know what you mean. We've been good boys recently though, haven't we?'

'Of course we have.'

'We haven't skipped any of the crap playlist songs, have we?'

'Not a single one.'

'And we haven't sworn on air recently, have we?'

'Nope.'

'So maybe next semester we *should* ask for an earlier slot. I think we deserve a wider audience, or at least an audience that's actually awake.'

'Too right, dude, too right.'

We were interrupted by the unfamiliar flashing red glow of the studio telephone. We had averaged about a call every four shows, so it was always an exciting time.

'Shit, shit, the phone, the phone!' I exclaimed.

'Go on then, Ross, pick it up.'

I did just that. 'Hello, KVCU?'

'...boom, boom...boom, boom...boom, boom...boom, boom...'

The voice continued indefinitely. I pressed the mute button and excitedly told Jak.

'I think it's the Hall Rapper, I think it's him!'

'Why, what's he saying? What's he doing?'

'Nothing really, he's just booming.'

I passed the receiver over to Jak's ear for a few seconds and then brought it back to my own.

'Shit, put him on air, Ross. Maybe he'll come to life then.'

I released mute and spoke into the phone.

'We're going to put you on air, OK?'

'...boom, boom...'

'Good. By the way, you didn't happen to run the Winter Warmer last weekend did you?'

'...boom, boom...'

'It's just that I could have sworn I saw you there, but I *had* just banged my head so maybe I just imagined it.'

'...boom, boom...'

'Yeah, I probably imagined it. Anyway, hold on a few more seconds and we'll get you on air, OK?' I then called over to Jak, 'Hey, get some instrumental rap shit of yours lined up, would you?'

'Sure thing.'

'...boom, boom...'

As soon as Jak's tune was ready to go, I faded out the Christmas music, cranked up the beats, and made the introduction.

'OK, we have a very special guest on the line now, all the way from Cheyenne Arapaho Hall!'

I put the call on air and waited.

'...boom, boom...I'm listenin' to your show...boom, boom...while I'm bonin' my ho...

'...boom, boom...I saved yo' ass in the race, Ross...boom, boom...then you showed, the fucker who's boss...

'...boom, boom...Merry Christmas one an' all...boom, boom...have a mother fuckin' ball...'

The phone cut dead, and Jak and I were left stunned. I muted our microphones while the music continued.

'Holy shit!' said Jak.

'Well,' I smiled, 'I think our chances of an earlier show have just flown out of the window.'

'Hi boys!' chimed April and Kristen as they entered the studio.

I welcomed them into our lair. 'Good evening, ladies! So, are you ready to go on air?'

'No way!' said April. 'We're just here to watch you guys do your thing and make sure you get back to the dorm safely in the dark.'

'How kind of you. Hang on a minute, I just need to put the next song on.'

Jak kept them entertained while I worked with the

controls. 'Can you believe it's Christmas? Finals are over, life is great, and *it's Christmas!*'

'You two are so excitable tonight!' said Kristen.

'Well, why wouldn't we be excited? We've got no work for the next few weeks, Santa Claus is on his way, and we both have such wonderful and special ladies in our lives.'

'Now you're making me want to throw up!' said April.

'He's right, April,' I added with the next track playing. 'What's not to be happy about?'

'Well,' she reasoned, 'there *is* the fact that I'm gonna be in California for the holidays while you're stuck here on your own.'

'I know, I know, but it's not for long. We'll get through it.'

'Why don't you just come with me then? To Encinitas? Jak's going to Kristen's place, so come home with me!'

'Well, I didn't want to disappoint you by telling you this, but I *have* been trying to get a ticket to fly out to be with you. But every single flight was completely sold out – I guess it's just impossible so close to Christmas. I'm really sorry it didn't work out.'

'Aw, that's a real shame. I was thinking how nice it would be to spend Christmas together, and for us to open our presents around the tree with my family.'

'Don't torture me! Maybe next year we can do that.'

'Yeah, maybe,' she sighed, while passing me an envelope. 'Unless you just want to use this ticket I bought for you instead?'